"An unforgettable classic with a hero who fulfills all your wildest fantasies, *Night Striker* is a treasure to be read over and over again!"

—*Romantic Times*

NIGHT STRIKER
Amii Lorin

Author of Five Million Books in Print

Winner of two *Romantic Times* Reviewers's Choice Award!

Arrogant, self-possessed, yet still innocent in love, she'd begged for her rescuer's kiss, unaware that the woman inside her would burst into flames at the first touch of his fiery mouth. Within weeks, Courtney Tremaine-Smythe had married the mysterious Rio McCord. But fears from her past haunted her and threatened to destroy the marriage conceived in sudden passion before it could grow into lasting love.

"Amii Lorin always gives her readers something special!"
—*Romantic Times*

NIGHT STRIKER

"What are you doing to yourself?" Rio demanded.

"I've got to rub it away," Courtney mumbled distractedly. "Don't you understand?" She sobbed. "I've *got* to rub it away!"

"What? What do you have to rub away? There's nothing there!"

Courtney glared up at him. "The feel of that beast's hand on me!" she shouted. "I must get it off!"

"Oh, Courtney." Sympathy and compassion gave Rio's naturally raspy voice a jagged edge. "It's gone," he murmured. Drawing her hand back, he exposed the irritated flesh. "You see? You've washed it aw..." Rio's voice trailed off as he stared at the purpling bruises on her shoulders.

"Are you sure?"

"Yes, it's off. There are bruises, but they will fade in time. As will the memory of it all," he promised.

Courtney shook her head sharply. "It will never fade. Never!"

Other *Leisure Books* by Amii Lorin:

COME HOME TO LOVE
SNOWBOUND WEEKEND/GAMBLER'S LOVE
TAWNY GOLD MAN/MORNING ROSE, EVENING
  SAVAGE
WHILE THE FIRE RAGES/THE GAME IS
  PLAYED
BREEZE OFF THE OCEAN/MORGAN WADE'S
  WOMAN

AMII LORIN

NIGHT STRIKER

LEISURE BOOKS · NEW YORK CITY

A LEISURE BOOK®

December 1991

Published by

Dorchester Publishing Co., Inc.
276 Fifth Avenue
New York, NY 10001

For my live-in lover of thirty-three years — my husband — Marv: Thanks for all the memories, hon.

NIGHT STRIKER

CHAPTER ONE

"Who *is* this man, Morgan?" Samantha Wade stared at her husband, a frown marring the perfection of her smooth brow. "Is he an undercover agent for the government or something like that?"

"No, darling, he is not an undercover agent or even something like that—at least not anymore." Standing by his desk, his hand grasping the telephone receiver, Morgan Wade smiled reassuringly at his wife.

"Not anymore!" Samantha exclaimed—in a very ladylike shriek. "What do you mean—not anymore?"

"Calm down, my love," Morgan soothed, a smile teasing his sharply defined lips. "As I told you. His name is Rio McCord. He and I were at Texas A&M together. Rio owns a horse ranch in West Texas. In fact, he's one of the best horsemen I've ever known." The smile on his lips grew reminiscent. "One of the best damned trackers too."

Walking to him, Samantha curled her fingers around one of his tightly muscled arms. "But, darling," she protested softly, "don't you think it would be better to leave this in the hands of the FBI and the local authorities?"

"The FBI surely," Morgan agreed—partly. "Your uncle has already notified them. But"—he shrugged—"what local authorities? We're not even certain exactly what locale they have Courtney in by now." His prominent features locked in anger. "Just because the van was spotted near the Texas border certainly doesn't prove they're actually *in* Texas."

Samantha revealed the depth of her concern by biting on her full lower lip. "I know that. That's why I don't understand why you want to involve this friend of yours. A friend, I might add, whom I've never met." Her oval nails dug into the long, hard muscle in his forearm—another indication of the tension gripping her. "I . . . I can't help feeling that you should leave it alone."

"Leave it alone!" Morgan's nostrils flared angrily. "Dammit, Sam! Until two weeks ago Courtney was a guest in this house! She is *your* cousin!"

"I know that!" Releasing her grasp on his arm, Samantha spun away to pace the braided rug on the hardwood floor, the fingers of one hand raking through the strands of mahogany-shaded hair that fell to the middle of her back. "And all I want is to have her returned safely!" As she pivoted to face him, her eyes pleaded for understanding. "Morgan, I'm terrified that these people will hurt Courtney; possibly even . . . ." Samantha's voice trailed away, as if she couldn't bear putting her fears into words.

His expression softening, Morgan crossed the floor to her in three long strides. "Don't even think of it, love." He slid his arms around her slender waist and drew her trembling body close to his. "We'll know more when they make their demands," he murmured into her hair, gentling her with long strokes down her spine. "Until then you must keep control of your emotions and imagination."

"I know." Breathing deeply, Samantha rubbed her face against the smooth cotton shirt that covered his warm, muscled chest, drawing strength from the solid feel of him. "But I'm so frightened. You don't know her, Morgan." Raising her head, she gazed helplessly into his concerned eyes. "Courtney is so very much her own person. She is so very"—she shrugged—"so very arrogantly independent."

"A family trait?" Morgan inquired dryly, his dark eyes alive with teasing mockery. "I seem to remember another young, very very arrogantly independent woman from the Tremaine-Smythe branch of the family tree."

Samantha laughed softly. "Horrible creature, wasn't I? Five years later I wonder whatever attracted you to me in the first place."

A blatantly wicked smile curving his hard lips, Morgan stepped back to gaze at her tall, elegant figure. "After all this time words shouldn't be necessary," he drawled, his smile widening at the color that washed her cheeks. "You know damn well what attracted me. Not only were you the most beautiful woman I'd ever laid eyes on," he admitted seriously, "but that same arrogance was a challenge I couldn't refuse." More than a hint of arrogance crept into *his* tone. "Come to that, I met the challenge very well—didn't I?"

Her laughter easy now, Samantha hugged him fiercely. Morgan's ploy to calm her had worked, as, indeed, *all* of the ploys he'd ever used to control her always had!

"About as well as I met yours," she concurred, arching one perfect eyebrow. "All right, darling, I'm ready to listen now." Her even tone was assurance of her renewed confidence. "Why do you feel this friend of yours can help us?"

Grasping her hand to keep her by his side, Morgan moved back to the desk as he answered her. "Two reasons," he said tersely, flipping open a leather-bound phone directory. "First, as I said, he's an expert tracker—of people as well as animals." Ignoring her soft gasp of dismay, he went on steadily. "And, second, he knows Texas, especially West Texas. *If* they are holed up somewhere in that state, Rio is the one to find them." His tone conveyed absolute belief in his assessment.

Samantha frowned. "Why haven't I ever met this Rio, Morgan?"

"Because he very recently decided to stop wandering the world and settle down." Morgan grinned. "Rio is like quicksilver, damn near impossible to pin down. Hell, *I* only found out that he was back in Texas by accident!" His long forefinger moved through the *M*'s in the phone directory. "I hope he's still there."

"All right, Morgan." Samantha gave in when he lifted one black, questioning eyebrow. "Do whatever you think is best."

Morgan was lifting the receiver before she'd finished speaking.

Stark terror choking her, Courtney Tremaine-Smythe slowly emerged from the drug-induced sleep. Her temples were throbbing, her throat was parched, her nerves were frayed, and every mus-

14

cle in her body was screaming a protest against the rough treatment that had been inflicted upon her for the last countless number of hours. In fact, the only relief during those horrendous hours had come when she'd finally been removed from the back of that bouncing van. And Courtney only vaguely remembered that!

Her mind still fuzzy from the drug, Courtney strained her eyes as she moved her head carefully. The exercise was useless; the darkness was complete. Swallowing in an effort to relieve the dryness in her throat, she tentatively jerked at the bindings securing her wrists. The leather bonds merely cut more deeply into her tender skin. Sighing in defeat, Courtney relaxed as much as was physically possible against the lumpy surface on which she was so awkwardly lying. If only she knew where she was, and why.

As the effects of the tranquilizing drug wore off, Courtney attempted to keep herself from falling completely apart by replaying the sequence of events of the previous hours over again in her fear-rattled mind.

It had begun with that phone call—which, of course, had been a trap, as Courtney now knew full well. . . .

On her own for the day, and happy to be so, the British socialite had gone to the brightly decorated restaurant in the Las Vegas hotel for an early lunch. Vacationing with her father, Courtney was enjoying the exciting resort. Male heads turned as she made her way across the dining room. Her tall, slender body, long blond hair, and classic features added up to aristocratic good looks. Unaware of the gentlemen's gazes, she ordered a lobster salad for lunch.

Having finished her salad, she was sipping a fresh cup of tea when the waiter brought a phone to her table. Frowning at the instrument, wondering who in the world would be calling her in Las Vegas, and why, she lifted the receiver and spoke into it briskly.

"Courtney Tremaine-Smythe here."

"Miss Smythe, this is Don Carleson." The unfamiliar, edgy-sounding voice deepened her frown; she didn't know a Don Carleson! "The golf pro out at the club," the man added with clarifying swiftness.

A shiver of apprehension slid down Courtney's spine; her father had gone out to the club to play golf hours earlier.

"Yes?" she responded in a clipped tone that masked her sudden uneasiness.

"I'm sorry I have to be the one to tell you this," the man said apologetically, "But I'm afraid your father has had a heart attack." At her soft, involuntary gasp, he hurried on. "He was stricken on the course a little while ago."

The apprehension coalesced into a tight knot of fear.

"Where is he?" Courtney's cool tone reflected her control and breeding.

"He's been taken to a private hospital not far from the club." There was a brief pause, as if the man were short of breath. "The ambulance left here just a moment ago. I ran right into the pro shop to place this call as they drove away."

"I appreciate your consideration, Mr. Carleson." Though her voice held steady, Courtney's fingernails slashed into the palm of her free hand. "Would you direct me to the hospital, please?"

"Yes, of course." Slowly, distinctly, he told her

16

the name and exact location of the private hospital, ending with: "I'm sure you'll have no difficulty finding it."

After scrawling her name and room number at the bottom of the check the waiter presented to her, Courtney scooped up her bag and hurried from the restaurant and through the hotel lobby.

As she pushed through the wide plate-glass entrance doors a taxicab shot in front of several others that were in line to pick up passengers, and came to a screeching halt inches away from the hotel doorman.

Frowning his displeasure at the breach of professional etiquette by the eager cabdriver, the uniformed doorman then turned to Courtney, smoothing his face into a polite smile.

"Cab, miss?" he asked respectfully.

"Yes, thank you." Sliding a bill into the man's hand, she stepped into the cab, instructing the driver where to go as the door closed beside her.

"I know where it is, lady," the driver assured her as soon as he'd heard the name of the hospital. "I'll have you there in no time flat."

Expecting something of a wild ride, Courtney was vaguely surprised when he drove the vehicle well within the speed limit. It wasn't until much later that she realized that her driver had no intention of being stopped for an infraction of highway safety laws.

The ride lasted well over a half hour and they had long since left the city limits behind before the driver turned the cab onto a private road. Riddled with concern for her father, Courtney glanced repeatedly at the diamond-encrusted watch encircling her slim wrist.

17

"Is it much farther?" she asked impatiently, glancing around at the desolate desert terrain.

"No, miss. We'll be there in a few minutes," the driver assured her tersely.

Too worried about her father to notice the nervous edge to the driver's tone, Courtney closed her eyes, breathing deeply to calm herself for whatever she'd have to face on arrival at the hospital. When the cab came to a sudden, jarring stop, she opened her eyes, expecting to see the clean lines of a small hospital. The sight that met her shocked gaze was a very ordinary looking, rather battered blue van and three men as nondescript as the tired-looking vehicle.

"Why have you stopped?" Courtney demanded imperiously.

Ignoring her question the driver pushed his door open. At the same instant the door beside Courtney was flung open.

"Out, lady." The harsh order came from the man holding on to the door.

"I certainly will not get out!" Courtney exclaimed, an altogether different type of fear rising in her throat. What did these men want? she wondered wildly. Money? God! Were they modern-day highway robbers? Infusing a coolness she was far from feeling into her voice, Courtney raised her chin haughtily. "I have very little money with me, if that's what you're after!" she lied coldly.

The man laughed nastily. "Wrong on both counts, lady." Leaning into the car he caught Courtney's arm in a bruising grip. "You most certainly *will* get out," he snarled, pulling her off the seat as he backed away. "And we're after a hell of a lot of money." With a final, brutal tug he yanked her from the car.

The moment her feet were steady on the sandy ground, Courtney began to struggle against the man's painful hold on her arm. "Let go of me at once!" she cried through the fear swelling in her throat. "I must get to the hospital! My father is very ill!"

With the help of the other men Courtney's struggles were swiftly subdued. Dragging her gleaming patent leather shoes in the yellow dirt, cursing and screaming all the way, she was forcibly moved to the back of the van. She twisted and fought frantically as the back panel doors were wrenched open. Rough hands brought her struggles to an end and a grimy hand was clamped over her mouth, sealing her protests inside her head.

"If it's any consolation, lady," one of the men growled at her ear. "Your old man is probably having a drink with his golfing buddies in the club bar right this minute." As he finished speaking, he grasped her around the waist and literally tossed her into the back of the van.

The breath was knocked out of Courtney's chest as she landed on the metal floor of the vehicle. A frightened moan burst through her lips along with the expelled breath as her forehead scraped the rough metal. Before she could regain her breath, her arms were yanked behind her back and her wrists tied securely. Seconds later her ankles received the same rough treatment.

"You—you can't get away with this!" Courtney panted, kicking out with her tightly bound feet and receiving a measure of satisfaction on hearing a curse when the spike heel of her shoe scraped against a body. But her satisfaction was short lived; she was struck across the face for her trouble.

"You bitch!" The man who'd forced her from

19

the car yelled close to her face. Courtney cringed at the rank odor of onions on his breath. "If you even try anything like that again, I'll—"

"Shut up and give her the injection!" A new voice ordered coldly from outside the van.

Sheer terror welled inside Courtney. "An injection!" she yelped. "Don't you dare inject me with anything!"

Hard hands grasped her around the hips, and Courtney began to wriggle wildly in an effort to get away.

"Get on with it, dammit!" the cold-voiced man snapped. "I want to get the hell out of here."

Though Courtney fought against it, cursing in an unladylike, violent way, all her efforts were in vain. The needle was plunged into her soft skin, and moments later she was plunged into oblivion.

The lucid moments Courtney had after that all contained a nightmarish quality.

Now, lying exhausted on a lumpy surface she assumed was some sort of bed, Courtney concentrated on remembering those brief moments of awareness.

She had awakened from the drug slowly, disoriented and wondering where she was and why she was so very uncomfortable. Memory had rushed back as her mind cleared. Slowly opening her eyes, Courtney had glanced around cautiously.

A man, obviously asleep, judging from the tenor of his loud snores, sat hunched against the door panels at the back of the van. By raising her eyes to the two small windows in the panels, Courtney could tell it was just about dusk outside. When she shifted her eyes to the front of the van, her gaze encountered two more even smaller windows, beyond which were outlined two heads, that of the driver and the man in the passenger seat beside him.

Who were these men and where were they taking her? Courtney wondered dazedly, blinking her eyes in an effort to clear her mind. Then, beginning to feel the strain on her shoulder muscles, she eased herself into a sitting position. Balancing awkwardly with the sway of the rapidly moving vehicle, she groaned aloud as she tumbled sideways into the metal side panels.

"Look alive, Ben!" The order came from the driver. "Our guest is awake."

As he straightened from his hunched position against the rear panels, the man the driver had called Ben stared at Courtney with calculating, beady eyes.

Biting her lip to contain the shudder of revulsion his avid stare produced, Courtney averted her eyes from his.

How long she sat there, her lips compressed, her body shuddering as it absorbed the jolts and bumps of the swaying van, Courtney hadn't the vaguest idea—it seemed to go on forever. Fear was a constant, a living entity that throbbed throughout her being. Speculation was her steadfast companion.

Where were they? Where were they taking her? What would they do to her when, if ever, they arrived at their final destination? The questions haunted Courtney through that wild ride, and through the hours of the night. She didn't consider asking them what they wanted. Although she had no idea of the terms, she knew she'd been kidnapped and would be held for ransom. Courtney didn't doubt that her father would meet their demands, whatever they were. The question was: Would they allow her to live after he'd met them?

She was cold: deep down cold, in her bones and in her mind. Shivering, Courtney huddled beneath the thin, scratchy blanket covering her. Fully alert now, she was struck by the realization that she'd been stripped of everything but her flimsy panties and lacy bra.

Damn them. Damn them. Damn them. Courtney's outraged mind condemned her abductors. Hadn't she been humiliated enough by being tossed around in that van and subjected to drug-induced sleep? Had they really thought it necessary to strip her of her clothing as well as her dignity?

All concept of time had deserted her. Although it seemed she'd bounced from floor to side panels for days, it had probably been no more than a few hours, perhaps less. Tired, frightened, and beginning to feel vaguely sick to her stomach, Courtney braced her aching shoulders against the side of the van and rested her head on the shuddering metal. Closing her eyes in an attempt to escape the unreality of her situation, she began to float in the nether world between wakefulness and sleep. Then all hell seemed to break loose.

There was a loud bang, followed by the wild lurching of the van. Courtney was thrown from one side of the vehicle to the other. Stunned but not unconscious, she lay listening to the driver spew out a string of obscenities as he brought the careening van to a quaking stop. Compressing her lips to contain the bile rising in her mouth, she closed her eyes as a storm of angry voices swirled around her.

"God damn it!" the cold-voiced driver cursed, "I thought you said all the tires were new!"

"They were! They are!" beady-eyed Ben shouted back. "You musta run over somethin' that slashed one of them!"

"We damned near bought the highway that time!" As the voice was a new one, Courtney assumed it was from the man in the passenger seat. "God! What were you doin', eighty-five?"

"Shut up and get out," Cold Voice snarled. "We gotta change the damned thing."

Courtney heard the sound of the two doors being angrily flung open; then Cold Voice called back, "Stifle the broad, Ben."

Keeping her eyes closed, Courtney concentrated on breathing evenly. Tension tautened her spine; she heard Ben scramble to her side and felt his moist breath feather her cheek.

"She's out cold," he shouted. "I think she rapped her head when the tire blew."

"She's not dead, is she?" Fear edged the tone of the cold-voiced man.

"Naw," Ben yelled. "She's breathing okay."

"You just keep an eye on her," Cold Voice directed from the front of the van.

Intent on her ruse of appearing unconscious, Courtney forced her tight muscles to relax. Lying in a limp heap, she felt the body of the van lift as the jack handle was cranked to the accompaniment of grunting curses. Then a new element of horror was added to the ongoing nightmare as she felt a hand slide along her thigh.

Biting down hard on her tongue to keep from crying out in revulsion, Courtney cringed inside as the hand moved over her hip and up her ribcage.

"So pretty, and so rich," Ben muttered thickly.

23

"And I bet those legs only spread for rich men too."

Her flesh shrinking from his touch, Courtney endured the disgusting feel of his hands on her body until she felt his fingers groping for her breasts. A moment before she would have betrayed her supposed unconsciousness by flinging herself away from him, the unmistakable sound of a stopping vehicle startled him into snatching his hand away.

"Damned truckers!"

Even as Ben cursed Courtney recognized the grinding and wheezing of a semi being brought to a halt.

"You guys need some help?"

As Courtney had not heard the sound of a door being opened, she assumed the trucker had called the offer from inside the cab of the truck. She was slowly drawing breath into her lungs when Cold Voice responded.

"No, we've just about got it. Thanks anyway."

Her nerves humming with tension, she released the hoarded breath in a pleading rush.

"Wait! Help me, plea—"

A sweaty hand was clamped over her mouth and a snarling voice hissed close to her ear.

"I'll strangle you, you stupid bitch!"

Her eyes wide, panic beating a mad tattoo in her pulse, hope and fear running in equal measure through her mind, Courtney strained to hear the masculine exchange outside.

"What the hell was that?" The trucker's voice held both amazement and suspicion.

"Nothin' important," the cold voiced man replied in a surprisingly indulgent tone. "My old

24

lady's sleeping in the back." His tone hinted at a shrug. "She gets nightmares."

Willing the trucker to ignore the excuse and investigate, Courtney sagged in defeat when she caught his uncertain response.

"Well, if you're sure . . . ?"

"Hey, fellah." Cold Voice actually laughed. "I've been married to her for over ten years. That's about as sure as I want to get!"

Hope shriveled and died inside Courtney when the trucker returned the laughter.

"I know what you mean. I got an old lady with some strange habits too. Ten four, buddy."

Everything inside Courtney went cold as she listened to the truck lumber back onto the highway. Would they kill her now? Terror ballooned in her mind. Dear God! Would they kill her and toss her body in some ditch alongside the road?

No. No, a tiny voice of logic argued. *If they kill you, they won't be able to collect the ransom.* Hanging on to that last glimmer of reason, she stared up at the man bending over her in threatening silence until she heard the other two men return to the cab of the van.

"That damned bitch nearly ruined everything!" Cold Voice snapped as he slammed the door. "Knock her out again, Ben."

Even though Courtney knew she should feel relieved at having escaped retaliatory punishment, she didn't. For all her cool sophistication, she abhorred the use of drugs to the point of obsession.

Once again she had struggled like a wild thing against the sleep-inducing injection. And, as before, she lost the struggle.

Now, many hours later, deprived of her clothing, Courtney huddled beneath the poor excuse for a blanket, waiting for the light of day, yet fearing what morning might bring.

Rio McCord was standing by the corral, his whipcord-lean body propped indolently against the railed fence, when the old Jeep came barreling into the yard, a plume of tan dust swirling in its wake.

Lids narrowed over brown eyes so dark they appeared black, he observed, from under the concealing brim of the well-worn black Stetson that was pulled low on his forehead, the man and woman who stepped from the Jeep and began walking toward him.

Lord, that is one gorgeous woman! Rio mused, deciding that everything he'd heard about Morgan's wife had been an understatement. Most men would likely forfeit half their remaining years on earth for one night in bed with that tall, strikingly beautiful redhead.

Most men perhaps, but not all men, and certainly not Rio McCord. Rio was very definitely *unlike* most men. In his opinion there wasn't a woman alive worth half of *his* remaining years.

The speculative thoughts inside Rio's mind were not revealed in his shuttered eyes or on his thin, harshly etched face. Rio had learned at an early age to guard his thoughts more greedily than everything else.

As Morgan and Samantha Wade came to a stop before him, Rio lazily eased himself away from the corral fence, straightening to his full height of six feet one inch. Lifting two fingers to the brim of his hat, he nodded respectfully at the woman, then shifted his dark eyes to stare levelly into Wade's even darker pair.

"Morgan." Extending his hand, Rio registered the startled expression that sprang into Samantha's face. The reaction to his voice seldom varied, yet it still amused Rio. One woman had claimed his voice sounded as if it came out of a throat filled with jagged-edged stones.

"Rio," Morgan murmured, returning the brief, firm handshake. Sliding his left arm around his wife's waist, he continued, "Sam, meet Rio McCord. Rio, my wife, Samantha."

"Mr. McCord." Sam smiled easily, thrusting out her slim right hand. As Rio slid his callused palm over hers, she said, quite seriously, "So, you're Night Striker."

The surprise that rippled through Rio's body was not betrayed by as much as the flicker of an eyelash.

"So I've been called," he grated softly. "Morgan's been talking, has he?" One black, neatly arched brow rose quizzically. "What did he tell you about me?"

"Very little, actually." Sam laughed softly. "And I must admit I had to badger that out of him." Her laughter ceased abruptly. "Courtney is my cousin, Mr. McCord."

"The name's Rio, Sam, and I understand." Releasing her hand, he glanced at Morgan. "Come into the house and tell me everything you know."

Rio led the way to the Spanish-style ranch house and first entered the walled patio through an archway, his boot heels clacking sharply on the flagstone flooring. Passing through another archway, he strode into the cool interior of the house, re-

27

moving his hat as he called, "Maria, coffee for three in the sala, please."

Rio led them across a wide, hardwood-floored entrance foyer and down two steps to a large, square living room. The room was comfortably elegant, Spanish-Mexican in decor, with splashes of brilliant, jewellike colors relieving the somber, intricately carved hardwood furniture. A huge natural-stone fireplace took up most of the far wall.

"Make yourselves comfortable," he invited with the absent wave of one broad hand. After Morgan and Sam were seated side by side on the ornate sofa, he stretched his length on the matching chair opposite them and fixed a calm gaze on Morgan's face, slowly shaking a cigarette from a pack and lighting it.

"Okay, let's hear it."

"The woman's name is Courtney Tremaine-Smythe," Morgan said quietly. "Her father, Charles, is Samantha's late mother's brother."

"Money?" Rio inserted.

"Of course." Morgan shrugged. "Old money, new money, and a lot of money in between."

"Go on," Rio drawled.

"She left the hotel in Vegas sometime around noon yesterday, directly after receiving a phone call. The call's a dead end. It went through the hotel switchboard, she took it in one of the restaurants. The hotel doorman was the last person to see her; he put her into a cab but did not hear what address she gave to the driver."

"FBI, local authorities?" Rio shot the question at him.

"Charles called them immediately," Morgan replied, "even though the contact gave the standard warning against doing so."

"Where did they get the make on the van?" Rio continued, "and how?"

"Through a flat tire, of all things." Morgan smiled faintly. "A trucker saw the disabled vehicle and stopped to offer assistance. The men working on the tire told him they had everything under control. He was about to pull out again when he heard a woman scream for help. When he questioned it, one of the men told him his wife was sleeping in the back and that she was prone to nightmares."

"It's possible." Rio shrugged.

"Sure," Morgan agreed, shrugging as well. "At any rate, the trucker wasn't about to argue, not with two men outside the van and who knows how many more inside. But he was suspicious."

"So he got the hell out of there," Rio guessed correctly.

"Right." Morgan nodded. "As soon as he got into a more heavily traveled area, he got on the CB and notified the authorities."

"And the van was heading for Texas." Rio sighed.

Morgan smiled. "Actually, it was already *in* Texas. The trucker placed it right over the state line." Raising his hand, he ran long fingers through his jet-black hair. "Rio, I've got a gut feeling that Courtney was the woman who screamed for help, and I believe the kidnappers are holed up right here in your bailiwick."

Reclining lazily, his overall appearance indicating sublime disinterest, Rio gazed at Morgan expressionlessly as he lit another cigarette. Slowly, he shifted his gaze from Morgan to Sam, who had remained silent through Morgan's briefing.

"Your uncle's British?"

"Yes."

"Of *the* influential Tremaine-Smythe family?"

Sam smiled. "Yes."

Rio's unrevealing gaze sliced back to Morgan. "Are there political overtones here?" Before Morgan could respond, he added sharply, "As in the possibility of some international repercussions?"

"No." Morgan's reply was prompt and decisive. "This is not the work of some terrorist group trying to gain political leverage. As a matter of fact, the experts theorize that this is the brainstorm of rank amateurs." His sigh was short on patience and long on disgust. "From what they've pieced together, they've concluded that this was a spur-of-the-moment snatch—the entire plan was so goddamned simple!"

"But effective," Rio retorted. "And the motive was . . ."

"Good old-fashioned greed," Morgan finished for him.

"A demand has been made?" Rio grated around the cigarette's filter, which was clamped between his teeth.

"They want three million dollars . . . in cash, of course."

"Who doesn't?" Rio's lips tilted up at the corners in the closest he'd come to a smile since entering the house. He regarded Morgan for several seconds, then shook his head slowly.

"You've got the Federal Bureau of Investigation," he said in that soft, not unattractive, gravelly voice. "And you've got state and local authorities. What do you want with me?"

Morgan's smile was both chiding and dry. "You know damned well what I want. I want to hire the legendary skills of the man known in *un*known circles as the Night Striker."

CHAPTER TWO

Fear, like the night, blanketed everything. Panic clawing at her throat, Courtney shivered, her senses straining for the slightest sound, the faintest flicker of light.

Nothing. Nothing. And then, intensifying her shivers into bone-shaking shudders, came the mournful cry of an unidentified animal. Her throat working spasmodically, her teeth digging relentlessly into her bottom lip, Courtney cringed into the lumpy mattress.

Dear Lord, would morning never come?

Terror tightened her chest, stiffened her limbs; Courtney was fighting a losing battle against choking sobs. Now, here, under the cloying blanket of darkness, she could allow herself the release of tears. Morning would come, as it always did, and with it her abductors.

Courtney's memory of the three men was sketchy. Eyes tightly closed in concentration, she conjured an image of the men as she'd first seen them.

Everything had happened too quickly for any lasting impressions. Courtney vaguely remembered the one man who'd sat up front and said little, as average in every way; average height, average weight, average face. Then there was the driver with the cold voice—that one she instinctively knew was the most dangerous of the three. Cold Voice was rather small, and wiry, with detached, dead-looking eyes set in a ferretlike face. But it was the third man Courtney was most frightened of; the man the others had called Ben. Ben with the overweight, lumbering body and avid, beady eyes terrified Courtney at a basic level. She knew if he was set free of all restraint, Ben would rape her. The knowledge of the threat Ben posed to her body chilled Courtney's blood.

First light was heralded by the twittering and rustling of small wildlife. Calmer now, Courtney lay listening to the sounds that preceded morning in unpopulated areas. The noises were not unfamiliar to her. She had grown up on a country estate, had accompanied her father on several photo-safaris. She was versed on the predawn murmurings of the wild.

As Courtney catalogued the morning arguments of the birds and the scurrying of tiny rodent feet, the complete blackness receded before creeping gray, which in turn dissipated into pearlescent pink. Surrounding features emerged from shadowy forms into solid objects.

Resentfully grateful to whoever had rearranged her bound wrists from back to front, Courtney shifted position on what she could now see was a narrow cot. Struggling to sit up, she shivered in the cool dawn air when the threadbare blanket slithered off her shoulders and onto her lap. Her eyes now clear of the blurring effects of the tranquilizing injections, Courtney examined her immediate surroundings.

The room was small and boxlike, measuring no more than eight feet by eight feet. The cot she lay on was shoved into one corner of the room, head-end below and to the left of a small, paper-shaded window. The shade was old, and torn, and thick with years of accumulated grime, which explained the absence of moonlight during the long night.

The furnishings in the room consisted of the cot, one straight-backed chair, and a chest of drawers that looked like it had been old when it came over on the *Mayflower*. In the opposite corner from the cot sat a paint-blistered, boxlike contraption with a hole cut out of the top surface. A delicate shudder washed over Courtney as she recognized what it was—an out-of-date, rickety-looking commode.

Wrinkling her nose, Courtney ran her gaze over the two door frames set into joining walls, the one opposite the cot, and the one facing it. The badly hung, warped doors were tightly closed. One of the doors, the one facing her, had an old-fashioned lock plate beneath the curved metal latch.

By simple deduction Courtney concluded that the lockable door led to the outside, and the other connected to another room in the structure. There was no way she could determine the size of the building, but by the fact of its crude construction, she surmised it to be quite small.

In contrast to the animal activity outside all was quiet inside. Not for an instant did Courtney entertain the optimistic idea that she'd been dropped off and abandoned. Those men who had forced her into the van—had it been the day before?—were around somewhere, probably still asleep. And, for all she knew, their numbers had increased.

What were their plans for her? The question created goose bumps on Courtney's shoulders and arms. Grasping the blanket with fingers numbed by the tight bindings on her wrists, she drew it up as she slid down on the cot, seeking warmth and rest. When her hands were level with her breasts a choking gasp broke through her compressed lips.

Her ring! Eyes wide, Courtney stared at her naked left hand. Her engagement ring was gone! Her gaze slid from her finger to her wrist; her watch was there! Lifting her arms awkwardly, she brushed her fingers over her earlobes; the diamond stud earrings were in place. Had her ring slipped off her finger during the scuffle when she'd fought against being loaded like so much baggage into the van? She frowned. Or had one of those men removed it while she lay unconscious?

The mere thought of being touched, even briefly, caused a sick, burning sensation in Courtney's stomach. Why take the ring and not the watch and earrings? It hurt to even think, but still, the questions persisted in teasing her mind.

Where was her handbag?

Fully aware she had not missed a thing in her initial perusal of the room, Courtney nonetheless sent her gaze over the area a second time. There were no signs of her clothes or handbag.

In addition to traveler's checks she'd had over four hundred dollars in cash in her purse. Was the money gone as well? Courtney felt positive that it was. So then, why leave the watch and earrings? Odd. Certainly, the ring was of much greater value than the other pieces, but the stones in them were flawless and worth quite a bit.

Very odd indeed!

Conscious of the ring's loss now, Courtney tentatively moved her fingers, her feelings mixed. She had grown used to the weight of the three-carat gemstone. The emotions that should have been attached to the symbol were simply not there. Courtney was not in love with the man who'd placed the ring on her finger seven months previously.

Her delicate eyebrows drew together above her aristocratically straight nose as she stared broodingly at her naked finger. Had Phillip been notified of her disappearance? she wondered. Was he, perhaps, en route to the States at this very minute? An image of her fiancé, frantic with worry, distracted her if only momentarily from the very real danger of her present predicament.

Dear Phillip. Courtney sighed. Dear, dear Phillip, so doggedly attentive, so very single minded in his pursuit of her, and so obviously upset and alarmed at their last meeting before she'd left England for the States.

Memory swelled of their last meeting, crowding all other considerations from Courtney's consciousness. It was a self-defensive mechanism, of course, a means of temporary escape from a reality too frightening to contemplate. Courtney grasped at the mechanism in silent desperation.

The meeting had taken place in the elegantly decorated morning room in her father's equally elegant house in Berkeley Square.

"Darling, you can't mean it!" His slender, impeccably attired body quivering with tension, Phillip leapt from his chair.

Courtney's smile conveyed compassion and sadness. "But I do mean it, my dear." The endearment had not been used as a sop to his sensitive male ego; Courtney genuinely liked Phillip Barrington. "I don't love you in that way, Phillip." Removing the diamond-and-platinum ring he'd given her at Christmas, she held it out to him.

"Dammit, Courtney!" Phillip exclaimed. "I thought we'd resolved that particular bone of contention!" Crossing to where she sat, he caught her hand in his. "You haven't met someone else? Some man for whom you do feel *that* way?"

"No, I haven't, but—" Courtney began impatiently.

"Well, then," Phillip interrupted forcefully, plucking the ring from her hand and sliding it onto her finger again. "I'm afraid I don't quite understand what this is all about, darling." Being very careful of his trousers, he knelt down before her. "I knew you were not in love with me when you accepted my ring, didn't I?" he murmured chidingly.

"Yes, of course, but—"

"Darling, nothing's changed," Phillip again interposed. "We've known each other forever, and what's more, we like each other." He arched light-brown brows. "Hmmm?"

Courtney had no choice but to smile and nod her agreement.

"All right, then, there you have it!" Phillip's own smile was utterly charming. "Love will come after we're married," he said persuasively. His argument and tone were the same as when he'd finally talked her into accepting the engagement over half a year before. "And you know the parents want it, don't you?"

As there was no denying that truth, Courtney nodded again.

"Then what is this all about, my sweet?" Rising gingerly, Phillip went back to the chair he'd been occupying when Courtney announced her intention of breaking their engagement. After meticulously straightening the crease in his trousers, he frowned questioningly at her.

"Oh! I don't know!" Now it was Courtney who jumped up to pace the floor. "I'm restless and"— she lifted her shoulders in an eloquent shrug— "and rather bitchy, I suppose." Raising a long-fingered, slender hand, she smoothed the gleaming mass of pale blond hair that fell well below her shoulders. "I thought that if I broke it off," she went on in a level tone, "I'd be freeing you to have a look around for a better deal." Courtney didn't bother to add that she'd feel easier about the whole thing also.

"But, darling, I don't want a better deal!" Phillip protested. "I'm quite happy with the status quo." Easing to his feet he intercepted her as she retraced her pacing steps across the Aubusson carpet. "As long as you drop me a postcard now and then from points of interest, I'll be perfectly fine while you're on holiday in the States with your father." Smiling benignly, he drew her into an undemanding embrace.

Closing her eyes, Courtney sighed.

As she shifted on the lumpy mattress, Courtney's chest expanded and contracted in memory. Then, suddenly alert and very much in the present, she inhaled again, deeply, her mouth watering with the scent she'd detected.

Coffee! Courtney's nose twitched and her stomach rumbled. Suddenly famished, she drew in a deep breath, savoring the aroma of—oh, heavens —not only coffee, but bacon as well!

How long had it been since she'd eaten? Salivating, Courtney wriggled her body into an upright position. She clasped the blanket to her chest, her nose twitching again. Oh, God, toasting bread! Her stomach issued a low growl and she waited in hungry anticipation. Were her captors planning to feed her?

The query chilled her. What if no one came with food for her? But surely they would not starve her? Or would they? Courtney moistened her lips. The action made her acutely aware of a growing thirst. A sudden pressure in the lower half of her body made her uncomfortably aware of another bodily function needing attention.

Courtney's glance sliced to the decrepit contraption in the corner. Ugh! A delicate shudder rippled the length of her spine. The . . . the thing didn't look too clean. Still . . . Courtney shrugged—the need definitely *was* there! Now, how to get someone's attention. Lifting her chin regally, she opened her mouth and yelled.

"Help!"

A moment later the door was flung open and beady-eyed Ben came lumbering in, Ferret Face at his heels. Both men stopped dead at the sight of her sitting calmly in the bed, the threadbare blanket held primly to her determinedly set chin.

"What the hell's all the yelling about?" Ferret Face demanded, his sharp-eyed gaze ricocheting off the four walls. Beady Eyes merely stood there, looking stupid.

"I'm hungry," Courtney announced succinctly. "And I need to use the facilities."

"You're going to need medical attention if you yell like that again," Ferret Face snarled, moving toward her menacingly.

Though she cringed inside, Courtney raised her chin higher in defiance; she'd be damned if she'd show these men how frightened she was! "I'm not being deliberately difficult!" she snapped—if a trifle weakly. "The situation is growing desperate!" She squirmed uneasily to give added proof.

His eyes narrowing on her wriggling form, Ferret Face came to a halt. "Ben, escort our guest to the—ah—facilities." A sneering smile revealed uneven teeth as he observed the horror filling Courtney's face.

"Your coffee, señor."

Rio smiled his thanks to the soft-spoken woman, then returned his attention to the man sitting across the kitchen table from him.

"You're positive it was them?" he asked in his raspy voice, eying the small, wiry man through the blue-gray smoke rising from the cigarette clamped between his teeth.

"Yeah, the stupid sons of—" the man broke off, shooting an apologetic glance at the placid housekeeper. "They left the end of the van sticking out of the lean-to." He blew noisily on his steaming coffee. "The trail leads into the hills."

"Figures." Rio grunted. "All right. Bring the Jeep and Hot Foot around in about fifteen minutes. I'll take off as soon as I've finished eating."

"Right." The wiry man nodded, gulped the last of his coffee, then, scraping his chair back, got quickly to his feet. He was at the kitchen door when he paused to glance back at his boss. "Ah, Rio, what about Tracker?"

"What about him?" Rio cocked one uneven eyebrow at his ranch foreman.

"He's gettin' a mite restless." Cleat Jamison grinned. "I think he's tired of being confined to sick bay."

Rio frowned. "The leg?"

"Good as new," Cleat assured him.

"All right, I'll take him along." A wry smile played over Rio's thin lips. "He's come in handy a time or two."

Fifteen minutes later Rio walked out of the ranch house and into the chill Texas predawn. His torso was covered in a faded blue cotton shirt. His narrow hips and long legs were encased in well-worn Western-cut jeans. His tan boots were scuffed and dusty. His Stetson had seen better days —much better days. He was wearing the typical uniform of the working cowboy, with one important addition. Riding low on his hips was a gun belt, the holster anchored to his taut thigh by a knotted thong. Nestled in the holster was a lethal-looking, long-barreled pistol.

A low whine greeted Rio's emergence from the house. With an easy, loping gait, he walked to where Cleat stood beside the Jeep, horse reins in one gloved hand, a dog's lead in the other.

"Ready to ramble, are you?" Rio murmured, reaching out with one leather-gloved hand to caress the narrow head of the quivering Doberman at the end of the lead.

The dog was large, for a Doberman, and sleek, its black hide gleaming in the defused light from the kitchen. At his master's touch another low whine trembled from his salivating jaws. Though he didn't lift one paw from the tan earth, his body moved with the excitement rippling through him.

41

"I think you have your answer," Cleat observed dryly, stepping away from the Jeep. Bending, he disconnected the lead from the dog's collar. "In, Tracker," he ordered mildly.

With a fluid bound Trapper's body left the earth, then landed dead center in the front passenger seat.

"How does he do that?" Cleat marveled, not for the first time.

Rio chuckled softly. "Beats the hell out of me." He laughed as he got into the Jeep and slid behind the steering wheel. "But I think he's demonstrated the soundness of that leg quite effectively," he drawled. "Don't you?"

"Yeah." Nodding, Cleat tied the horses' reins to the back of the Jeep. "He's too damned smart for an animal by half," he muttered, backing away from the vehicle. "You know where you're goin' now?" Cleat asked.

Rio paused in the act of turning the key in the ignition to cock his head and level a dry look at his foreman.

"Your directions were very concise," he chided mockingly. "If I get lost, I'll send up a smoke signal." The smile that curved his lips as Cleat turned beet-red could only have been described as wicked.

Before shifting around to the front again, Rio slowly ran a narrow-eyed glance over his horse, Hot Foot, dancing behind the motionless Jeep. The beautiful animal stood at least fifteen hands high. Rio knew that Hot Foot, hand picked and hand trained, would respond immediately to his command in the same fiercely loyal way that Tracker would.

Rio trailed his gaze from Hot Foot to the back

42

bench seat in the Jeep, his glance encompassing the bedroll propped against his own saddle and the rifle lying under the bedroll. His perusal of gear completed, he shifted position and started the engine.

"Might as well get comfortable, ole buddy," Rio advised the avidly panting dog. "We've got a long ride before going to work."

As if he understood his master perfectly, Tracker circled the seat, then curled his slender body into a ball on the worn leather.

"Good hunting," Cleat called as Rio set the Jeep into motion.

"Thanks." Rio tugged the Stetson lower on his forehead.

With the trotting horse in mind, Rio teased the gas pedal with his booted foot, all his concentration centered on the bumpy, dusty, unpaved road. He hesitated briefly when he came to the intersection of his own and the county owned road. He paused, then drove under his SHADOW C RANCH sign that marked the entrance to his property.

Though he accelerated slightly after pulling onto the secondary road, the ride became smoother on the macadam and required less of Rio's attention. Controlling the Jeep with casual expertise, he mused on his direction and his own crews' investigative work in pinpointing the location.

Rio had dispersed the four separate crews the previous afternoon, after accepting Morgan Wade's request for help in finding his wife's kidnapped cousin. One of the teams had scoured the area from the air with the ranch helicopter. Two others had set off in four-wheel-drive vehicles.

Cleat and two other men had gone out on horseback. All had communication devices.

The helicopter crew had spotted the van. The pilot had relayed the location to the driver of one of the Jeeps, who, in turn, had alerted Cleat—who just happened to be closest to the designated area.

On investigation Cleat had observed the van from a discreet distance. As reported, the van had been driven into the ramshackle lean-to attached to an equally decrepit abandoned ranch house situated in a fold of the mountain foothills. The kidnappers had literally taken to the hills. Darkness was already settling in by the time Cleat confirmed the make of the van so any attempt at scouting out a trail had to be put off till morning.

Morning was now sending tentative shades of pink into the eastern horizon as Rio tooled the Jeep in the direction of the ranch he knew well as the Henderson property.

Sadistic bastard!

Trembling with the rage searing her body, Courtney clutched the blanket to her breasts and screamed curses at both men while refusing to move.

The man was an absolute sicko, she fumed, and she wasn't going to allow his foul mind to derive amusement from humiliating her this way.

Ferret Face's twisted form of early-morning fun and games was over, because Courtney's screams showed him that she insisted on privacy while seeing to her body's hygiene. She'd been screaming since Ben had actually put his grimy hands on her to 'escort' her to the commode, and now the boss issued his order in that chillingly cold voice.

"Enough, Ben. Cut her bonds and get her some

44

hot water." That sneering smile tugged at his lips at Ben's grunt of disappointment. "We don't want to soil the merchandise, do we?" Arms crossed over his narrow chest, he stood watching her implacably while Ben carried out his order. After Ben returned to the room with a basin of steaming water and a towel, and set both on the rough surface of the rickety chest of drawers, he motioned Ben out of the room again with a jerk of his head. Before following Ben, he favored Courtney with another of his sneering smiles.

"You have exactly ten minutes to wash up before 'Hot-to-Trot' there brings your breakfast. Better rustle your rump, honey." Chuckling in what Courtney thought was a decidedly evil way, he strolled from the room.

Shivering in her panties and bra in the morning chill, Courtney performed the fastest sponge bath of her life. Being careful of the red welts inflicted on her wrists by the leather cords she'd been bound with, she scooped water into her cupped hands and splashed it over her face, moistening her lips and mouth with the hot water.

Even though her watch had stopped sometime during the night, she was certain no more than six or seven minutes could have elapsed when Ben came lumbering back into the room, bearing a tray of food and a leering grin.

Feeling every bit as exposed as if she were completely naked, Courtney dived for the cot and the concealment of the threadbare blanket.

"Have you ever heard of knocking?" she snapped icily, glaring at him.

"Why bother?" Ben's beady eyes crawled over her form outlined clearly under the thin covering. At the evidence of a shudder she couldn't repress, his grin widened. "I've seen it all before," he said thickly. "I undressed you." He laughed as Courtney blanched. "Got a few good feels in while I was doing it too," he continued tauntingly, lumbering to where she now crouched on the cot. "You're the first woman I ever touched whose skin felt like silk."

Courtney had the sensation that tiny bugs were cavorting under her skin. In an instant's flashback of memory she could feel his hand roving her body during the minutes she'd pretended she was unconscious in the van. Knowing he had touched her again while removing her clothes created an empty, sick feeling in her mind and stomach.

"You had no right to touch me!" Courtney exclaimed fiercely, hate blazing from her glittering blue eyes.

"Sez who?" Ben retorted smugly. Holding the tray of food just out of her reach, he licked his lips and taunted, "I'll let you have this food for another feel."

"Go to hell, you bloody swine!" Courtney spat, drawing her legs protectively to her chin. "I'll starve first!" As he began moving closer to the cot, she warned, "I'll scratch your eyes out if you touch me again!"

Ben's beady eyes actually seemed to light up with anticipation. "You want to fight, huh?" he jibed hopefully. "I like when a woman fights me, it gets me all kinds of excited."

Disgust and fear ran in relays along Courtney's nerves. Eying him warily, she watched as he headed for the chest of drawers to free his hands of the tray. "Don't you dare!" she croaked—her throat had gone suddenly dry. His only response was a frightening laugh. A coldly snapped order from the doorway wiped the look from his face and the laughter from his lips.

"Let her the hell alone, Ben." There was an edge to the words that stopped Ben in his tracks. "The food's getting cold, give it to her and then get out of here." Confident that he would be obeyed, Ferret Face turned away from the doorway.

"You're not going anywhere," Ben said in a tone pitched for her ears only. "I'll get a feel, more than one." He lowered the tray to the foot of the cot. As he straightened, he smiled in a way that sent an icy chill down Courtney's back. "I'll get more than a feel. We're gonna have us a real wrestling match." Chuckling nastily he shuffled out of the room.

Oh, dear God. Motionless with dread Courtney stared at his retreating back. A violent shudder ripped through her trembling body. What was she going to do? Her mind racing in circles, she sent her gaze on a frantic search around the room for a means of escape.

Inching stealthily from the cot, she tested the window. It was not only locked but nailed shut as well. Dragging the thin blanket with her like a toga, she crept to the other door in the room. That also was securely locked. A fine film of perspiration sheened her body as she crept back to the cot. Her stomach lurched as her gaze collided with the food on the tray.

There were two pieces of unbuttered toast, now cold. On a paper plate lay three strips of undercooked bacon, the edges thick with congealed fat. There was a chipped earthenware mug of coffee as black and thick as tar. Swallowing bile, Courtney drew the tray closer to her; she had to

47

eat to keep up her strength—which she felt positive she was sorely going to need.

Courtney was longing for a cup of hot tea; with a
grimace she sipped at the rancid coffee. If nothing
else, the brew was wet and quenched her now
raging thirst. How long had it been since she'd had
anything to eat or drink? she wondered, gingerly
picking up the greasy bacon strips and hiding
them from view between the two slices of toast.

In between chewing each bite methodically and
washing the mess down with swallows of cold coffee, Courtney recalled what had happened the
day before. She now had a flashing memory of
surfacing from the drug to the realization of being
tied to the back of a mule. Even in her groggy
state of mind she'd been aware of the intensity of
the heat and her own raging thirst. She recalled
crying out for water, and then the sweet coolness
of liquid trickling down her throat. A reflexive
shudder moved her body as she felt again the
plunge of the hated needle that sent her tumbling
back into oblivion.

Fortified by the food, Courtney pushed the tray
to the foot of the cot and stared defiantly at the
partially open door to the other room. She was
trapped and she knew it. There would be no escape. Her only hope was that her abductors would
release her after her father had met their demands, but even that hope held only a very dim
glimmer. She could identify and describe in detail
every one of her abductors, including the man
who'd driven the cab.

As the summer sun rose in the eastern sky,
bright rays pierced the grimy windowpanes, flood-
ing the small, airless room with stifling heat.
Wrapped in the blanket, crouched at the head of

the narrow cot, Courtney stared fixedly at the doorway.

Intellectually, she knew her chances of ever being released were slim. Even if she were released, Courtney didn't allow herself the luxury of believing she'd be set free in the same mental and physical condition she'd been in when she'd entered that cab.

Through the four-inch opening between the door and warped frame, she could hear the men talking in the other room. Although their voices were too low for Courtney to make out more than a word here and there, she knew they were discussing her. The knowledge increased the tremors quaking through her slender body.

The unpleasant sound of Ben's laughter wafted into the room, reinforcing the decision Courtney had reached while eating.

The unhealthy glow deep in Ben's eyes as he'd taunted her before leaving her to eat, convinced Courtney of his determination to possess her physically—and soon. Not for one minute did she delude herself. When he took her, Ben would be brutal.

Swallowing the brackish coppery taste of fear, Courtney shuddered outside while resolution set into concrete in her mind.

She would die rather than suffer that man's invasion of her body.

By the time the sun was high enough and warm enough to scorch his skin through the soft material of his shirt, Rio had been in the hills for well over an hour.

He had not been on the road long before he'd deserted the macadam to shoot across country, cutting his actual traveling time almost in half. After his arrival at the Henderson property, which was literally falling down, Rio had ascertained within minutes that it was completely deserted; the van and its driver were gone. Not many minutes more, and very little of his tracking ability were required for Rio to pick up the kidnappers' trail into the hills.

Sitting easily in the well-worn saddle, Rio held the reins loosely in one hand, allowing Hot Foot to pick his way delicately as he bore his rider up the uneven terrain. Tracker, his pointed ears at attention, trotted tirelessly by the side of the horse.

"Morgan was right, old friend," Rio confided to the bright-eyed dog.

Tracker tilted his sleek head to gaze adoringly up at Rio, jaws opening slightly as he panted, for all the world giving the impression that he was grinning in agreement. Rio grinned back.

"These clowns *are* rank amateurs," he continued softly. "A first-year Cub Scout would have little trouble following this trail." A derisive smile played over his thin lips. "Or in reading it either."

Rio himself had read the signs at once. Five animals had entered the hills from the back of the Henderson property: three horses and two mules. If the woman was astride one of the horses, that meant two men and two pack animals. On the other hand . . . Rio opted for the other hand. If he was reading the signs correctly—and he invariably did—that meant there were three men on horseback, and two pack animals, one of them packing supplies, the other packing a hostage.

Though he'd kept his own speculations to himself while questioning Morgan Wade the previous afternoon, the possibility that the kidnappers had

50

crossed the border into Mexico had occurred to Rio. Now he strongly doubted it. They were close, Rio could feel it in his bones . . . and though he'd often wondered where these intuitions of his came from, Rio never questioned them anymore.

An hour later Rio's shirt was clinging damply to his back and Tracker was panting for real. Leaning forward in the saddle, he ran his palm over Hot Foot's sweaty coat. The animal trembled in response to the caress.

"We'll rest soon," he murmured, positive in his own mind that he could follow through on the promise.

Following a trail that looked as if it had been made by a stampeding herd of buffalo required very little of Rio's concentration, so he amused himself by thinking about his friend Morgan's wife.

Samantha. Rio rolled the name around in his mind. Beautiful—the name and the woman. A sardonic smile teased his lips. A cool, controlled man could happily kill for the right to call such a woman his.

Tracker cocked his head at the soft chuckle that whispered from the throat of his master. Catching the dog's action from the corner of his eye, Rio chuckled again.

"Of course, you do realize that if I had serious designs on that ravishing creature, I'd have to knock off Morgan to carry them out?" he asked the eager-eyed animal solemnly. "And knocking old Morg off would be no minor accomplishment." A shadow of a smile twitched his lips. "Not impossible, mind you, but a long way from minor." Tracker's head swiveled around when Rio chuckled again. "Lucky for Morgan that I don't have designs on his woman. Knocking him off would put a hell of a strain on our friendship." A frown drew his dark eyebrows together. All Samantha had told him by way of a description was that Courtney was tall, slender, and blond. "I wonder what the cousin looks like?" he said reflectively.

God, if my skin looks as bad as it feels, I very likely resemble a harridan by now, Courtney thought despairingly as she drew her palm down one cheek. Though her skin was wet with perspiration, drawn from every pore by the intense heat in the closed-off room, it still felt gritty. *What it needs,* she wailed mutely, *is a drink of moisturizer.*

She slid her fingers into her hair, grimacing at the feel of the lank strands. She could do with a brush as well! Dropping her hand to the cot, she wriggled uncomfortably under the now heavy-feeling, scratchy blanket. If the covering had failed miserably to keep her warm during the night, it was making up for the omission now! Still, the threat of bodily injury or death wouldn't have made her relinquish the threadbare protection.

Sighing, Courtney fought the leaden pull of her eyelids. The heat was making her extremely sleepy, and she longed for the blessed relief of oblivion. Stark terror kept her from seeking escape in sleep.

Since serving her breakfast, and warning, Ben had come into the room twice to torment her. The first time he'd come on orders from the cold-voiced, ferret-faced man, who was obviously the head kidnapper, to rebind her wrists and ankles. Ben had taken full advantage of his assignment by running his filthy hands over her arms and shoulders after he'd secured her wrist bindings, and stroking the length of her legs after he'd fastened the leather cords to her ankles.

The second time Ben entered the room, Courtney wiggled into as tight a ball as humanly possible, glaring her hatred and loathing for him out of fiery blue eyes. He was carrying a metal cup of water in one bearlike hand.

"The boss says it's time for your midmorning tea, your highness," he taunted, lumbering to the side of the cot. "Can't have you dry up and blow away from us, can we?"

The water had a brackish, mineral taste. Courtney gulped it down greedily, longing for more when the cup was empty. As she'd lowered the cup from her lips, Ben had grasped her by the hair to hold her steady and, swooping like a bird of prey, fastened his thick lips onto hers.

Gagging, Courtney had twisted her body violently, raising her bound wrist to hit him with the cup. All her resistance had earned her was the degrading action of his fleshy hand clutching at her body through the thin blanket. She was spared further debasement by a shout from the other room.

"Hey, Ben, Dub says you're to get out here and help with the damned animals!"

As the voice was only vaguely familiar to Courtney, she had to assume it belonged to the man she thought of as average, and that "Dub" was the given name of Ferret Face. Regardless, she was thankful for the call, whomever it came from, for it freed her of the obviously aroused Ben. Muttering a string of obscenities, Ben shuffled heavily out of the room.

Courtney kept her eyes open, fighting sleep by

replaying the two nerve-shattering scenes over and over in her mind.

"Well, well, look at what we've got here," Rio murmured to himself, sitting statue still on the back of the heaving horse. Eyes narrowed, he scanned the crude two-room cabin that was nestled in the bush slightly beyond a small, narrow canyon. The place appeared deserted but the bray of a mule betrayed its occupancy.

From his concealed observation point Rio studied the lay of the land carefully, imprinting every rock, bush, and cranny on his memory. Then, his reconnaissance complete, he withdrew to the far end of the canyon. Selecting a spot safe from detection, Rio dismounted and prepared to wait out the daylight.

After the animals were cared for, and watered at a small pool formed from a trickle of water that ran over the rocks, he opened the bedroll, ate the cold beef sandwich and crisp apple his housekeeper had packed for him, sipped appreciatively at the tepid coffee, and stretched out.

Less than thirty minutes later, the rifle by his side, the holstered pistol within reach of his hand, and Tracker curled up on his other side, Rio tilted his Stetson forward to cover his eyes, and promptly fell asleep.

For Courtney, simply surviving the noon meal was an ordeal she never wanted to repeat.

The ritual of the morning—release wrist and ankle bindings, use disgusting receptacle, wash hands and face, eat revolting food—was carried out to the letter. The only difference was that this time Dub didn't bother tormenting her with the threat of surveillance during her toilette. Ben was dispatched immediately after he'd removed her bonds; the "average" man brought the food tray to her.

It was after she'd finished eating the garbage Dub had called a sandwich that the horror began all over again. The horror entered the airless room under the guise of the lumbering Ben.

Even applying all the considerable self-control Courtney possessed, she could not contain the shudder that shivered through her at the sight of his thick, leering lips and gleaming, avid eyes. The visual evidence of her revulsion drew a snicker from his throat.

"You're afraid of me," he muttered, halting near where she cowered at the head of the cot. "That's good, I like that." Bending awkwardly, he grabbed her by the hair, jerking her upright painfully. His thick, wet lips peeled back to reveal small, yellowed teeth. "Tonight," he whispered on a heavy breath, "after the others are asleep, we're gonna get it on."

Fear vied with fury in Courtney's mind and fury won. Ignoring the sharp pain it caused, she shook her head violently. "If you don't let me go, I'll scream for Dub!" she warned in a dry squeak.

"Dub, is it?" Ben snarled, yanking her head back to expose her arched throat. "When the time comes, I can take care of Dub!" Bending lower, he fastened his open lips on her vulnerable neck. "I can't wait to get at you!" he mumbled against her cringing skin an instant before he sank his teeth into it.

Arching her body frantically, Courtney bucked like a horse gone berserk. Nausea rose to burn in

55

her chest, nearly choking the scream that burst from her throat.

"No! No! Get away from me!" When Ben's dirty hand grasped one breast, she shouted shrilly, "I can't stand it! Somebody please help me!"

There was the pounding of feet against the plank floor, then a command: "Dammit, Ben, I told you to let her alone!"

Courtney kept the wracking sobs at bay until Ben had left the room and Dub had angrily pulled the door closed behind the both of them. Then, burying her face in the smelly, lumpy mattress, she surrendered to the hot tears and shattering chills that tore through her body.

By God, if I get the opportunity, I'll kill him, I swear it! Courtney repeated the vow over and over again like a litany.

"Phillip, will you please sit down! Pacing the room will not get her back any faster." Charles Tremain-Smythe frowned at the young man circling the spacious sitting room in the opulent hotel suite.

"I know that, but I feel so bloody useless!" Phillip Barrington came to a halt at the wide window that overlooked the swimming pool fourteen floors below. Slanted rays from the glaring afternoon sunshine struck sparks off the stone set into the ring he held between his thumb and forefinger. "Shouldn't we have heard something by now?" The face he turned to the older, calmer man was scored with lines of strain. He had not slept since leaving London the previous afternoon.

"I'm positive we'll hear any and all news immediately the authorities find her," Charles replied soothingly. Rising from his chair with unstudied elegance, he crossed the room to the window. "That is, unless this Rio McCord finds her first." A brief smile touched his lips, easing the austerity of his aristocratic face.

"Who is this Rio McCord? What do you know of him?" Phillip questioned suspiciously, his frown darkening into a scowl.

"I know nothing of him," Charles answered candidly. "But Morgan not only trusts the man implicitly, he has a great deal of faith in the man's ability to find people. And"—he held up a detaining hand when Phillip would have spoken—"*I* have a great deal of faith in Morgan."

"That may well be," the younger man murmured sourly. "I for one think you'd do well to put your faith in the authorities." As the beginnings of a frown drew Charles's brows together, Phillip forestalled an argument by continuing, "I hope, since you've agreed to the kidnappers' demands, they'll release Courtney as soon as they get their money."

"I hope the same." Charles sighed. "Yet I'm not encouraged that they will."

At dusk a built-in alarm went off in Rio's head. He came fully awake at once, alert to his surroundings and the slightest of rustling noises. By the time darkness had shaded the hills from deep purple to near black, he was ready to move. Hot Foot was saddled, the bedroll was tied in place, the gun belt was buckled securely around Rio's narrow hips, soft moccasins had replaced the scuffed slanted-heeled boots.

"Time to go to work, boy. The key word is *quiet.*"

Tracker pricked his ears at the soft command; then, quivering with readiness, he followed his master as he silently blended into the night.

Employing all the expertise he'd acquired in Asia and South America, Rio approached the cabin with the silent stealth that had earned him the nickname "Night Striker" from his covert contemporaries. Shaking his head in disbelief at finding the entrance door to the cabin wide open, he knelt beside Tracker.

"Stay." Rio covered the dog's bony head with his palm as he whispered the command. "Wait." He was gliding away again as Tracker's bottom made contact with the ground.

Reconnoitering, Rio circled the cabin, coming up to the far end of a crudely-knocked-together, three-sided structure that housed the animals.

At the first uneasy movement by one of the animals he slipped silently inside the manger, murmuring in a shaman's chant, soothing and settling them before they had time to become alarmed.

There were five animals in the crude manger, three horses and two mules—exactly as he'd figured. That meant there were three men to contend with. Pleased with the odds, Rio was smiling grimly when he heard the murmur of conversation from beyond the far end of the structure. Whispering past the last two animals, he came to a noiseless halt at the rough board wall.

"What do you think Ben's doing in there?" a slurred voice wondered aloud.

"Huh!" The snort came from another equally slurred but cold voice. "I know damn well what he's doing. If I know Ben, by now he's got his fat hands all over that high-class dame's body."

"Lordy, she's somethin', ain't she?" The first

58

voice slurred away to a sigh. "But don't you think we ought to get Ben off her?"

"Hell, yes!" The one with the cold voice agreed. "And we're gonna too." There was a pause and a gurgling sound. "Just as soon as we finish this bottle." There was another pause, and a different sound to the gurgle, and then the voice heated up on a string of curses. "What the hell do you think you're doin'? You jerk! Go into the trees to do that!"

There was a whining mumble, then the shuffle of booted feet stumbling drunkenly over the uneven ground. The smile on Rio's lips turned feral as he melted back into the darkness; the animals didn't make a nicker of protest as he whispered by them. Slipping around the end of the manger, he followed the direction the kidnapper had taken into the trees.

Rio came silently up behind the man as he was zipping up his pants. A moment later the inept kidnapper dropped like a stone to the pine-needle-cushioned ground, felled by the stiffened edge of Rio's chopping hand.

Using the tape he'd slid into his pocket earlier, Rio securely bound the unconscious man's wrists and ankles. Not many minutes later he was performing an instant replay on the other man. Then, his lips twisting with disdain, he quietly saddled one of the horses and led it to the front of the cabin. Kneeling once more beside the quivering dog, he slipped the reins between Tracker's powerful jaws.

"Hang on to the leather, boy, and stay put."

Even as he issued the soft order, Rio was blending into the darkness of the open doorway. The brief exchange he'd overheard by the lean-to had

59

given him an inkling of what he'd find inside. Every muscle in his body tensing, Rio cursed to himself in several languages in a bid to keep his mind clear of conjecture.

Tension humming along her nerves and tautening her muscles into painful knots, Courtney crouched on the cot staring wide-eyed at the closed door. The evening meal had passed without incident, despite the fact that the food offered had been every bit as revolting as the preceding two meals. Fortunately for her sanity the cold-voiced Dub had stood guard outside the bedroom door throughout the reenactment of the morning and noontime ritual.

But full darkness had now settled on the land, and revived terror stalked through Courtney's mind with the memory of Ben's muttered threat.

"Tonight, after the others are asleep, we're gonna get it on."

Courtney's midriff ached from the clenching and roiling in her stomach. Her head pounded from the effort of straining to hear every tiny noise. Her eyes burned from maintaining an unblinking gaze on the door. At least, she thought wearily, she'd had the foresight to raise the window shade while free of her bonds. In contrast to the night before, pale moonlight lent some illumination to the shadowy room. The waiting was making her ill.

How long before the others turned in for the night? The question revolved in her mind sickeningly. How long before that slimy creature slithered into the room? Merely speculating about the odious Ben sent waves of horror washing over Courtney's entire being. Then, with a barely noticeable scraping, the door was slowly opened, and the waiting was over. Ben's low growl reached her even as she opened her mouth to scream for Dub.

"You might as well save your breath—they're both outside."

"But they'll be back!" Courtney's high pitched voice betrayed her fear.

"Not for a good long while." He snickered, moving closer to the cot. "They're halfway into a bottle I just happened to have with me." Grabbing the blanket, he tore it from her and flung it aside.

Resolution covered Courtney's mind like a shroud; she would have to die—but not without a fight!

Courtney struggled against Ben with all the strength of a demented person. It was a losing battle, and a painful one. Her resistance only served to make Ben more brutal than he'd been before. Concerned only with his lust, he would maul her, inflicting bruises on her tender skin and scars on her mind.

Tearing the bonds from her ankles with vicious fingers, he clutched at the delicate flesh of her inner thigh. "You're gonna learn what it feels like to have a man between your legs, Miss High-and-Mighty," he snarled, forcing her thighs apart to kneel between them. Grasping her bound wrists with one hand, he drew them up, over her head, laughing nastily as she twisted and arched her hips to get away from the disgusting feel of him. "Yeah, you're gonna bump and grind for me, sister." Courtney jerked violently, crying out in protest when he pushed the heel of his hand between her thighs.

They were both breathing heavily, Courtney from fear and inflamed rage, Ben with consuming lust. Neither one heard the soft click of a pistol being cocked. Courtney became aware of a change in the situation when Ben froze. A soft, raspy voice chilled the air.

"Take your grimy hand off the woman, you scum bag."

CHAPTER THREE

Ben snatched his hand away from her body as if from a red-hot stove plate.

"Now let go of her hand." The quietly rasped command was obeyed instantly.

Her body bathed with the sweat of exertion, her breathing ragged and uneven, Courtney lay absolutely still while her rattled mind grappled with this new, and possibly even more dangerous, threat.

The intruder stood just beyond the pool of moonlight that washed the cot with its pale glow. All that was visible of him was the lower half of his arm and his hand, which was wrapped securely around the butt of a long-barreled pistol, glimmering a deadly blue-black. The tip of that barrel was touching the back of Ben's oversized head!

Motionless, fighting a fresh surge of panic, Courtney felt the muscles in Ben's legs tense, as if to spring. Somehow, someway, the intruder felt or sensed the tensing also.

"Yes, do it," the raspy voice coaxed softly. "Give

me an excuse for killing you." When Ben again froze in place, the intruder laughed—unpleasantly. "No? I didn't think so. Pity." He jerked the revolver. "All right, slob, back away from her and get off that cot . . . very slowly, and very carefully."

Ben carried out the order to the letter. Barely breathing, Courtney strained to see the intruder as Ben withdrew, instinctively positive the man was infinitely more dangerous than all three of her abductors. The ensuing action had Courtney boggling in disbelief.

The moment Ben cautiously backed away from the cot, the intruder's arm arced up, and then down with incredible swiftness. The pistol struck Ben's skull with a dull thunk; Ben's body struck the floor with a loud crash.

The panic ballooned inside Courtney's mind, tightening her chest, blocking her air passages. Without conscious thought she began moving, inching back on the cot into a crouching position. Her movements did not go undetected.

"You have nothing to fear from me, Miss Smythe." For all its softness the raspy voice reached Courtney's ears clearly. "I've come to take you out of here."

The rush of relief was weakening. Hanging on to the last of her composure by a very thin thread, and sheer will, Courtney dragged a calming breath into her constricted lungs.

"You . . . you're from the FBI or police?" she finally whispered.

"No, ma'am."

"But—" Courtney swallowed, almost afraid to continue.

"I'm Morgan Wade's friend," he inserted sooth-

64

ingly. "Morgan . . . ah, asked me to look for you."

"Morgan!" Courtney could have wept with relief. "Oh, thank God! I . . . I . . ." Searching her mind for adequate words, she fell back on the trite but sincere. "And thank you, Mr. . . . ?"

"McCord. Rio McCord. And you're welcome." A trace of humor lightened his tone. "Now I think we'd better get out of here." His leg came into view in the moonlight as he nudged Ben's unconscious body with a moccasined toe. "I don't know how long fatso here will be out of it."

With his observation the tension was back. "There are two more of them!" Courtney informed him, her gaze flashing to the open doorway as she scrambled off the cot.

"Not to worry," Rio murmured, turning away as she scooped the blanket from the floor. "The other two are in the same never-never land as that thing on the floor." Even in the darkness Courtney could see his head move, as if he were searching for something. "I don't suppose you have any idea what they did with your clothes?"

"No." Beginning to shiver in the chill night air, Courtney drew the blanket around her. "They are not important. I just want to get away from this place."

"Right." His movements silent, Rio glided toward the doorway. "Let's move. I have a horse saddled and waiting for you."

Rio shot one look around the room, then stepped through the doorway. "I'll have a look in here for your things," he called back softly from the other room. She was about to follow him, but a mere moment later he stepped through the doorway, a neatly folded bundle in his arms.

"I found your clothes and handbag." Crossing the room, he cast a wry glance at the unconscious Ben as he dropped the articles on the bed. "That animal will likely be out for a while," he observed dryly. "But I think I'll immobilize him just the same." Moving with that swiftness Courtney could barely follow in the dimly moonlit room, he secured Ben's ankles and wrists with tape he removed from his pocket. "Be as quick as possible, please," he advised softly as he left her to dress.

For a woman who never dressed in less than an hour, Courtney set a record for herself, pulling on the silk blouse, stepping into the badly crushed suit skirt, and shrugging into the matching jacket. Ignoring her pantyhose, she slid her feet into the high-heeled leather pumps, scooped up her purse, then hurried from the room. Rio was standing at the entrance door, his back to the room.

"Ready?" he asked without turning.

"Yes." Courtney's eyes darted around the trash-littered room as she walked to the door. The curl of disgust on her lips eased as she strode from the cabin into the cold night air. A low, menacing growl stopped her in her tracks.

"Behave yourself, boy," Rio murmured from beside the patiently waiting horse. "Come on, Ms. Smythe, Tracker won't hurt you."

Courtney moved toward Rio cautiously and was practically on top of both man and horse before she could discern the large dog. The dog was standing at the right front leg of the horse, reins clamped tightly in his long jaws, tethering the animal securely. Prudently Courtney gave the canine a wide berth as she circled around to Rio.

The cleared area in front of the cabin gleamed silvery white in the glow from a melon slice of moon. Coming to a stop less than a foot from her rescuer, Courtney got her first real look at him. The sight of him provoked contrasting feelings of reassurance and trepidation.

He was taller than he'd appeared in the shadows of the small bedroom, and he had the type of lean body that indicated hard strength. In the watery illumination his hair was an indescribable dark color, as were his eyes. But it was his face that gave Courtney pause. The features were sharply defined, the lips thin, the jaw unrelenting, giving the impression of rocklike hardness and fear-inspiring ruthlessness. Unthinkingly Courtney took one step back. A shiver ran the entire length of her body as he swept it with a narrow-eyed glance.

"You can't ride dressed like that," he said flatly, indicating the straight skirt hugging her hips and thighs.

"I'll manage," Courtney replied stiffly, imagining herself hiking the garment up around her hips.

"Like hell you will." Moving with the mercurial quickness he'd displayed in the bedroom, Rio leaned forward to grasp the hem of her skirt at the side seam. With one sharp tug of his long fingers the seam came apart to the top of her thighs.

"What are you doing?" Courtney gasped. She tried to step away, but was not quick enough. With a ripping noise that sounded loud in the stillness, he tore open the seam on the other side of the skirt.

"Freeing your legs," Rio drawled laconically—after the fact. Moving to the side of the horse, he cupped his hands. "Come on, I'll give you a leg up. We've got to move."

"That won't be necessary," Courtney said tightly, ignoring his cupped hands as she ap-

67

proached the animal. Out of the corner of her eye she saw him shrug and step back as she stepped into the stirrup and swung gracefully into the unfamiliar feel of the Western-style saddle. As she reached forward to gather in the reins, Rio plucked them from Tracker's mouth.

"I'm afraid you're going to have to keep your seat by hanging on to the saddle horn." Rio's voice came to her even more softly as he walked away. "I need the leather to lead your horse out of here." He gave a gentle tug on the reins to start the animal moving.

Courtney was an excellent horsewoman and at any other time would have had little difficulty in "hanging on" to the horn to retain her seat. But now, very close to the edge of both mental and physical exhaustion after her ordeal, she had little choice but to hold on for dear life.

The going was far from easy over rough terrain in the meager light from a moon playing hide and seek with a few errant clouds. Holding her nerves together, and her body erect in the saddle, became a challenge Courtney was determined to meet. Traversing the canyon was a test she very nearly failed. She was relieved when Rio brought his horse to a halt.

Courtney frowned in confusion. Where were they? she asked herself bleakly. She could see no signs of habitation anywhere. They were still in the hills. A low murmur and a shadowy movement to her right attracted Courtney's attention.

Rio stood beside his horse, gentling the animal with crooning murmurs.

"Steady, boy, we're going home now." Stroking the arched, quivering neck of the horse with one hand, Rio lifted a wide-brimmed hat from the saddle horn and put it on his head, settling it low on his forehead with one swift tug. As he turned to face her, he scooped a garment from on top of the bedroll. "You'd better put this around your shoulders," he advised, walking toward her horse. "The nights can get pretty cold in these mountains."

Though Courtney was already feeling the truth of his statement, she shook her head. "I'm fine," she insisted, noting the lightweight shirt he was wearing. "You keep it, my jacket is quite warm enough," she lied evenly, hoping he could not discern the goose bumps coating her thighs—what good would his jacket do her legs, at any rate?

"Suit yourself." Shrugging into the waist-length jacket, Rio unfastened a coil of rope from the saddle before turning back to her. "I don't want to lose you on the way down," he murmured dryly, tying an end of the rope to the harness. "Ready?" Tilting his head back, he stared directly into her eyes.

"Yes." Though her voice was faint, it held steady.

Rio turned away at once. Sliding his moccasin into the stirrup, he literally stepped into the saddle in one smooth, blurring motion.

"Okay, Tracker. Get us the hell out of these hills."

As if he understood his master perfectly, Tracker loped to a few feet ahead of Rio's horse. Alternately sniffing the ground and lifting his long head to glance around watchfully, he led the way down the trail they had made early that morning.

Her insides cringing at every noise, Courtney could not prevent herself from glancing over her shoulders periodically in fear of seeing her abductors in hot pursuit. At regular intervals scenes from her captivity flashed through her mind, especially those terrifying moments when Ben had tortured her with his lecherous and sickening attentions. Less than an hour after they'd taken to the trail, Courtney was trembling violently from cold and reaction.

Incredible! A smile tugged at Rio's thin lips as the observation shot through his mind for perhaps the tenth time. If he had thought Samantha was some kind of woman—and he most definitely had—her cousin Courtney was absolutely incredible.

Following Tracker's lead with automatic ease, Rio savored the memory of the way Courtney looked as she'd stepped into the revealing glow of moonlight. Her skin had the shimmer of white satin. Her hair, unbrushed and tangled, had the sheen of gleaming gold. Her mouth, free of artificial color, and trembling, had the allure of luscious wild strawberries.

Now, as he had then, Rio was filled with an urgent need to crush the wildness out of those trembling lips, making them his. The one need spawned another, hotter need in the part of his body that pressed against the saddle.

Damn! he reflected, acutely uncomfortable. How had one family managed to produce two such ravishingly beautiful women? No wonder Morgan had worn that oddly amused expression on hearing Samantha describe her cousin simply as tall, slender, and blond!

Rio's eyes narrowed dangerously at the memory of the scene he'd witnessed on entering that bedroom. How many times had that scene, or one similar to it, been enacted during Courtney's captivity? Rio tensed, experiencing again the scorching fury he'd felt in the cabin. Even in the pale moonlight he'd seen the sweat that slicked her body from her struggle with the would-be rapist.

Had that fat slob succeeded in violating Courtney's beautiful body? The speculation locked his features into granite. In the hours she'd been held hostage in that stifling room, had he, and possibly all three of the kidnappers, raped her?

Closing his eyes briefly, Rio felt an angry regret at having left the kidnappers alive. For one flashing instant he was tempted to go back and finish the job as he would have in the jungle.

Rio shifted in the saddle to check on Courtney and raged inwardly at the kidnappers as his sharp glance noted the rigid set of Courtney's jaw and spine. Experience told Rio that she was hanging on to both the horse and her composure by a very thin thread. How long would it be, he reflected, before that thread snapped, leaving her dangling and exposed to the buffeting winds of reaction and shock?

A low, whining sound from Tracker's throat drew Rio around in the saddle just as the dog was leading them into the back of the Henderson property. Rio felt like whining with joy himself.

As Rio had confidently expected, the Jeep was exactly where he'd parked it early that morning. He reined in Hot Foot and dismounted, then bent to run his palm rewardingly over the dog's head and down his quivering neck.

"Good work, Tracker," he congratulated softly, turning to grasp the reins of the other horse.

As he gazed up at Courtney, Rio felt a tightening in his chest. Her eyes were drooping with weariness and her face was dead white with shock. When she shook herself alert valiantly, the tightness spread to his throat. This cousin of Samantha's was some gutsy woman, Rio decided in admiration.

By the time the horse stopped jostling her aching body around in the unfamiliar saddle, Courtney's mind had long since lost any notion of where she was or why she was there in the first place. She was so very cold, and so tired, that, at that moment, she would gladly have died—just to get the rest.

"Where are we?" she asked dully, focusing her eyes and attention on Rio.

"Not much of anywhere." He reached up to grasp her around the waist. "But at least we're out of the hills," he added encouragingly, sliding her effortlessly from the saddle into his arms. He felt the chill on her skin the instant her body touched his. "Damn, you're freezing!" he muttered, cursing under his breath.

Carrying her to the Jeep, he settled her onto the front passenger seat, then reached into the back for the blanket that was always kept there.

"This isn't too clean," he said in a rough but concerned tone. "Still, it will warm you." Tucking the blanket around her, he demanded impatiently, "Why didn't you call out . . . tell me how cold you were?"

Snuggling into the sweet warmth of the scratchy old Army-issue blanket, Courtney managed a weak smile. "I was too busy clinging to that saddle horn, and clamping my teeth together to keep them from rattling out of my head," she retorted as he slid into the seat beside her.

Rio's soft laughter flowed over her like a soothing balm, sparking a curious curl of response deep inside that Courtney was beyond understanding in her muddled mental condition. All she comprehended was that the feeling was rather pleasant.

"I like your style, lady," he observed seriously, firing the Jeep's engine. "You'd do to ride the river with."

"Thank you," Courtney murmured, surrendering to the pull of her weighted eyelids; reflection was simply too much for her to handle at the moment. "I think," she added in afterthought, in a fuzzy, half-asleep mumble.

Rio's soft laughter was the last sound Courtney heard before drifting into a semiconscious fog.

Courtney was floating on swiftly moving clouds that kept colliding with other, jagged clouds, jarring her, tossing her to and fro. Sinking deeper into the strangely scratchy cumulus, she drew herself together in an attempt to ride out the buffeting of atmospheric pressure. As she broke through the clouds' flat bottom she jerked erect, eyes flying wide at remembered terror.

"Steady." Rio's voice, as scratchy yet comforting as the blanket around her, chased away the demon of memory. "You're safe, Ms. Smythe." The assurance was backed by a strong arm that shot out protectively, preventing her from flinging herself against the windshield.

"I was falling!" Courtney's breath was expelled on short, ragged puffs. "I had no control!" A shudder tore through her body. *"I had no recourse!"* Courtney knew as well as the man sitting beside her that she was no longer referring to her dream.

"I know the feeling." Rio grunted in understanding. "I've been there."

"I hated it! I hated the feeling of helplessness. And I detested the feel of that man's hands!" Hearing the growing note of hysteria in her voice,

73

Courtney clamped her lips together; feeling the tremors increasing in her shuddering body, she hugged herself to contain them.

But reaction had taken over and the shudders overpowered her clasped arms, and the need to purge in words broke the barrier of her lips.

"I was so frightened," she babbled on. "I've never been so very frightened. I wanted to kill!" Courtney closed her eyes, agonized by the remembrance of the bloodlust she'd felt. "I was actually consumed with the need to kill that disgusting man!"

Courtney was no longer aware of riding in the Jeep. In her mind she was back in the mountain cabin, experiencing all the sensations and emotions that had terrified her throughout her captivity. A sharply voiced command snapped her back into the here and now.

"Stop it, Courtney!"

Her breathing stabilizing, Courtney opened her eyes, unconscious of the fact that her rescuer had used her given name for the first time.

"I'm sorry." Swallowing convulsively, she imposed control over her screaming nerves by sheer strength of will.

"Don't be," Rio grated softly. "But don't let it destroy you either." Bringing the Jeep to a stop, he turned to face her, an understanding smile softening the harshness of his set features. "We're here, in *my* territory. You are safe now."

Not knowing Courtney had been rescued, the fourth kidnapper placed a call. What little color there had been on Charles Tremaine-Smythe's face drained as he listened intently to the muffled voice over who knew how many miles of telephone wire.

"You're stalling, Smythe, and we're not waiting any longer."

"No, really!" Charles protested, slicing an anguished look at the FBI agent standing with his back to the wide window. "My people cannot get the money to me before noon tomorrow!"

"Okay," the filtered voice snarled. "I'll get back to you sometime tomorrow morning with instructions for the drop."

"Wait! Don't hang up!" Charles's tone was edged with panic. "I insist you let me talk to my daughter!"

"You insist!" The caller laughed nastily. "The ring was proof that we have her. But you want more proof?" The caller laughed again, sending an apprehensive chill down Charles's spine. "How about one of her earrings?" he asked insinuatingly. "Still attached to her ear?"

"God, no!" Charles gasped, grasping the receiver to prevent it from slipping from his sweat-slicked palm. "I'll have the money by noon, I swear it." His aristocratic features tautened at the snicker that preceded the dial tone as the line was disconnected.

Standing on the other side of the telephone table Phillip seemed to have readied himself for a physical blow. "For heaven's sake, what is it, Charles?" he demanded hoarsely. "What did he say?"

His appalled eyes fixed on the watchful gaze of the agent at the window, Charles repeated the conversation. The agent crossed the room to Charles as he spoke, gently removing the receiver from his clutching grasp. The instrument rang an instant after the agent had dropped it onto the cradle.

Charles's stricken gaze flashed to the phone, then back to the agent.

"Answer it," the agent directed quietly.

Snatching up the receiver, Charles brought it to his ear and drew a deep breath before saying, "Tremaine-Smythe here." After listening intently a moment he sighed. "I'm sorry. Yes, I'll tell him."

"The tap?" The agent guessed correctly.

"Yes." Charles nodded in a defeated manner. "He couldn't get a trace. The call wasn't long enough."

"Dammit!" Phillip exploded, in a way that was completely out of character. "You people must do something!"

Unaffected, yet sympathetic, the agent smiled gently. "We are doing everything possible, Mr. Barrington. There are teams of our people scouring the area where the van was reportedly spotted. There are other teams chasing down every clue we've received on the phony cabdriver, and still more pursuing every lead we've picked up, regardless of how far out or far fetched." The agent shrugged helplessly. "A phone trace would have been of inestimable help . . . but, these men are obviously wise to that."

"Well, I still say—" Phillip argued doggedly; Charles cut him off in mid-bluster.

"Leave it, Phillip, please." Looking as though he'd aged ten years within the last few days, Charles walked slowly to the couch, lowering himself heavily to the cushion. "My brave, beautiful girl," he murmured, as if to himself. "Oh, Phillip, I only pray God I get to see her beloved face again."

It was close to midnight when the phone rang in the office-study.

"Wade here," Morgan snapped tensely into the receiver, clasping the trembling hand Samantha stretched out to him.

Rio came directly to the point. "I have her, Morgan. She's here at the ranch."

Relief washing through him, Morgan tugged on Samantha's hand to draw her close to his work-toughened body. "Courtney's safe with Rio, darling. They are at the ranch." Morgan felt his own throat thicken at the sob that was wrenched from his wife's. Holding her tightly to his side, he returned his attention to his silent, patiently waiting friend.

"What's her condition, Rio?" Morgan asked in the same terse tone.

"Shaky," Rio replied briefly. "Reaction has set in and she's in a mild state of shock."

"I'll leave as soon as I've notified her father," Morgan said briskly, smiling reassuringly into Samantha's tear-brightened eyes.

"No, Morgan." Though soft, Rio's tone relayed flat adamancy. "She's out on her feet, and not up to traveling. I'm going to put her to bed and let her sleep until she wakes naturally. Then I'll bring her to you." A hint of humor touched his voice. "Delivery is part of the job."

"Hang on, Rio," Morgan requested, lowering the receiver and covering the mouthpiece with his palm; Samantha had demanded to know what was going on.

"Rio says that Courtney's exhausted," he explained quickly. "He thinks it would be best if we let her sleep. He'll bring her here when she has slept herself out." When Samantha frowned her

77

disapproval he shrugged. "We know she's safe now, love. We can wait one more day."

"I want to talk to her at least," Samantha insisted, reaching for the receiver. Smiling in understanding, Morgan handed it to her.

"It's Samantha, Rio," she said in a tear-clogged voice. "May I speak to Courtney, please?"

"I'm afraid not, Samantha," Rio responded gently. "She's in the shower. She insisted on it the minute I brought her into the house. Said she had to be clean. Under the circumstances, I think that's understandable, don't you?"

"Yes, of course, it's just that I . . ." Samantha's voice wavered. "You're positive she's all right, Rio?"

"She's all right, Samantha," he responded confidently. "I give you my word."

Though she had no previous knowledge to go by, Samantha knew instinctively that Rio's word was all that anyone ever needed. Sighing softly, she accepted the added day's wait. "All right, Rio, we'll look for you sometime tomorrow."

"We'll be there," he promised. "Now, would you put Morgan back on, please?"

"Shoot, Rio," Morgan said as he raised the receiver to his ear once again.

"I've got some directions for you to pass on to the authorities, friend. I left some garbage in the hills for them to pick up."

Briefly but concisely Rio gave Morgan the exact location of the Henderson property and the trail he'd followed into the hills, detailing guiding landmarks. "Got that?" he asked when he'd finished.

"Got it," Morgan replied. "But will the garbage still be there when the collectors arrive?"

78

Rio laughed softly. "They won't be going anywhere."

"Rio, you didn't . . . ?"

"No, Morgan, I didn't." Rio's sigh was heavy with self-disgust. "I wish I had, but I didn't."

His expression thoughtful, Rio crushed out the half-smoked cigarette after replacing the receiver. Then, shrugging off the nagging certainty that he really should have eliminated the kidnappers, he strode from his in-home office. Let the authorities handle them, he mused. He had a shocked, exhausted houseguest to worry about.

Courtney had been so very intent on cleaning herself off that she'd barely noticed Cleat when he'd stepped from the shadows as Rio brought the Jeep to a stop. Indulging her pleas for an immediate bath or shower, he'd left Tracker, Hot Foot, and the other horse in his foreman's capable hands and escorted her into the house and directly to the largest guest room. Courtney had homed in on the bathroom like a missile. That had been approximately fifteen minutes ago.

Running a hand around the back of his neck, Rio decided he could do with a shower as well. But he wanted to reassure himself first that Courtney was comfortable. Dragging a velour robe for her from the depths of his closet, he left his own room to stride across the hall to the guest room. The door he'd deliberately left open still remained so. Even before he entered the room Rio heard the sound of water rushing from the shower head.

A frown drawing his dark brows together, Rio stood statue still, staring at the closed bathroom door. Was she all right? As the question sprang to mind, Rio wondered at the sharp stab of alarm it elicited. Dismissing the tension that suddenly gripped him, he turned abruptly and strode from the room, tossing the robe on her bed from the doorway.

Rio was not the man to tarry in the shower—he believed one bathed to become clean, not shriveled. Even so, prodded by the pale, desperate-eyed image of Courtney as she entered the bathroom, he knocked three or four minutes off his usual shower-and-shave ritual time.

With his damp hair lying in sculpted waves around his face and neck, and belting a mid-thigh-length terry robe around his otherwise naked body, Rio crossed the hall, eyes narrowing at the open door.

Damn, what was the woman doing? he railed inwardly. Though the sound of running water had ceased, the bathroom door was tightly closed. The velour robe was still lying where he'd tossed it. Picking it up he moved to stand less than a foot from the door, ready to hand the robe to her the moment she opened it.

"Ms. Smythe?" he called softly. When his call was met by silence, Rio grew really apprehensive.

"Ms. Smythe." His voice was stronger now, serrated with concern.

There was silence. Nothing. And then, a soft, whimpering sound, like a small animal in pain. Rio stepped to the door and yanked it open. The sight that met his eyes turned his spine to ice.

"Courtney!" The exclamation exploded from his constricted throat. "What in God's name . . . ?"

She was standing in the center of the floor, her wet hair gleaming in the glow of the indirect lighting, the water dropping off the ends mingling with the flow of tears coursing down her cheeks. She had wrapped a bath sheet around her slender body and, with one corner of it, was rubbing her shoulders and arms with wild-eyed determination. Where she'd rubbed her beautiful, pale skin was already dark pink and abraded.

A strange twist of emotion very like fear clawed at Rio's insides, and cursing softly, he dropped the robe and closed the space between them in one stride, stilling her action by grasping her wrist.

"What are you doing to yourself?"

"I've got to rub it away," Courtney mumbled distractedly, pulling against his hold. "Don't you understand?" She sobbed. "I've *got* to rub it away!"

"What?" Rio demanded, frowning darkly. "What do you have to rub away? There's nothing there!"

Flinging her head back, Courtney glared up at him from sapphire-bright eyes. "The feel of that beast's hand on me!" she shouted. "I must get it off!"

"Oh, Courtney." Sympathy and compassion gave Rio's naturally raspy voice a jagged edge. "It's gone," he murmured soothingly. Drawing her hand back, he exposed the irritated flesh. "You see? You've washed it aw . . ." Rio's voice trailed off. Eyes narrowing dangerously, he stared at the purple bruises on her shoulders and upper arms. He tore the towel from her hands, cursing viciously at the sight of the ugly marks Ben's brutal hands had inflicted on her perfect breasts and satiny thighs.

"That son of a—"

"Are you sure? Is it off?"

Amazed at the intensity of the fury raging in him, Rio draped the large towel around her and

81

led her from the bathroom. His voice a husky whisper, he murmured assurances.

"Yes, it's off." He brushed the wet strands of hair from her cheeks with incredibly gentle fingers, marveling at the tremor that ran the length of his arm. "There are bruises," he murmured. "But they will fade in time." Giving in to temptation, he allowed his fingers to drift to her eyes to brush at the tears flowing over the red-rimmed edges of her eyelids. "As will the memory of it all," he promised.

Courtney shook her head sharply. "It will never fade. Never!"

Her vehemence spawned the question that slipped past his guard. "Were you violated, Courtney?" With a confusing sense of shock, Rio held his breath as he waited for her answer.

"No!" Her head moved again in that sharp, negative way. "I wouldn't be here, alive, if I had been."

Rio didn't pretend for an instant that he didn't understand. "Don't talk like that!" he snapped, fury racing through him again. "You have everything to live for. You're a beautiful woman." Reflexively he grasped her arms, drawing her to within inches of him.

"Am I?" She sobbed. "Am I, Mr. McCord?" Sniffing, she brought her hands up between them to swipe ineffectually at the increasing flow of tears. "I don't feel beautiful. I don't even feel real." She gulped for breath around the wrenching sobs. "I feel like a thing, Mr. McCord. A *thing!*"

"You are not a thing, dammit!" Rio grated, tightening his grasp to steady her. "You're a woman, an exceptionally lovely woman."

Courtney stared at him with anguished eyes.

"Would . . . would you kiss me, Mr. McCord?" she pleaded. "And make me feel like a person instead of a thing?"

In the subdued bedroom lighting Rio's narrowed eyes sketched her face. Even with the puffiness around her eyes from weeping, and the strain of exhaustion pulling at her pale face, she was unbelievably beautiful. She had gnawed at her lips while rubbing her arms, drawing a flush of color to their fullness. The wash of tears lent an inviting slickness to her trembling mouth.

Wild strawberries. Rio shivered with the effort of imposing his will against the hot need rushing through his veins.

"You're tired," he rasped thickly. "You'll feel differently after twelve solid hours of sleep."

"No! I won't feel different!" Courtney closed her eyes as if in acute pain. "I feel subhuman. Do you have any idea what that feels like?"

Her anguished cry set a reel of memory spinning in Rio's mind. For an instant he was back in that bamboo cage in the jungle, teeth bared and snarling like an animal at his torturing, tormenting captors. Oh, yes, he knew what it was like to feel dehumanized. After his escape he had coldly meted out slow, agonizing death to cleanse and reclaim his soul. All Courtney was asking was to be kissed and caressed as a woman instead of a "thing."

And Rio wanted to kiss her, had in fact been aching to since his first glimpse of her in the moonlight. His fingers flexing into her soft flesh, he fought the temptation with an effort that extracted moisture from his brow.

"Mr. McCord, please, help me." Courtney was begging now, begging in a soft, sobbing tone that stabbed at his heart. "Oh, please, kiss me, love me the way a man loves a woman he thinks of as beautiful."

The lure of her soft, begging lips proved stronger than even Rio's considerable willpower. Lowering his head slowly, he touched his mouth gently to hers.

CHAPTER FOUR

The soft, comforting kiss Rio had thought to bestow singed his lips like a branding iron. Courtney's mouth was both the promise of heavenly attainment and the hell of unattainable satiation. One kiss was a joyous torment. A million kisses would never be nearly enough.

With a low groan Rio released her arms to slide his hands down her back, pressing against her delicate spine to urge her closer. A sighing whisper fluttered through Courtney's parted lips to tease his mouth and senses as her pliant body melted and flowed into his.

Muttering a curse against his own weakness, Rio crushed her soft lips with his hard mouth, drinking the essence of her in like a man with an uncontrollable thirst. She was wild strawberries, and warm honey, and sweet, exotic, forbidden fruit. Defying reason, Rio nibbled hungrily.

Driven by need, he slid his lips from hers to test the satiny texture of her cheeks and ears and the secret spot behind the delicious lobe. Courtney's whimper of pleasure as she curled her arms around his taut neck caused a flare of pain in his loins.

"Oh, you are beautiful, Courtney," he murmured into the curve of her neck as he trailed a string of moist, biting kisses from her ear to her arched throat. "And you are every inch a woman —never doubt it."

Berating himself for having taken advantage of her in her shocked, exhausted state, Rio moved away. As his crushing hold loosened, Courtney's tightened. Clinging to him, she arched her body into his.

"Don't stop, Mr. McCord, please don't stop." Breathing raggedly, Courtney skimmed her parted lips over his tension-tightened cheekbone.

"Dammit, Courtney! The name's Rio." Pulling his head back, Rio glared down at her with eyes burning like coals in his strained face. "And I must stop. You need rest and—"

"I don't need rest!" she cried angrily. "Damn you! I need to feel alive, vital, real!" Tugging on his hair, she drew his face to hers. "Make me real, Rio. Breathe your life into my dead body."

"Oh, God, Courtney, forgive me," he groaned, molding his mouth and body to hers.

Digging his fingers into her hair, he kissed her deeply, parting her lips wider and still wider, feeling a desire unlike anything he'd ever experienced before.

With her soft moans urging him farther into madness, Rio plunged deeper and deeper, extracting the flavor of her and drawing it into himself. His hands, restless and damp with sweat, roamed her back over the soft nap of the terry-cloth towel, until he grasped the material and dropped it to the floor.

The creamy warmth of her skin set a torch to Rio's body, and to the last of his good intentions. Fired by a demanding desire to know her, to love her, he skimmed his palms the length of her back, stroking her hips, her thighs, then lifting her to his naked body.

Fully expecting Courtney to withdraw in renewed fear from the intimate contact, Rio was shocked into momentary stillness when, murmuring encouragement, she parted her thighs while seeking his mouth with hers.

This time it was her mouth that ravished, her tongue that sought the smoky taste of his, her hands that grasped to feel all of his body.

Crazily spinning pinwheels of flashing lights exploded inside his head, and groaning in triumph and defeat, Rio drank the fire from her mouth as he urged her back, onto the bed. Even as she settled on the smooth bedspread, Courtney was holding out her arms, grasping hold of him to drag him down to her.

Sprawling half over her, Rio went again and again to the wellspring of desire that was her mouth. Sometimes sweetly tender, others deeply passionate, he kissed her over and over in a desperate attempt to smother a fire that only raged more wildly out of control.

As the passion consumed him, Rio learned every inch of Courtney's body with his hands and his mouth and his tongue. Spurred on by her whimpering murmurs of pleasure, he kissed and tasted her from her hairline to the slender arch of her foot and back again, feeding his own needs while building hers.

His breathing reduced to harsh gasps, his body slick with perspiration, Rio banked his own raging need in his determination to make Courtney feel "alive."

When Courtney came to the realization of how very much alive she was, she became every man's dream of the perfect love partner. Writhing beneath him, exciting him to the edge of endurance with her softly moaned pleas, she was all woman.

Rio brought her to completion the first time with his mouth. Grasping her by her hips, he absorbed the shudders that rippled in cascading waves through the length of her body with his own, making her pleasure his as well.

Refusing her rest now, he returned to her mouth, to tease and torment, until she was a gasping, pleading flame, burning for him, breathing for him, begging for him.

Anticipating the luxury of thrusting into the velvet softness of her, Rio slid between her legs, thrilling to the sensations sent through his body by the brush of his hair-roughened thighs against the satin smoothness of hers.

Watching her flushed face and cloudy eyes through passion-slitted lids, Rio lifted her hips with his splayed hands and began entering her slowly, savoring every nuance of pleasure. When she shifted suddenly under him, Rio assumed it was for her own fuller enjoyment, not because of any discomfort. Then, the need to bury himself in the softness of her overwhelming his control, he thrust his hips into hers.

Courtney's sharp outcry of pain froze Rio deep inside her, and brought an oath of amazement to his lips.

"Sweet Lord! Courtney, am I the first man?" Rio

knew the answer, of course. Even though he had disregarded the instant of resistance, he had recognized it for what it was.

Courtney Tremaine-Smythe was a virgin—or at least she had been until a moment before Rio's deep thrust.

"Courtney, baby, I'm sorry!"

Hearing the note of self-condemnation in Rio's softly spoken apology, Courtney opened her eyes and smiled up at him. Besides coming after her in the mountains, he had given her so very much. He had given her both pleasure and pain—but the pain as well as the pleasure had proved to her that she was not a frozen creature, but a warm, attractive woman.

And, in the deepest reaches of her mind, Courtney knew the frozen creature had existed long before the brutish Ben had ever touched her. Ben had merely added another layer of ice. Warmer now than she'd ever been, she likened herself to the fairy-tale sleeping princess, only she'd been wide awake, watching the world go by in a virginal state, waiting, waiting, for the one person capable of making the physical expression of love the perfect act of her expectations. Until now she had waited in vain, arrogantly determined to have all or nothing.

Her smile fading, Courtney studied Rio's harshly etched features. His was certainly not the face of a Prince Charming. But his face revealed character, and strength, and compassion, and vibrant, exciting life. Her drifting gaze settled on his strongly defined lips.

How could she have known? She wondered in awe, basking in the heat radiating through her.

When she'd asked him to kiss her to reaffirm her identity as a member of the human race, however could she have known that the frozen woman inside would go up in flames at the first touch of his fiery mouth?

At her lengthy silence Rio started to withdraw. Startled out of introspection, Courtney reacted to his movement by clasping her legs around the long, hard muscles of his thighs.

"No, Rio, don't!" Raising her arms, she cradled his frowning face in her hands, drawing him down to her parted lips. "The pain is gone," she whispered, outlining his lips with the tip of her tongue. She smiled as he drew his breath in on a soft hiss. "Would you now deny both of us the pleasure?"

As if he could not stop himself, Rio lightly kissed her lower lip. "But you're so damned beautiful," he said with a groan. "And I hurt you."

"Yes, you did," she admitted. When he stiffened, she stroked his tongue with hers. "But I'm alive, Rio. Really alive."

"You are that." Rio smiled with the release of tension. "Oh, God, baby! You are the most alive woman I've ever met." His kiss sent the sexual tension swirling through her again. "This man," he murmured excitingly, "could happily burn to a crisp in the fire of your very alive body."

Courtney smiled as his breath warmed her lips, then gasped as his hand found her breast, then moaned as his slowly undulating hips moved his body more deeply into hers.

"Pain?" he asked roughly, jerking his head back to study her expression.

"Pleasure." Courtney sighed. Gazing up at him she frowned in confusion. "Unbelievable pleasure," she murmured wonderingly.

Rio laughed softly, excitingly, heating her lips and her skin and her desire with his warm breath. "For me too," he whispered sexily, gliding his tongue along the sensitive spot on the inside of her lower lip. "Being inside you is like being sheathed in hot, wet velvet."

"Ohhh," Courtney moaned, closing her eyes to better enjoy the stabbing motion of his teasing tongue. "I never . . . never thought it would be like this!"

"Like what?" Rio prompted, sinking his teeth delicately into her lip. "Talk to me, beautiful woman, tell me what you're feeling."

Even though his hard body was on top of her, Courtney was experiencing the oddest, most delightful sensation of flickering, like a flame, inches above the mattress. Raising her heavy eyelids, she gazed in bemusement into the corresponding flame that leapt in the depths of Rio's midnight-dark eyes.

How strange, she mused, mesmerized by his compelling face, taut with desire. This man was a virtual stranger to her, and yet she felt not the slightest shame or embarrassment at sharing this most intimate act with him. Raising her hand lazily, she caressed his harshly etched features with her fingertips, absorbing each bone, every mark, into her skin. There was a thin white scar that arched his dark eyebrow, and was picked up again in a short, scoring line along his prominent cheekbone.

How had he gotten that scar? Even as she formed the question, the answer slammed into Courtney's mind. A knife! Someone had slashed out at Rio with a blade! Good Lord! How had it missed his eye? An image of Rio with one eye scarred into uselessness flashed into her mind. Responding automatically to that image, her fingers clenched on his dark skin.

"Feeling remorse, Courtney?" Rio asked tightly, turning his head to press his lips to the fluttery pulse beat at the inside of her elbow.

"No! Oh, no!" Courtney denied hoarsely. "That scar . . . Rio . . . ?"

"The scar is old, and forgotten," Rio murmured, stroking the now hammering pulse with the tip of his tongue. "Do you find it repulsive?" he asked, too quietly.

"Repulsive?" Courtney frowned. Then, indignantly, "Certainly not! But, what if it had caught your eye?"

"But it didn't," he chided, "so forget it." Stroking, stroking with his tongue, his mouth moved up her arm and over her shoulder. "Are you feeling shy with me, beautiful woman?" he murmured into the curve of her neck.

"Shy?" Courtney's frown deepened. "No." Her fingers speared into the silky strands of his hair. "Why do you ask?"

"Do you have any idea at all what you're doing to me, remaining still with my body inside yours?" he countered softly, raggedly.

"Oh!" Courtney gasped. "I'm sorry!"

"I'm not." His lips moved in a sucking action up the side of her neck and over her cheek to her mouth. "I'm rather enjoying the agony of anticipation."

Her humor sparked, Courtney laughed freely, and moved her hips invitingly. His low groan stilled her movement.

"Oh, Lord! Don't stop, beautiful woman." As she resumed the motion, Rio moved his body rhythmically with hers. "Now make it perfect, Courtney," he ordered coaxingly. "Talk to me. Tell me what you're feeling."

"Hot, so very hot!" Courtney said with spontaneous honesty. "And tense—inside, outside—an exciting tension. Free, and loose, yet strangely tight."

"Hmmm, yes." Rio's lips played touch-and-go with hers. "Yes, you are wonderfully loose, and excitingly tight." A low groan whispered into her mouth as he slowly increased the rhythm of his body. "It gets better," he promised.

"How—how could it possibly get better than this?" Courtney gasped, fighting for breath. Tension was mounting unbearably along her every nerve ending as he steadily increased the measured strokes into her body. "I don't know if I could bear it if it gets much better!"

Blindly following impulse, she raked her nails down his back, marveling at the steellike cords of muscle her fingers skimmed over.

"Yeah," Rio groaned into her mouth. "Oh, yes, I like that!" He was quiet a moment as he synchronized the rhythm of his tongue with his body. When she quivered in response, he laughed softly. "Better and better, hmmm?" he murmured in a darkly sensuous tone.

"Oh, yes! Oh, God, yes!" Clinging to his now slick back, Courtney sought his lips with hers. Their mouths fused, they melted together to reach perfect harmony, perfect union.

As Rio increased his rhythm in that final drive toward completion, Courtney sank her teeth into his shoulder to keep from crying out with the intensity coiling ever tighter inside. Yet, when ec-

93

stasy gripped her, she flung her head back to cry his name hoarsely.

"Rio!"

Rio's answer was silent, yet eloquent. His body shuddering, his breathing harsh, he crushed her mouth with his.

In the long, long moments after passion, while the earth slowly righted itself on its axis, and thumping hearts and gasping breaths returned to normal, Courtney and Rio lay entwined, stroking each other softly, not yet ready to give up the afterglow of loving.

When he felt her shiver, Rio tightened his embrace. "You're cold, and you're tired." With the gliding motion she'd come to recognize as natural to him, he sat up, taking her with him. "Let me put you under the covers. You must rest."

Feeling wonderfully taken care of, Courtney smiled at him sleepily. "What I really *must* do is use the bathroom," she murmured, inhaling the musky, all-male scent of him appreciatively. "If you'll hand me that towel, please?" Even as she spoke of moving, she snuggled into the warm strength of him.

"Not the towel," Rio corrected, reluctantly disentangling himself from her. "There's a robe here somewhere." Sliding off the bed, he moved to the foot end. "Ah-ha," he grunted, bending to scoop the velour robe off the floor. Straightening, he held it open and shook it lightly. "Come put this on, Courtney," he ordered softly. "I can hear your teeth chattering from here."

Courtney obeyed him instantly, scrambling from the bed without giving a moment's consideration to the fact that she never obeyed orders from anyone. Closing her eyes, she leaned back against

94

him as he wrapped her in the smooth material that, for all its warmth, was not nearly as comforting as his embrace. Her sigh of contentment was met by his delightful, gravelly laughter.

"Go," he commanded, grasping her shoulders and aiming her toward the bathroom. "I'll straighten the bed."

This time Courtney's sigh was heavy with disappointment. She was practically out on her feet, and she knew it, yet she wanted nothing more than to stand there indefinitely, anchored to the lean hardness of Rio's body. When it became obvious that she was not going to move on her own, Rio escorted her to the bathroom door.

"Don't set up house in there, beautiful woman," he teased. "And don't close your eyes." Pushing the door open, he gave her a gentle shove. "Because if you do, I'll probably have to sweep you off the floor." Rio met her frown of confusion with a chiding smile. "You're nearly unconscious now," he explained. "If you close your eyes, you'll be asleep before your body hits the floor. Your lovely body has too many bruises now," he said harshly, reaching out to stroke her cheek with one long finger. Concern deepened the lines scoring his face from the edges of his nose to the corners of his mouth. "Don't be shy, Courtney," he urged tightly. "If you need help, yell."

Feeling absolutely cosseted, and loving it, Courtney favored Rio with a breathtakingly tender smile. "I will," she promised, shutting the door quietly.

The smile in place, she turned, then gasped in horror at the bedraggled urchin reflected in the mirror that ran the entire length of the bathroom wall. Was this the woman Rio had referred to as every inch a beautiful woman? Appalled, Courtney stared at the less-than-beautiful vision in the silvered glass.

Her hair was a wildly tangled mass framing her face and spilling onto her shoulders. Staring into the dreamy eyes in the mirror, Courtney frowned at the indigo-shaded smudges under her eyes and, now that the flush of passion had faded, the excessive lack of color in her cheeks. Rio was correct in his judgment, she mused wryly. If she should close her eyes, she very likely would be asleep before her body hit the floor!

Thoroughly captivated by Courtney's smile, Rio stood staring at the bathroom door in bemusement. Despite the ravages of exhaustion from her recent ordeal—*and* intense lovemaking—she remained the most stunningly beautiful woman he had ever gazed upon—or wanted.

And want her he did! Even now, after what was the most powerful sexual experience of his life, Rio could feel the stirrings of renewed hunger in both body and mind.

Approaching the bed, he stopped, narrowed gaze riveted to the rumpled, sea-green spread. The stain was small but glaringly obvious, the once bright-red color of life darkening as it dried.

Blood. Courtney's blood. Proof positive of her chastity prior to his invasion.

As he stared at the coin-sized spot, Rio's body swayed with the overwhelming urge that swept through his mind. Irrationally, unreasonably, he felt compelled to tear the spread from the bed and display it in triumphant pride.

The compulsion was ridiculous, if not downright crazy; yet, even as Rio attempted to convince him-

96

self the compulsion was crazy, he had to curl his hands into fists to keep from performing the act.

Lord! It wasn't as if Courtney had been his first woman or virgin. A man did not number his years to near forty without knowing both, even a man as selective as Rio. And, though it was true he had always had a particularly soft spot in his heart for the virgins he'd known, Rio had never before felt this overwhelming urgency to possess and protect.

The sound of the opening bathroom door snapped him out of the muddled confusion of his thoughts. Coming to an instant decision, Rio whipped around, strode to Courtney, and swinging her into his arms, walked purposely from the guest room to the sanctuary of his own bedroom across the hall.

Long after Courtney's breathing confirmed her state of exhausted sleep, Rio lay awake, holding her relaxed body close to his, glaring at the window that faced east as if daring morning to come one second sooner than scheduled.

A frown of concentration drawing his dark brows together, Rio studied Courtney's face as if to imprint her features on his memory.

When daylight came, and she woke, he would escort her to the Wade ranch in Nevada. Rio had never, even as a child, attempted to avoid facing reality. Now his reality was that Courtney Tremaine-Smythe was not only of a different country, but a different world, from a working horse-ranch west of the Pecos. Come daylight he would take her back to her own people. Until then he would hold her close, and yet closer, in an effort to fill the unfamiliar emptiness yawning inside him.

Dawn was encroaching on the horizon and Rio was losing the battle against the weights tugging on his eyelids when he was brought to alert awareness by the arousing feeling of Courtney's slim fingers hesitantly exploring the swirls of dark hair on his chest. Angling his head, he pressed his lips to her golden hair.

"What woke you?" he murmured into the silky strands that tickled his mouth—and fancy.

"I haven't the vaguest," Courtney responded sleepily. "Perhaps it was the need to touch you." Sighing, she rubbed her cheek over his chest. "Just to make sure you were still here."

Enduring the near pain of contracting muscles in his chest, and his stomach, and parts due south, Rio inhaled the sweet female scent of her. "I'm still here," he assured her huskily. "Go back to sleep." A ripple of sensation rushed through his body when her fingers caught on a few hairs as she fingered, then lifted, the medal he always wore around his neck.

"A talisman?" Her cheek slid excitingly over his skin as she moved to get a closer look at the coin-shaped medal.

"Not altogether." Rio smiled. "It has some sentimental value."

The chain holding the medal scraped his neck as she twisted it to examine it. "From a lady?" she demanded curiously.

"No." Rio laughed softly. "My father—the secretly superstitious Irishman."

"What does it represent? I can't make it out."

"St. Patrick."

"St. Patrick?" Courtney pulled back to stare up at him. "Why would an American wear a talisman of the patron saint of Ireland?"

"To keep the snakes out of the hair on my chest?" Rio asked innocently.

"Indeed!" Courtney arched one perfectly shaped brow elegantly, but the twitch of amusement at the corners of her lips ruined her effort at haughty disdain.

"It works too," Rio continued seriously. "There hasn't been a viper in the bush since my father slipped the chain over my head the day I left for the army."

"You were in the service?" Courtney asked interestedly, prudently ignoring the bit about vipers.

Rio smiled sardonically. "Like every redblooded American boy. I served my time right out of college and ROTC."

"Hmmm, fascinating."

As Courtney's fingers had now discovered the quickly hardening male nipples hidden within the springy curls, Rio wasn't sure whether she was referring to his statement or his body—but then, since a much more vital part of his anatomy was hardening just as quickly, he didn't really care much. Gliding his hands down her back, he gripped her enticingly rounded derrière.

"Courtney"—Rio's breath was expelled on a groan—"do you know what you're doing?"

Raising her head, Courtney gazed at him with the same innocence he'd shown her moments before. "Searching for hidden vipers?"

"You keep on and you're going to find something a lot more dangerous than a viper," he teased.

"I was so hoping you'd say that." Slowly, deliberately, she lowered her mouth to the hardened nipple.

The touch of her lips to his body sent a shaft of sheer pleasure rocketing through Rio's nervous system. He drew her slender hips into line with his, making her aware of the physical reaction she was eliciting from him.

"Maybe you should have gone back to sleep when you had the chance," he suggested thickly.

Courtney jerked her head back to stare at him in amazement. "Do I appear stupid to you?" she demanded imperiously.

"Not likely," Rio drawled. "Why do you ask?"

"I would have to be utterly stupid to prefer lying unconscious to this." Watching him closely, Courtney slowly rotated her hips, grinding her body into his.

"Oh, Jesus . . . Courtney!" Rio's body arched in reflex. "I . . . I . . . oh, Lord, yes!" The words were torn from his throat as, parting her thighs, she moved to straddle him.

Conflicting emotions stormed Rio's mind while sweet hot passion surged through his body. What was it about this particular woman that she could arouse him so very quickly, so very urgently? he wondered in a fleeting instant of lucidity. Then, as her silky thighs caressed the bunched muscles of his, rational thought retreated before the hot advance of rampaging need. Grasping her hips, he attempted to impale her, only to be frustrated by her quickly shifting body.

"Want to play games, do you?" Rio growled, releasing her hips to bring his hands up to capture her face.

"Yes, please." Her smile sensuous, Courtney allowed him to draw her face to his.

The gently cradling hold of Rio's hands changed dramatically the instant Courtney's mouth settled on his. With a convulsive kick he felt painful power surge into his manhood. Reacting instinc-

100

tively, he tangled his fingers in her hair to anchor her mouth to his. When she moaned and opened her mouth in response, he thrust his tongue deeply into the sweetness of her.

As had happened earlier, wild erotic lights danced behind Rio's eyelids before deciding to take a swim through his racing bloodstream. Despite his attempt at restraint, the urgency overpowered his control. He lifted her, then slowly settled her over him as he arched his body to thrust into the moist, sheathing velvet of hers.

"Rio! Yes, please!"

Courtney's outcry was a delicious spur to his urgency. Responding to it, he thrust up while pulling her hips down.

"Lean to me, Court," he ordered harshly, straining to drive his body more deeply into hers. As she lowered her slender torso to him, Rio shuddered with intense excitement at the sight of the desire flushing her face and clouding her eyes. "Yes, like that," he rasped encouragingly as her dusky nipple brushed his lips. "I want to taste you," he murmured thickly, closing his lips around the diamond-hard bud.

Giving in completely to the rioting clamor of his senses, Rio lavished attention on her perfect breasts, kissing, gently biting, suckling, first one, then the other, in equal measure. And all the while his body arched rhythmically into hers to the inflaming music of the sounds of pleasure she was making deep in her throat.

Fighting to hang on to the last shred of control to ensure her pleasure, Rio was quivering on the edge of ecstasy when he felt her tighten around him.

"Give in to it, beautiful woman," he urged

roughly. "Let go and soar with me." Gasping for breath, he gave one final thrust that raised his hips high off the mattress, attaining his own satisfaction at the exact instant he speared into hers.

His body shuddering, his teeth tightly clenched, Rio drank in Courtney's cry of repletion, and absorbed her rippling tremors into his own throbbing completion. When her trembling body collapsed onto his, he held her to him with an embrace at once fiercely protective and tenderly possessive.

How long they lay locked together physically and spiritually, he had no idea. For himself, he felt he could remain buried in the satin warmth of her forever. But, concerned for her comfort, he lifted her from on top of him to ease her onto the bed beside him, drawing her close.

"Go back to sleep now, wild lover," he advised softly. "You need more rest."

Courtney was quiet for so long, Rio believed she'd drifted back to sleep. Surrendering to the weariness dragging at his mind, he closed his eyes, only to have them flip open again when, seconds later, she spoke.

"Was I a wild lover, Rio?" she asked in sleep-slurred tones.

"Excitingly wild, satisfyingly wild," he replied in a voice husky with remembered pleasure. Amazingly, excitement curled in him again as Courtney, murmuring contentedly, stroked his chest with the tip of her tongue. His hands had begun moving in a reciprocal stroke down her spine when her voice froze him, inside and out.

"Then would you be willing to pay for that wildly exciting satisfaction?" she asked with stunning calm.

"What form of payment would you demand if I were willing, Ms. Smythe?" he inquired in a cold, remote tone.

With a convulsive jerk of her body Courtney reared back into a sitting position, her face pale, her eyes wide with shock.

"Rio, you misunderstand!" she cried.

"Then educate me," he half snarled, refusing to give in to the urge to fill his palm with her heaving breast. "What do you want?"

"Food, you odious beast!" Courtney articulated loudly. "Rio, I'm positively famished!" As if she had the uncanny power to read his mind, she grasped his hand and drew it to her breast.

"Oh, Jesus . . ." Rio cursed in an undertone for long seconds, all the while caressing her satiny skin with infinite gentleness. "Courtney, I'm sorry. Of course you're hungry." Reluctantly sliding his hand from her breast, he rolled away from her and sprang from the bed. "Come to that, my stomach is beginning to feel as if my throat's been cut! Sit tight, beautiful." Grinning at her, he pulled a pair of faded jeans from a dresser drawer and stepped into them. "I'll forage around in the kitchen and see what I can rustle up for us."

"But, Rio, wait!" Scrambling off the bed Courtney followed him to the bedroom door. "Can't I help you in some way?"

"Sure," he drawled lazily, swinging the door open. "You can get back into that robe, and take my brush to that mop of yours." At the startled expression widening her eyes he explained, "That tangled mop is every bit as inviting as your sexy body. Tame it, honey." Stepping over the threshold he shot her a blatantly sensuous smile. "Or I'll just have to tame it, and you, myself."

As he strode to the kitchen a burst of soft laughter rumbled in Rio's chest as Courtney's sweetly voiced rejoinder wafted back to him.

"I sincerely hope you're the type of man who keeps his promises, Mr. McCord."

Rio and Courtney ravenously devoured the hastily gathered repast of slices of cold roast chicken wrapped in warmed tortillas and chunks of canned pineapple, and washed it down with large earthenware mugs of darkly rich, steaming hot coffee.

Sitting cross legged on the bed opposite her, the remains of the meal between them, Rio drank the last of his aromatic brew while his gaze drank in the incredible beauty of her. In the now bright morning sunlight, Courtney's hair gleamed with varying shades, from ash blond to bright gold, all the way to the curled ends that tumbled over her shoulders to cover her breasts. Her eyes sparkled like many-faceted gemstones. Her cheeks glowed pink and dewy fresh from the shower she'd indulged herself in while he'd been in the kitchen. Her body curved invitingly, even through the luxurious pile of the velour robe.

Throughout his perusal of her, Rio was acutely aware of Courtney's eyes slowly taking his measure. When he raised his gaze to hers, she met it directly.

"Were you pleased with what you saw?" she asked boldly.

Rio's lips parted in a rare, teeth-flashing smile. "You are one fantastically beautiful woman, Courtney Tremaine-Smythe," he praised softly. "Beautiful in appearance. Beautiful in spirit. And beautifully wanton in bed." His smile growing dangerously sensual, he watched a flush of pleasure tinge her soft skin.

"Now it's your turn, wild lover," he taunted when the color had begun to fade from her cheeks. "Were *you* pleased with what you saw?" Before she could respond, he added, "And don't feel you have to be kind." His smile tilted into a devil grin. "My shaving mirror never lies."

"I'm rarely kind," Courtney retorted cuttingly —then spoiled the effect by grinning back. "And you are certainly not a matinee idol," she observed candidly.

"Thank God!" Rio laughed outright.

"Be quiet, it's my turn," Courtney scolded. "But there is a rugged who-gives-a-damn aura about you that intrigues, and goes well with your rather harshly delineated features . . . you know?"

Rio's deep laughter exploded in the early-morning quiet. "Only the British!" he gasped. "Only the British can manage such a left-handed compliment so elegantly—and make you love hearing it!" He met her gaze with shrewd intensity. "That is no aura, lady. I don't give a damn about a hell of a lot."

Courtney wet her swollen lips and smiled softly. "Has life been hard on you, Rio McCord?"

"No harder than I've been on it," he returned cynically. "Has life been easy on you, Courtney Tremaine-Smythe?"

"Up till recently, yes," she admitted. "I've had the usual number of bad moments, you understand, but hard?" She shook her head. "No, I'm afraid life has been extraordinarily easy on me."

"And then, so soon after 'recently,' I storm your defenses into the bargain."

"Oh, but the storm was beautiful, Rio," Courtney protested. "And long overdue." With a cool disregard for the food tray separating them, Courtney leaned forward to caress his cheek with her fingertips, following the creases from nose to mouth. "You were so gallant, and so very understanding of what I was feeling, and I do thank you most humbly, Rio McCord."

The realization that she was dead serious galvanized Rio. Sweeping the tray from the bed, he gathered her into his arms, taking her with him as he sank to the mattress.

Before his head touched the pillow, Rio had her mouth open under his, devouring her with a hunger that put his appetite for food to shame. In the back of his mind was the knowledge that before many more hours had passed he would be relinquishing Courtney into the care of her family.

Just once more, he promised himself. He would make love to her just one more time, and then he would let her sleep. Not comprehending the sense of desperation gripping him, Rio skimmed every inch of Courtney's body with his hands and mouth, knowing her—in every sense—more intimately than he'd ever known any other woman.

Curiously, Courtney's hands and lips moved every bit as avidly over his body, arousing him to a point almost beyond endurance, and answering a need, buried deep inside, that Rio wasn't even aware he'd had.

As their lovemaking flared into a pulsating inferno, all Rio was aware of was his gut-wrenching response to her, a response that drove him on and on in a quest to wring every ounce of sweetness from her.

Even before their breathing had leveled off, still clinging to each others' perspiration-bathed bodies, they finally slept. The harsh West Texas sunlight was powerless against the depth of their satiated slumber.

Less than four hours later Rio came awake instantly to the touch of his housekeeper's hand on his shoulder.

"I'm sorry, señor," she murmured, her eyes strangely sad. "It's the phone for you. Mr. Morgan Wade." Her lips curved in a soft smile as she ran a shy glance over Courtney's form, held within his possessive embrace. "Shall I tell him you are still asleep?" she asked hopefully.

"No." Rio's tone conveyed firm conviction. "Tell him I'll be there in a moment."

Sighing, but nodding her head in understanding, the sad-eyed woman retreated from the room.

Moving away from Courtney carefully, Rio slipped silently from the bed, then paused to stare at her regretfully a long moment. A smile played at the corners of his mouth; he realized she was everything he could ever ask for in a woman. But she was not for him. He had seen too much of the wrong side of the world, committed too many unforgivable acts. And yet that was not the reason he would be returning her to her family.

Courtney Tremaine-Smythe belonged in the drawing rooms of the privileged class. Rio McCord belonged to the earth—most especially the dry, West Texas earth. Except for a physical hunger for each other, that would, if indulged, probably fade swiftly, they had little in common.

With a final sweeping glance at her sleeping face, Rio turned from the bed, his movements soundless as he stepped into his jeans. Without a backward look he strode from the room.

CHAPTER FIVE

When Rio left the bed, Courtney awoke with a start and, for a moment, panicked. Then she remembered Rio—strong and loving—and she smiled as she headed for the shower. When Rio returned to the bedroom she was completely dressed, her weariness disguised by expertly applied cosmetics.

Entering the room silently, Rio came to a dead stop at the vision of her, bathed in the sunlight streaming through the windows. Her glorious hair was pulled back off her face and coiled into an intricate French chignon. The hairstyle exposed her aristocratic bone structure to advantage, lending an elegant, sophisticated image that was in direct contrast to the wildly disordered picture Rio carried in his memory. He disliked it at once.

In the seconds before Courtney detected his presence in the room, Rio skimmed her tall figure with an encompassing glance, his sharp-eyed gaze missing nothing.

Her suit, restored by Maria, made a bold statement for the advantages of exquisite taste and an unlimited bank balance. Everything about her, from the neat coil of her hair to the handworked leather of her narrow-heeled shoes, spoke eloquently of cultivated refinement. Courtney Tremaine-Smythe was a lady, in the purest definition of the word.

The smile Courtney bestowed on him, when she caught sight of him, took Rio's breath away—along with something else—something he was not yet ready to examine or identify.

"Good morning," she said softly. Her smile widened. "Or should I say, good afternoon?"

"Afternoon, I'm afraid," Rio murmured, frowning. "But not late enough in the afternoon. You should have slept longer." He went to his closet and was reaching his hand inside when her response momentarily froze him in place.

"I was cold . . . after you left the bed."

The simplicity of her statement caused a gentle ache in the depths of Rio's soul. It was past noon, in summer, in West Texas, and already the temperature was flirting with a higher than hundred degrees reading. His eyes closing briefly, Rio accepted her admission for what it was. Courtney had confessed to missing the warmth of *him*, not his body.

Ruthlessly blocking the rush of emotions her confession generated, Rio calmly chose a suit and shirt before turning slowly to face her.

"I left the bed to answer the phone." His smile was as remote as his carefully controlled expression. "The call was from Morgan. Your father is at the ranch, waiting anxiously for your arrival."

"Oh! Oh, good Lord! I haven't given a thought—haven't even considered . . ." Courtney's voice trailed away, along with what little color there was in her cheeks. "Poor father! He must be frantic by now." Guilt stricken, she looked at Rio imploringly. "We must leave for the ranch at once."

"Not quite at once." Rio's smile revealed none of the feelings churning inside him. "Maria has breakfast ready for you. You can eat while I shower and dress."

Though it was obvious Courtney felt impatient about the delay, she gave in gracefully. "Yes, of course." Her elegant body erect, she started for the door, then paused to glance at him over her shoulder. "Have you eaten?"

"Yes." It was an outright lie that didn't bother Rio in the least. Suddenly the appetite he'd awakened with was gone—just as the woman he'd awakened next to was gone, replaced by an exquisitely beautiful stranger.

"You go ahead, I'll be with you in a few minutes." Tossing his clothes onto the rumpled bed, he walked to the bathroom. "The kitchen is at the end of the hall." Stepping inside, he closed the door quietly.

Hours later, Rio watched Courtney as she slept peacefully on a seat inside Morgan Wade's private Learjet. In repose, Courtney's body revealed the weariness eating up the last of her reserves. Her skin gleamed with an unnatural, whitish color and there was a defenseless, vulnerable look about her that caused an ache of conscience in Rio's mind.

After her ordeal in the mountains, Courtney had needed rest, many hours of rest. Instead, she'd had brief periods of sleep between bouts of sexual calisthenics and now, here, on a less-than-comfortable seat in a small airplane.

The plane had been waiting for Courtney and

Rio at the landing strip Rio maintained on his ranch; Morgan had dispatched it to Texas early that morning. To Rio's mind the Learjet was unnecessary. Rio owned his own plane—a good one, if not a Lear. But Morgan had insisted and Rio gratefully accepted the jet.

What he could not accept was the news of the absence of any human or domestic animal presence at the cabin in the mountains when the authorities had arrived there early that morning.

Rio was no novice to the art of immobilizing a man. He had known that, without assistance, the kidnappers were not going anywhere under their own power. All of which indicated a simple conclusion: There was a fourth kidnapper—and Rio McCord should have known it.

Damn! Self-disgust left a bitter taste in Rio's mouth. How had he overlooked such a simple factor? There *had* to be a fourth man—because there had to be a contact.

Good thing you retired when you did, ole son, Rio chided himself scathingly. *If you hadn't, you'd probably have had your ass shot off by now.* To overlook the rudimentary element of a contact! Jesus! His expression grim, Rio shook his head in wonder. Then, understanding that hindsight was as useful as self-pity, he closed his eyes and went immediately to sleep.

The light touch of Courtney's hand on his forearm woke Rio a short time later.

"We'll be landing in a few minutes, Rio," she said softly when he opened his eyes. "The pilot is circling the air strip at the ranch."

Moments later they were on the ground, taxiing toward the small building that housed the sleek plane. As the plane approached the hangar, Rio could discern a group of people standing in front of it. Rio spotted Morgan immediately, simply because he stood a head taller than the others, and was the only one wearing the flat-crowned, flat-brimmed Andalusian hat Morgan preferred. And then he identified Samantha by the bright beacon of her flaming red hair. The other two members of the group, both men, were strangers to Rio, but obviously not to Courtney.

"That is my father, standing beside Sam," she said quietly. Then, with a sharp gasp, "And Phillip!"

Although Rio had a gut feeling he knew the answer, he asked the question anyway. "Your brother?"

Courtney turned from the miniature window to his expressionless face. "No." Her tone steady, she went on, "My fiancé."

A shadow of a curl he could not contain played over his lips. "I see."

"No! Rio, you must understand, I—"

"But I do understand, Ms. Smythe." Rio's voice rasped harshly. "The circumstances were more than a little unusual." His shrug effectively halted the argument she had opened her mouth to launch. The plane came to a smooth stop, and flipping the lock on his seat belt, Rio stood with lazy grace. "They're waiting." Stepping back, he executed a courtly bow. "After you, Ms. Smythe."

Before Rio's eyes, Courtney underwent a complete metamorphosis. Gone was the smiling, soft-spoken, wild love partner of the night and morning hours. In that woman's stead was the cool, haughty daughter born of the manor.

Like a creeping disease the gentle ache in Rio

spread outward, encompassing his vital organs, interfering with his breathing process.

Imposing his will over emotion, Rio straightened his spine and followed Courtney from the plane. In the emotionalism of reunion Morgan was the only one of the group to note Rio's presence. The smile that quirked Morgan's lips spoke eloquently of appreciation and relief. Rio accepted the smile with a barely perceptible nod.

Standing on the fringes of the group Rio coolly observed the tall, distinguished man who was obviously Courtney's father draw her into his arms.

"My dear, my dear," Charles murmured, unabashed by the tears evident in his eyes. "I was so dreadfully afraid for you." There was a muffled response from Courtney, then Charles studied her face. "You are unharmed?" he asked anxiously.

"I am fine, Father," Courtney assured him gently. "Really."

"Courtney?"

Rio's eyes narrowed on the slender, fair young man who had spoken her name uncertainly.

"Oh, Phillip!" Turning to him, Courtney stepped unhesitatingly into his open arms. "How wonderful to see you."

Every muscle in Rio's body tightened as Phillip embraced Courtney, and an instinctive urge for violence threatened to outweigh his common sense when the young man's lips took hers. Fortunately Samantha chose that moment to greet her cousin.

"Oh, please, Phillip, let me get a hug in!" Samantha chided, laughing and crying at the same time.

The tension in Rio's body eased as Phillip relinquished his fiancée into the arms of her cousin.

From Samantha, Courtney was turned over to Morgan, who gathered her close to murmur his delight at having her back.

While his attention was centered on Courtney, laughing up into Morgan's face, Rio was aware of her father moving toward him.

"Mr. McCord?"

"Yes?" Reluctantly, Rio shifted his narrow-eyed gaze from Courtney to the man responsible for her presence on the earth.

"Charles Tremaine-Smythe, sir." The clipped British accent didn't quite conceal the emotion woven through his tones. "I fear I owe you a debt of gratitude I'll never be able to repay," the older man continued, offering his hand.

Clasping the pale, delicate-looking hand, Rio was surprised to discover a handshake of solid strength. "You owe me nothing, sir. I'm glad I could be of assistance, Mr. Tremaine-Smythe," he added dryly.

"Charles, please, Mr. McCord," the older man urged sincerely.

"Rio, please"—Rio's lips tilted at a hint of a smile —"Charles."

"Why are we standing around here?" Morgan demanded, planting an avuncular kiss on Courtney's brow that shot sparks into Rio's dark eyes. "Let's get out of the sun and back to the house." Draping his arm around Courtney's shoulders, he caught Samantha's waist with the other. "I've got a case of champagne chilling to celebrate the occasion." Flashing the devilish grin that had melted many a female heart, Morgan led the group to the two cars parked to one side of the hangar.

Rio was about to announce his intention of returning to his ranch immediately when Charles,

114

reading his attitude with amazing accuracy, fore-stalled him in a firm tone.

"Please, join us, Mr.—"Charles smiled warmly—"Rio. It is due to you that this celebration is possible."

On the point of adamantly declining Charles's invitation, Rio caught sight of the infinitesimal spasm of annoyance that scurried over Phillip's face. Smiling sweetly—an expression that would have instilled a dread of warning into the heart of anyone who knew him well—Rio graciously accepted, lazily falling into step with the older man.

As they approached the vehicles, a brand-new estate wagon and a five-year-old Jaguar, Samantha said, airily, "I'll drive the family back in the wagon, darling. You can bring Rio in the Jag." Sliding away from his encircling arm, she turned, her hand held out for the car keys.

The expressive look Morgan gave his wife was a curious mixture of indulgence and admonition. "Play light-foot on the pedal, Red," he cautioned softly, dropping the keys into her palm.

"Morgan, really!" Exasperation heightened the trace of a British accent in Samantha's tone. "I have no desire to knock off my family by running the car into a damn ditch!"

The accent, coupled with the American slang, drew soft laughter from Morgan. "I'll follow behind you, just the same," he taunted, motioning Rio toward the Jaguar.

"Sam isn't a good driver?" Rio probed softly as Morgan tailgated the station wagon.

"Sam is an excellent driver," Morgan corrected, slanting a grin at Rio. "But, she is also a fast driver." He shook his silver-salted dark head. "I don't know what comes over her, but whenever she slides behind the wheel of any vehicle, whether it's this beauty or the oldest four-wheeled heap on the property, she imagines herself on the track at Indy."

Morgan's observation elicited one of Rio's rare, breathtaking smiles. "I've been hearing things about Sam for some years now." Rio offered the information casually, watching his friend closely.

"What 'things'?" Morgan's black eyes narrowed as he sent Rio a warning, sidelong glance.

Rio grinned. "Oh, mostly how very beautiful Morgan Wade's woman is." He chuckled softly. "On inspection I'd say it was a bit of an understatement."

"More than a bit." Morgan returned the grin, while keeping his eyes on the road and the wagon in front of him.

"I also heard that you nearly lost her a few years back," Rio went on. "Childbirth, wasn't it?"

"Yes." The change in Morgan was instantaneous and almost frightening. Tension tightened the smooth skin over his high cheekbones and added a serrated edge to his tone. "I was never so damned scared in my life, Rio," he confessed hoarsely. "Not before or since." A visible shudder rippled down his spine at the memory. "I felt a bloodlust to kill—doctors, nurses, everyone separating her from me." Collecting himself by inhaling deeply, he smiled with wry self-amusement. "I was ready to tear that entire hospital apart with my bare hands."

"You love her very much, don't you?" Although Rio posed it as a question, it was not one; he knew the answer.

"No, old son, I don't love her." The tension eased from his features as Morgan smiled. "Trite as

116

it probably sounds, I absolutely worship the ground that lady walks on."

They were quiet for some minutes, each with his own thoughts. Morgan's musings were pleasant, for a gentle smile teased his chiseled lips. Rio, on the other hand, frowned with the effort of comprehending a love so strong and deep. Was that kind of romantic love really possible? he wondered cynically. Or was his friend living in a fool's paradise? Unbidden, an image, too sharp, too clear, of Courtney, her hair wildly tangled around his fingers, her mouth hot and eager on his, rose to cloud Rio's thinking. In an attempt to banish the vision, and the resultant physical reaction to it, Rio spoke abruptly.

"Twins, weren't they? Boys?"

"Hmmm." Morgan nodded, then laughed. "And sometimes I feel positive they have the devil's blood in them. Of course," he tempered, "I can't say they're solely to blame. Sara has spoiled them outrageously since the day Sam and I brought them home." Morgan thus serenely indicted the woman who'd been the Wades' housekeeper from the day Morgan's mother married his father. And, after Morgan's mother, Betty, died in a car accident, Sara had taken on the role of surrogate mother to the two-year-old Morgan.

"How is Sara?" Rio asked, smiling in remembrance of the only woman who'd ever had the temerity to take him to task for his life-style.

"Bossy as ever." Morgan's smile was tinged with sadness. "Although a little of her fire dimmed when Jake died."

Rio nodded in understanding; Sara had been devoted to her husband Jake. "Jake was a good man." Sighing soundlessly, he slid his hand inside

117

his jacket to retrieve a package of cigarettes and held it out in offering to Morgan.

"Yes, he was." Morgan accepted the offer; then, after drawing deeply on the cigarette, he exhaled sharply. "At least he went quickly. The doctor said Jake was dead from that hemorrhage before his body hit the ground."

"There are worse ways to die." Rio agreed.

"And you've seen most of 'em, haven't you?" Morgan shot him a knowing look.

Rio smiled cynically. "I've looked at death a time or three. It's never pretty." A fine trail of smoke rose before his eyes. "And sometimes it's downright messy. But, either way, it's final as hell." He was pensive a moment, then rasped with soft violence, "I should have made it final for those bastards in the hills."

"Was she raped, Rio?" Morgan asked, very softly.

"No." The steel of conviction laced Rio's tone; no one knew better than he how chaste Courtney had been when he'd found her. "She'd been pawed and she was bruised and shaken, but she hadn't been violated."

With his mind's eye, Rio could see the bruises on Courtney's slender arms and legs, and on her silky breasts. His muscles tautening, he crushed out the cigarette, then immediately fired up another. Impatient with the memories that persisted in teasing his mind and tormenting his body, he spoke.

"So, what's the story on our inept kidnappers?"

Morgan shrugged. "There was a fourth man, of course."

"Don't remind me," Rio drawled disgustedly.

"You did what you were asked to do, Rio." Morgan, aware of the portent of fury in his friend's

118

oversoft tone, continued evenly. "The authorities can handle it from here."

"I suppose." Tension eased as Rio exhaled slowly. "Any theories?"

"Yeah." Morgan paused as he turned onto the drive to the house, shifting as the Jag began climbing the slight incline in the wake of the station wagon. "They figure that, for whatever reason, the fourth man went into the hills sometime before dawn and, after he'd freed his trussed-up partners, they lit a shuck for the Mexican border." As he finished speaking, Morgan brought the car to a smooth stop in the driveway behind the wagon. "Hopefully the authorities will round them up before long, once they have descriptions from Courtney."

"Hopefully," Rio repeated vaguely, his gaze clinging to the woman under discussion as she alighted from the wagon. Even pulled back into a bun, Courtney's hair gleamed like gold in the late-afternoon sunlight. Rio felt his hands itch with the desire to yank the pins from her hair and slide his fingers through the silky strands.

"Rio?"

Morgan's voice jerked Rio out of the forming fantasy. Tilting his head, he smiled wryly at the discovery that Morgan was out of the car, frowning in at him. "I'm right behind you, Morgan," he assured him, pushing the door open and stepping out onto the paved driveway.

"I was afraid you'd drifted off to sleep," Morgan jibed as they approached the entrance to the large L-shaped ranch house. "I know your habit of grabbing z's when the opportunity presents itself."

"I could use some," Rio admitted blandly. "I'm about out on my feet." He shrugged as he preceded Morgan into the house. "I wanted to go directly home. Mr. Tremaine-Smythe insisted I stay."

"The authorities are going to want to talk to you," Morgan said, ushering Rio into the living room.

"They know where to find me," Rio responded laconically, his manner belying the tension riding him again at the sight of Courtney once more enfolded in Phillip's embrace. *If he kisses her again, he's going to find himself on the floor, hurting like hell,* Rio vowed silently, sauntering into the room as if he hadn't a care in the world.

Courtney felt exhausted, and on the verge of tears. Rio had not so much as glanced at her since they'd deplaned.

Well, what had *you expected?* she charged herself bitterly, squirming delicately inside Phillip's possessive embrace. Rio was an unlikely candidate for avowals of deep affection on the basis of a one-night stand—or even an extended affair! Nevertheless, he might at least *look* at her!

"Champagne, darling?"

Startled out of her reverie Courtney forced a smile for Phillip. "Yes, thank you." Accepting the glass she sipped at the wine before asking, "When did you arrive in the States, Phillip?"

"Early yesterday morning." He grimaced. "Very early yesterday morning."

Cognizant of Phillip's propensity for sleeping until midmorning, Courtney made a soft sound of commiseration. "Poor, darling, such a bother."

"But not at all!" Phillip had the grace to flush. "I mean, naturally I had to come over!"

Courtney patted his glowing cheek. "There's a

120

dear. Now, I think I'd like to sit down." Turning toward an inviting couch she missed the glittering, narrow-eyed glare drilling her from the other side of the room.

"But, darling, wait! You're not completely dressed." Phillip halted her with a touch on her arm.

"I beg your pardon?" Though Courtney's tone was pitched as low as his had been, Phillip could not help but note the edge of hauteur in it.

"Your ring." Displaying her missing engagement ring he grasped her left hand.

"But how . . . ?" Courtney began, then smiled dryly. "Of course. They sent it to father, didn't they?"

"Yes," Phillip responded, slipping the ring onto her third finger.

An urge, a compulsion, something, made Courtney glance up. A gasp rose to clog her throat when she found herself caught by a flame leaping in the depths of Rio's dark eyes.

He's angry . . . no, he is furious! Courtney thought, a rush of excitement heating her body. Does the idea, the very meaning, of the engagement ring bother him? Breathing slowly, she glanced at Rio again and felt all the energy drain out of her. Rio had turned away.

What was left of the afternoon and the evening hours dragged intolerably for Courtney. All through the endless questioning by her family, and then by the FBI agent who arrived after dinner, Courtney longed for solitude and sleep. When, finally, Samantha escorted her to the guest bedroom and left her with a hug, Courtney flung her clothes off and dropped like a stone onto the bed. She was dead to the world within minutes.

And it seemed mere minutes later when a knock drew her from a dream in which a pair of dark eyes smiled instead of glared at her. Courtney was struggling into a sitting position when the gentle knock sounded again on the door.

"Yes?" she called softly, smothering a yawn with her palm.

"It's me, Courtney." Samantha peeped around the door. "I wanted to make sure you were still breathing. It's after one."

"In the afternoon!" Courtney exclaimed.

"Yep." Samantha grinned. "I've brought your breakfast," she announced unnecessarily, bumping the door wide with her hip and entering the room, a large silver tray in her hands. "Would you like it in bed or over there?" Sam indicated the samll table placed before a wide window.

"On the table, please." Yawning again, Courtney slid off the bed. "The coffee smells delicious." She inhaled appreciatively. "I hope you brought two cups."

"I did." Samantha laughed.

"Good. Pour out, then, I'll be with you in a moment." Pulling on her satin robe Courtney headed for the bathroom. After splashing her face with cold water, and brushing her teeth, she exited the room, a soft smile for her cousin curving her lips.

"Thanks again for unpacking my things, Sam." With a flick of her wrist Courtney indicated her nightgown and robe.

"It kept me busy while we were waiting for you," Samantha said, returning the smile.

Silence fell in the room while they sipped at the hot coffee; then Sam glanced directly at Courtney. "You are all right," she asked carefully. "Aren't you, Courtney?"

"Yes, darling, I am all right," Courtney assured her firmly. "There were a few bad moments when I was positive I'd never leave that disgusting cabin alive," she went on candidly. "But I was not raped, Sam."

The breath whooshed out of Samantha in relief. "I was an absolute basket case," she admitted. An expression of wonder widened her eyes. "And to think I didn't want Morgan to call Rio." She shook her head in self-despair. "If it weren't for him"—a delicate shudder moved her shoulders—"who knows what might have happened!"

"Yes," Courtney whispered, forcing composure to features that ached to crumble with tears. "If it weren't for Rio." *I would still be a virgin. I would still be innocent. I would never have known the rapture of his lovemaking,* she added to herself. Fixing a smile on her dry lips, she asked brightly, "Where is Rio, by the way?"

"Oh, he left for Texas this morning, long before anyone else was awake." Samantha paused to swallow her coffee, then corrected herself. "Anyone but Morgan, that is. Morgan drove him to the plane."

"I see." The sense of desolation was shocking in its intensity. Wanting to cry out in pain at his desertion, Courtney lowered her gaze to her breakfast because Samantha would surely detect the agony in her eyes. In a bid for time to collect herself she automatically lifted, then lowered, her fork, methodically chewing the food she didn't taste.

The plate was almost clean when Courtney decided her composure was as solid as it was going to get. "Tell me about Rio, Sam," she requested coolly, amazed at the steadiness of her hand as she refilled the cups. "I really didn't have a chance to get to know him." That is if one could overlook sharing the most intimate acts with him—and not merely once, but numerous times, she anguished silently. The first time could possibly be excused; the circumstances had been unusual, as Rio had pointed out. But what of the subsequent acts? What excuse could she manufacture for those? Courtney suddenly felt exhausted again.

Pressured, stressed, she shivered with relief when Samantha's cultured voice drew her from introspection. Later, Courtney promised herself; she would deal with the examination of self later. Her tone low with inner strain, she apologized for her inattention.

"I'm sorry, Sam, but would you repeat what you said? I . . . I'm afraid I was distracted and didn't hear you."

Samantha's smile held a depth of understanding only another woman could feel for Courtney's mental state. Replacing her cup on the saucer she reached across the table to grasp Courtney's hand.

"Please, don't," she said softly. "Darling, there's no need to apologize to anyone, least of all me. I'm family, remember? And so is Morgan. We want you to feel free here, to rest and try to put the memory of it behind you." Blinking suspiciously she squeezed Courtney's hand. "Will you do that?"

Forget? Good Lord, she would never forget! Courtney's mind raced. That frightening ride through the night. That filthy cabin in the hills. Those horrible men. That beastly Ben. Rio! Dear God, Rio! Why had he returned to his ranch so quickly? She needed him! Didn't he know how very badly she needed him now? Or did he simply not care?

124

The muscles working in her throat, Courtney closed her eyes, fighting desperately to reassert her composure.

"Would you like me to leave?"

"No!" Courtney's eyes flew wide. She couldn't be alone, not yet, and Rio had gone. Turning her hand, she clasped Samantha's in a crushing grip. "No, don't go. Talk to me, Sam, please," she pleaded. "Just keep talking. I can't bear my own thoughts at the moment."

Samantha launched into a monologue before Courtney had finished her plea. Her tone light and airy, she commenced chattering on every and all subjects that sprang to mind, from the antics of her sons to the vagaries of Wall Street. The even cadence of her voice was balm to Courtney's nerves, and slowly the tension lessened in her chest. The coffee had long since grown cold in the china cups when Samantha wound down, then stopped speaking altogether.

Calm now, if not serene, Courtney again pressed her fingers against Samantha's. "Thank you," she murmured simply.

"Better?" Sam studied her anxiously.

"A great deal, actually." Courtney managed a brittle chuckle. "At least I no longer have the terrifying feeling that I might shatter at any moment."

Setting her chin determinedly Courtney slid her chair back and stood up. Following her example Samantha rose also, a questioning arch peaking one dark red brow.

"I'm going to dress," she answered Sam's mute query. "I'm sure father is worrying by now."

"And Phillip?" Samantha asked, in a carefully modulated tone.

Courtney sighed. "And Phillip," she concurred wearily.

Samantha stared into Courtney's troubled eyes; then, shrugging, she asked, "You aren't comfortable in the engagement, are you?"

"No." Courtney raked her fingers abruptly through her sleep-tumbled hair. "I tried to give the ring back to him before coming over here." She smiled piquantly. "He wouldn't have it. Why do you ask?"

"Because it's obvious you're not in love with him," Sam said bluntly.

"But I am fond of him . . . deeply fond," Courtney countered.

Samantha smiled pityingly. "Oh, Courtney— fond? You're willing to settle for *fond?*"

"I've never met anyone else. . . ." Courtney's voice faded, became faint, as her conscience chanted: *Liar, liar.*

"But that hardly means you won't!" Samantha objected strongly.

Courtney's nerves were quivering. She could feel Rio, *taste* him, as if her senses had absorbed the essence of him into her system.

"Is love so very important?" she cried, consciously denying the ache of longing inside. "Phillip and I grew up together. We've been friends forever. We understand each other. Isn't that enough?" she demanded, more of herself than of her cousin.

"Is it?" Samantha chided gently. Circling around the table she drew Courtney into an embrace, murmuring, stroking, in the same way she comforted her children when they were hurting. "Darling, I'm sorry. I have no right to question or badger you, especially now, after what you've just gone through." She sighed. "But, oh, damn, I want you to be as happy as I am, and Phillip . . . well . . ."

"Phillip is a long way from being another Morgan," Courtney finished for her. *And even farther away from being another Rio,* she acknowledged to herself.

"Yes." Stepping back, Samantha smiled.

"And does Morgan share your less than enthusiastic opinion of Phillip?" Courtney managed a weak smile in return.

Samantha's smile dissolved into trilling laughter. "Morgan hasn't offered an opinion. He does have this frustrating habit of keeping his own counsel! That's the reason I couldn't answer your question about Rio."

"What?" Courtney was suddenly alert.

"Right after we sat down," Samantha reminded her. "You asked me to tell you about Rio, and I said I really didn't know all that much about him *to* tell." She lifted her shoulders in a helpless shrug. "Morgan is about as communicative as a dead telephone line!" An impish glow flared in her green eyes. "I'm dying of curiosity about Rio myself. Maybe, just maybe, if we both work on Morgan, we can pry some information out of him."

Tilting her head Courtney stared at Samantha. "I can't get over the change in you, Samantha Denning Wade. You are so completely different from the Samantha I knew before you married."

"I hope the difference is an improvement," Samantha teased.

Courtney pursed her lips. "It is, rather. Even in your early twenties you were so regal, so"—she shrugged—"So very self-contained and impervious to everything and everybody."

"Somewhat as you are now?" Samantha suggested softly.

Courtney stared at her in startled blankness a moment; then she laughed, the first easy laughter Samantha had heard since her return.

"You know, you're right!" Sliding her arm around Samantha's waist, she hugged her briefly. "Being the younger by almost four years, I always tried to emulate you, be exactly like you." Removing her arm, she started for the bathroom. "It would appear that I've succeeded." She laughed, pausing at the doorway.

"Not quite," Samantha chided. At Courtney's arched look she taunted, "I'm desperately in love with the man I married."

The verbal dart hit home. Reflexively Courtney glanced down at the sparkling diamond on her finger. Samantha was right, of course, she thought tiredly. She had no choice but to return the ring to Phillip.

A frown marring her smooth brow, Samantha crossed the room to Courtney. "Forgive me," she urged contritely. "I've upset you, and I never meant to."

"No, no." Courtney shook her head, sending the gold strands of her hair flying like spangled sunbeams around her shoulders. "I know you're right. I've always known it. I can't possibly marry Phillip."

Especially not now, she thought pensively, stepping into the bathroom; *not since Rio.*

Rio. Even with the hot water cascading over her head in the shower, Courtney shivered at the thought of his name. Rio, with his raspy, nighttime voice. Rio, with his silent, shadowy movements.

128

Rio, with his rangy, long, muscled body, and his hot, searching mouth.

Tasting his hunger, feeling the stroke and thrust of his tongue, Courtney parted her lips with a sigh of longing. The rush of water into her mouth quenched the heat rising in her body and drowned the too real dream.

What a fool she was! Sputtering, she switched the water off and stepped out of the shower. Patting her body dry, she lectured herself bracingly.

She was looking at Rio through newly misted eyes, seeing him as the hero, bigger than life; her knight in shining armor. It had to stop. Rio McCord was a man, if not quite like other men. So he had been gentle with her, so he had been compassionate and understanding—so what?

What did she expect of the man? Hadn't he given her enough?

The towel dropped from Courtney's hands. Her eyes stinging with hot tears she skimmed her reflection in the mirror. Rio had given her much more than compassion and understanding. Rio, a man she had never seen before that night, had proved to her that every secret hope she'd held about the possibility of beauty in the act of making love was true.

No, Rio had taken nothing from her, he had given. And then only after she had begged him to make love to her! She, Courtney Tremaine-Smythe, the arrogant young woman who had breezed through life with the best of everything, now felt bereft of everything.

She had no earthly right to expect anything from Rio McCord, no right at all. She knew that, and the knowing hurt like hell!

The young woman grew pale, while her eyes

brightened with the threat of tears. Staring at her own reflection Courtney shook her head in mute denial. She rarely ever wept! What was happening to her? She didn't feel like herself! But if she wasn't herself, who was she? She needed to be around people—people who knew her, knew Courtney Tremaine-Smythe! Swallowing a sob she forced herself to dress very slowly, very carefully, in exactly the manner Courtney was known to do.

She was all right. Of course she was all right! She'd had a bad time of it, but now it was over. *I need time, that's all, time,* she thought, buttoning the silk shirt she had pulled out of the closet. *The memory will fade,* she insisted silently, stepping into raw silk slacks, even as the bruises on her body were already starting to fade.

Bruises. Ben. His hands, grabbing, kneading, her breasts, her thighs! Oh, God! *Rio, take me out of here, away from him! I'm so cold, so frightened!*

The harsh, uneven sound of her own breathing startled Courtney out of her trancelike state. In amazement she realized that she was cradling her body with arms wrapped tightly over her breasts. Her teeth were clenched, and she was shivering uncontrollably.

How long would it continue to haunt her? How many times would she be caught like this, unaware, unprotected? An urge to run, somewhere, anywhere, swept through her. But where could one run to get away from the images of memory?

Panting as if she'd already run to the point of exhaustion, Courtney sent her haunted gaze scurrying around the room. There was nowhere to hide, no corner to crawl into. Her glance collided with the bed—and held. She had felt safe in *his* bed. The memories had receded in *his* bed. Terror was held at bay in *his* bed.

Courtney's arms tightened around her breasts convulsively. His arms had given haven. His mouth had banished fear. His body had been the tutor of memory-blanking pleasure.

Rio.

CHAPTER SIX

The stain was gone.

His stance rigid, his expression grim, his eyes narrowed into slits, Rio stared at the pale-green bedspread. There wasn't the faintest trace of the coin-sized spot. Maria took her role of housekeeper very seriously.

Yet, with his mind's eye, Rio could still see the red stain, and feel again the riot of sensations he'd experienced at the sight of it. And the sensations were awesome in their power. Foremost of the emotions bedeviling him was blatant masculine pride. He, Rio McCord, had accomplished the feat Courtney's fiancé, the elegant Phillip, had not managed to pull off!

The back side of the heady emotion was chagrin; Rio was all too cognizant of the mental state Courtney had been in at the time of her initiation into full womanhood.

And there were myriad other emotions vying for recognition: anger, contrition, frustration, and the oddest sensation that felt very similar, too similar, to grief.

Rio was not by nature introspective. He'd come very early in life to an understanding of self. Acceptance had followed understanding. What he was, he was—and what he was not, he was not—until Courtney Tremaine-Smythe. The advent of Courtney into his life had created inner conflict Rio was positive he could easily live without. Yet the conflict was there, riding him as tenaciously as a cowboy hellbent on winning top money at the rodeo.

Frowning, Rio walked to the bed and tore the spread from it; then, turning abruptly, he strode across the hall and into his own room. As neatly as Maria had, he smoothed the covering over his bed.

The work completed he stepped back, a derisive smile pulling at his lips. An empty gesture, perhaps, and yet, in his mind, the spread and the lovemaking were connected. He wanted her, wanted her so badly his bones ached, and until the wanting ceased to torment him, he'd sleep wrapped in the spread of their first time together.

"By some he's called Night Striker."

Courtney was too much of a lady to gape, yet now she sat open mouthed in surprised reaction to Samantha's calmly delivered statement. One week had transpired since Rio had escorted her to the Wade ranch. Within that week she had been to Las Vegas for further debriefing by the authorities, had returned her engagement ring to a disgruntled Phillip, had assured her father she would be fine if he remained in the gambling city for some relaxation, and had returned to the ranch the day before.

Now, stretched out on a lounge chair by the Wade pool, Courtney gaped at her serenely smiling cousin.

"Close your mouth, darling," Samantha teased. "You're creating a draft."

"Night Striker?" Courtney repeated softly, envisioning Rio the first time she'd seen him, standing in the shadows in that boxlike room in the cabin.

"Night Striker," Samantha reiterated, grinning at the wary expression stealing over her husband's face. Her statement had been in response to a question from Courtney about Rio. Courtney's query had not been made casually; it had been the opening move in the game plan contrived by the two women to pry information out of Morgan.

"But why on earth would anyone call him that?" Courtney's gaze turned in unison with Samantha's to pin Morgan to the lounger he was sprawled upon.

"Why do I have this nasty suspicion that I've been set up?" His eyes shuttered, Morgan glanced from Courtney to Sam.

"Very likely because you have," Samantha retorted sweetly. "We are both consumed with curiosity about your friend, my love, and you are the only person at hand who can satisfy that curiosity."

Impatient, yet cautious, Courtney forced herself to relax while avidly observing the byplay between Samantha and Morgan.

"Samantha," he said warningly, "I told you before, several *times* before, that Rio's business *is* Rio's business."

"There, you see?" Jerking into a sitting position Samantha swung her gaze to Courtney. "Didn't I tell you?" Her eyes beginning to glitter like gemstones, she whipped her head around to glare at

Morgan. "For heaven's sake, Morgan, we aren't asking you to divulge state secrets, you know! You claim the man is your friend, yet I never even heard his name mentioned until a little over a week ago! And we've been married for over five years!"

Morgan shifted his deeply tanned, leanly muscled body on the padded lounger. Again his gaze flashed from his wife to her cousin. Both countenances were set in lines of determination. His hands lifted slightly off the lounger, then dropped back.

"Okay," he muttered. "What do you want to know about him?"

"Everything!" Courtney and Samantha demanded simultaneously.

"Oh, Lord!" Morgan closed his eyes and groaned. "As if I didn't have my hands full with the redhead! Now I get her blond counterpart!"

"Stop stalling, darling." Settling back comfortably, Samantha favored her husband with a dazzling smile. "Spill your guts," she ordered pleasantly.

Morgan's expression grew pained at Samantha's terminology. His black eyes glowing like hot coals, he observed, "I think you and I are going to have an in-depth discussion about your language very soon, Mrs. Wade."

"Everything I know, I learned from you," Samantha reminded him serenely. "Now let's hear all about Rio."

A spark of pain ignited in Courtney's chest at the loving banter between her host and hostess. Samantha and Morgan were so blatantly, so very unselfconsciously, in love! The unconcealed evidence of their love had struck Courtney at once,

135

on her first arrival at the ranch a month previously. On that initial visit she had cynically decided that Samantha and Morgan were putting on an act, a performance designed to impress Samantha's British relatives. Now Courtney knew better.

Courtney also realized that the spark of pain she'd felt at odd moments while in Samantha and Morgan's company contained elements both of envy and longing. Sighing for an unnamed something she'd missed in life, she riveted her attention on Morgan as he began to reminisce.

"I met Rio at Texas A&M," Morgan commenced, a faraway look on his face as he stared through a fine stream of smoke rising from the cigarette between his fingers. "I think we gravitated together naturally because neither one of us had any interest in sports." He grinned. "At least not as participants."

"I would have thought the opposite to be true," Courtney commented, skimming his well-knit athlete's body with unabashed admiration.

Morgan laughed softly. "Well, it wasn't really that neither one of us wasn't interested exactly, we simply didn't have the time. Both of us were carrying schedules heavy enough to break an elephant's back." He crushed out his cigarette and then settled back, as if for the duration. "And, as many of our courses coincided, we kept running into each other in lecture halls. Then one afternoon, after one particularly boring session, we left the hall griping about the professor and wound up in a bar off campus." A smile twitched the corners of his mouth as his voice trailed away.

"Morgan!" Samantha drew him into the present sharply. "What happened then?"

"We both got smashed," Morgan answered,

laughing, "and sealed our new friendship with Jack Daniel's, a lot of Jack Daniel's. It didn't take us long to discover we had much more in common than a few college courses," he went on soberly. "The most important thing being our land."

Though his statement was obviously old news to Samantha, Courtney, fully aware of Morgan's many and varied business interests, shot an inquisitive look at him.

"I'm a cattleman first, Courtney," Morgan answered her mute question. "I always have been. And, that day I learned that Rio was, first and foremost, a horseman. And, also like me, he had taken on the backbreaking study load to get through school in the shortest amount of time possible." A reminiscent smile tugged at his lips. "You might say we were drawn together at that time because we were both homesick for the range."

"But what does that have to do with the nickname 'Night Striker'?" Samantha asked, clearly exasperated.

"Shut up, darling," he ordered mildly. "You badgered me into this true confession, now let me tell it my own way."

Courtney silently supported Morgan's position; she personally was soaking up every word. Impatience eating at her, she endured the moments of delay necessitated by his lighting a fresh cigarette. When, at last, Morgan continued, Courtney was thrown into confusion by what she considered an unrelated observation.

"His father is Patrick McCord, you know."

Courtney frowned but not Samantha.

"Patrick McCord!" Samantha exclaimed, bolting upright on the lounger. "*The* Patrick McCord?"

137

"The Patrick McCord," Morgan repeated with relish, grinning in satisfaction at having stunned his wife.

"Ho-ly mackerel!" Samantha muttered in an awed tone.

"Have I missed some vital bit here?" Her frown deepening, Courtney glanced from Samantha to Morgan. "Who, exactly, is Patrick McCord?" Even as she voiced the name, memory stirred, not of a person, but of a medal, nestling in the dark curls on Rio's chest. And of Rio's soft laugh as he told her the medal was a gift from his father, the secretly superstitious Irishman.

"Oh, I'm sorry, Court," Samantha responded for Morgan. "Of course you wouldn't know. Patrick McCord's name is synonymous with oil in Texas," she explained.

"And quite a few other places," Morgan inserted dryly. "He is known affectionately as 'the flamboyant Irishman,' " he added on a chuckle.

Rio's father? Courtney smiled vaguely in bewilderment, attempting to equate *flamboyant* with the silent, self-contained Rio.

"Rio doesn't look at all Irish!" she blurted when the equation proved impossible for her.

"That's for damn sure!" Morgan laughed. "He's got more the look of his Conquistador ancestors than he does the leprechaun."

"His mother is Spanish?"

"Was," Morgan corrected Courtney gently. "His mother is dead, but yes, his mother had undiluted Spanish blood." His lips tightened into a grim line. "When she ran off with Patrick, her family declared her dead. She had no contact with them until the day she actually did die, six or seven years ago. Patrick adored her, so did Rio."

138

In the small moment of silence that followed Morgan's explanation, Courtney achingly wondered what being adored by Rio would be like. Heaven, she decided, sheer heaven. Morgan's voice, as he resumed his narrative, drew her from longings of celestial perfection.

"Luz was beautiful," Morgan mused, a smile softening his lips. "I met her at graduation. She had creamy skin, and dark, soulful eyes, and a soft, caressing voice. And all Patrick's millions were useless against the illness that ravaged her lovely body." A sigh moved his chest. "After her funeral Patrick went on a two-week rip. Rio finally dragged him, roaring drunk and sobbing, out of a bordello in a dusty little town across the border." The smile that touched his lips held more sadness than humor. "The funny part was, one of the girls told Rio that Patrick hadn't bedded any one of them, but that he'd talked of Luz incessantly to *all* of them."

Courtney's heart contracted at the picture Morgan's words drew so clearly. How sad that a man who could have afforded the most expensive of counselors, had paid prostitutes to listen while he'd poured out his grief for his wife! With sudden sharpness the thought hit Courtney that Rio probably did indeed favor his father, in temperament, if not in appearance. The only difference being their methods. Instinct assured Courtney that Rio would suffer the loss of a loved one as deeply as his father, if not more—only Rio would suffer in silence and solitude. Morgan confirmed her belief when he continued speaking.

"It was an extremely bad time for Rio as well as Patrick," he told them solemnly. "I'll never forget how shocked I was when I saw Rio at the funeral.

139

He had aged ten years in two." Morgan was quiet a moment, then he amended, "Of course, the change in him wasn't all due to his mother's death. His occupation was beginning to take its toll."

"Night Striker." Samantha's murmur was not a question.

"Yeah," Morgan concurred, drawing harshly on yet another cigarette.

"Well, for heaven's sake, go on!" Samantha voiced the plea hovering on Courtney's lips.

"I know very little about it." Catching sight of the utter disbelief mirrored on their faces, he added earnestly, "I really don't! Hell, I doubt if more than a handful do."

"Mor-gan!"

"Samantha, all I can tell you is that Rio was employed by private corporations in a covert capacity."

"Private corporations! Covert capacity? I don't under—"

"What he means is," Courtney interrupted softly, "Rio earned his probably exorbitant salary by getting a corporation's employees out of any trouble they might have got into in some foreign country or"—Courtney smiled wryly—"created the trouble himself, whichever way his employers wanted it. Right?"

"That about sums it up," Morgan drawled. "And, as Rio preferred to do his 'thing' at night, his —ah—companions dubbed him Night Striker."

Night Striker. Courtney rolled the sobriquet around in her mind. Yes, it fit him; hadn't he struck in darkness up in those hills? Instinct assured Courtney that there were probably deeper connotations to the nickname than Rio's penchant for

140

working in the nighttime hours—*striker* hinted at acts she didn't even care to think about.

"By comparison, designing haute-couture clothes for wealthy women seems rather dull and dilettantish," Courtney murmured at length, unconscious of the sigh that whispered through her lips.

"Dull and dilettantish! Really, Courtney!" Samantha exclaimed. "There is absolutely *no* comparison. I mean, who would even want to be some sort of female James Bond!" Morgan's bark of laughter earned him a glaring glance from Samantha. Then, ignoring his continuing chuckle, she went on, "I think your work is very exciting. And don't frown," she scolded as Courtney's brows drew together. "Do you have any idea how many women envy you your talent? You are an exceptionally gifted designer!"

"If you'll pardon the opinion," Morgan inserted. "Of what importance is this discussion? As he is officially retired from the cloak-and-dagger game, Rio is now merely a horse rancher." He grinned. "By comparison, designing haute couture sounds rather exciting."

"Morgan's right, you know," Samantha agreed promptly. "What brought on this feeling of inadequacy, Court?"

"Oh, I don't know." Courtney sighed. "I suppose I had an attack of the guilts. I was so utterly helpless, and Rio handled everything so effortlessly. Masculine envy, perhaps."

"Understandable," Morgan grunted. "Rio is something."

How extraordinary! The observation was still ringing in Courtney's mind long after she'd retired to her room for the night. The conversation had ended shortly after her explanation to Sam when the twins—the Wades' version of the dynamic duo—came tearing onto the patio, raring to go after their nap.

Though delightful, watching Morgan roughhouse with his sons increased the twist of envy and longing in Courtney's heart. By anyone's definition of the word Morgan was all male. Yet, with his wife and sons, he was gentle and tender, revealing a sensitive understanding of their emotional as well as physical needs.

Courtney readily admitted that she was jealous of the life her cousin had wrought for herself. She was not jealous of Morgan, the man, though she had grown very fond of him already. No, Courtney was jealous of the deep love and rich companionship Samantha had realized from marriage. And Courtney no longer felt even a twinge of regret for having broken her engagement to Phillip. After the past week at the Wade ranch she decided that, unless she could have a relationship even remotely close to what Samantha and Morgan shared, she would rather not marry at all.

As Courtney's father had an unprecedented run of luck at the craps table in Las Vegas, her visit with Samantha and Morgan was extended several times. After the second phone call from Charles begging for "just a few more days," Courtney turned to her hosts with an apologetic smile.

"He's still running hot," she explained wryly. "If you'd prefer, I could join him there."

The vigorous objections made by both Samantha and Morgan brought a thickness to Courtney's throat and a sting to her eyes. And, as events unfurled, having Samantha close proved not only beneficial to Courtney, but necessary.

As the hot summer days melted one into another, and Courtney and Samantha became closer friends, the residual trauma of Courtney's recent experience lessened. There were, of course, the odd moments when the memory—too sharp, too clear—flared and she found herself cold and shivering. At those moments Samantha was there, talking to her, drawing the coldness out, instilling warmth and confidence. One of those moments came on an extremely hot afternoon when Morgan came storming into the house, his black eyes glittering, his expression frightening in its fierceness.

"That son of a—"

"Morgan!" Samantha's startled yelp drowned his string of curses. "What or who put a burr under your saddle?" she demanded, releasing the twins into the care of the housekeeper, Sara.

"The law has picked up one of the kidnappers," he said, in the closest thing to a snarl Courtney ever wanted to hear. "The bastard worked for me!"

"One of *our* men?" Sam fairly screeched.

"Not one of the permanent crew, no." Morgan's abrupt movements betrayed the rage searing his lean body. "It was one of the extra men I hired for spring roundup." Sheer amazement left his face blank for a moment. "And do you want to hear what his name is?" he asked, unnecessarily. "Henderson! Henderson, for Crissake!"

Sitting stiffly, as if glued to her chair, Courtney was feeling both associated fear and fuzzy confusion. Why had learning the man's name so enraged Morgan, she wondered vaguely, rubbing her hands up and down her suddenly chilled arms.

Samantha partially answered Courtney's mute question.

"Henderson," she repeated musingly; then, eyes widening, "The Henderson property was the name of the place where Rio's men spotted the van!" she exclaimed.

"Exactly," Morgan gritted. "And where the kidnappers went into the hills. The Las Vegas police got a positive identification on him. Henderson was the man driving the bogus cab that picked Courtney up at the hotel. He was also the man who stayed behind to make contact with Charles."

"And the man who set the kidnappers free," Samantha inserted.

"Hell, yes," Morgan snorted disgustedly. "No wonder he had no difficulty finding that cabin in the dark. His family built the damn thing! And *he* probably grew up crawling all over those damn hills!"

"Wh—What about the other men?" Courtney asked starkly, an image of the leering Ben looming large in her mind.

Morgan stopped pacing and gave a concerned glance at the sound of terror lacing Courtney's voice. Moving to stand in front of her, he placed his hands over hers to halt their chafing movements.

"There is nothing to be afraid of, Courtney," he said softly. "You are completely safe here." A hint of steel underlined his soft tone. "I protect my own." A smile eased the harshness as he added, teasingly, "And that includes my own's relatives."

Gazing into his now smiling black eyes, Courtney chastised herself for cowardice. She had to put the memory of that time behind her! Forcing herself to relax, she smiled back at him.

"But is there any information about the other men?" she asked with hard-fought-for calm.

"No." Morgan shook his head as he straightened. "Henderson claims they split up after they crossed the border. The authorities are inclined to believe him. But don't worry, the other three will be found; stupid outlaws usually are. And talk about stupid!" Swinging around, he cocked an eyebrow at Sam. "Do you know where the Rangers picked him up?" Since he obviously didn't expect an answer, he didn't wait for one. "That jerk was hiding in that pile of rotting lumber on his property! I suppose he figured the law would never dream of looking for him there—at the scene of the crime, so to speak." Shaking his head, Morgan strode out of the room.

"Are you all right?" Samantha asked softly after the dust had figuratively cleared from Morgan's passage.

"Yes, I'm fine." Smiling at Samantha, Courtney repeated aloud the dictate she'd silently given herself. "I must put the memory of it behind me."

A few days later Courtney came to the jolting realization that putting the memory behind would be not only difficult, but impossible.

On awakening, Courtney lay in the deliciously air-cooled room, staring at the open beamed ceiling. She had fallen in love with the place—not just the apricot-and-cream bedroom she now occupied, but the entire ranch. The ambiance, the casual, easygoing pace of the ranch, appealed to her, after the more formal setting she was used to.

But it was time to go home. Courtney had reached the decision the night before. Now, her smile fading, she reiterated it. If she could extract her father from the gaming rooms and golf courses, she planned to be back in England before the week was out. She had work to do; it was time to start on next year's fall line—even if it was frivolous and unimportant.

Disturbed by her thoughts, Courtney shifted restlessly. It was not the realization that her work was less than world shattering that made her uneasy, but the man the thoughts brought to mind.

Courtney did not want to think of Rio. Most of all she did not want to remember the haven and heaven she'd discovered in his arms. Intellectually, she understood the traumatic needs that had initially driven her to seek reassurance of her worth as a woman by begging him to love her. Emotionally, she felt shattered by the effects and after effects of their lovemaking.

Which was precisely why Courtney did not want to think of Rio.

Secretly, to herself, Courtney could admit that she was very close to obsessed with the man. No matter how often she told herself her feelings had more to do with hero worship than any deeper emotion, she continued to think of him constantly, and with painful longing.

And so Courtney knew it was time to go home, to put the distance of miles as well as culture between them. Rio had walked away from her without a word or backward glance; it was past time she did likewise.

She was, Courtney reminded herself, the daughter of a very wealthy, prominent man. And though she had gained her reputation as a designer working for her father, it did not lessen her talent. She was good at what she did, and she knew it. It was time to get back to her life.

Her decision reaffirmed, Courtney swung her

legs out of the bed and stood up, only to sit down again immediately. The room, or her head, was spinning and her stomach churned warningly. Clutching the edge of the bed she drew a deep breath; then, her eyes flying wide, she sprang to her feet and dashed for the bathroom. When the roiling in her stomach ceased, she hung over the sink, shaking her head slowly in silent denial. She couldn't be pregnant! She simply could not be! Yet even as she rejected the idea, Courtney faced the very real possibility that she was indeed pregnant.

Courtney was well aware that only one mating was required to create a baby. She had also duly noted the absence of her flow at the completion of her normal cycle earlier that week. Optimistically she had assured herself that the missed period was a direct result of the trauma she'd suffered. The wrenching sickness had ripped away the veil of optimism.

The condition would have to be confirmed, of course—but only to make it official. In her own mind Courtney needed no official confirmation; she knew she had conceived Rio's child.

After brushing her teeth and showering, Courtney dressed in comfortable summer-weight slacks and a brightly patterned cotton shirt—one of her own designer outfits—and stepped into a pair of wedge-heeled sandals that bore the mark of an equally famous Italian designer. Smoothing her hair back into a simple braid, she applied a light covering of makeup, then left the bedroom; all traces of her earlier nausea gone.

Courtney announced her decision to spend the day in Las Vegas while she sat across the kitchen table from Samantha as they breakfasted together, Sam on bacon, eggs, toast, and coffee, Courtney on

Sara's delicious homemade biscuits and herbal tea. Samantha took Courtney's announcement enthusiastically.

"It will do you good to get out and mingle with other people," Samantha said in a mother-hen tone. "I'd offer to go with you, but I just spoke to Babs Carter on the phone and agreed to meet her for lunch in Ely. I was going to ask you to join us, but . . ." She shrugged. "Do you remember Babs, Court?"

"The madcap?" Courtney laughed softly. "Of course I do. Who could ever forget her?" Sipping her tea, she imagined the bubbly young woman as she'd looked the last time Courtney had seen her. "How is she?"

Samantha grinned. "Babs will be forever Babs. And her husband is still head over heels in love with her. They have three children now, two boys and an adorable little girl." There was a wistful sound to Samantha's tone as she mentioned the girl.

Sam's wistfulness was echoed mutely inside Courtney's mind. How had both Sam and Babs, who had been best friends from their teens, managed to find men—wonderful men—who obviously adored them? Into Courtney's mind came a vision that brought a sting to her eyes. She could actually see a small child, a girl, with dark hair, and dark eyes, and the occasional smile that stole one's breath and heart.

"Courtney?"

Courtney reluctantly surrendered the vision for reality. Her dream-clouded eyes clearing to deep sapphire, she smiled at Samantha, who was staring at her with concern.

"Yes?" she asked brightly.

148

"Are you all right?" Samantha demanded suspiciously. "You had the strangest expression for a minute there."

"Yes, I'm fine." Courtney infused a carefree note into her tone. "I was remembering some of the outrageous stunts Babs used to embroil you in," she lied blandly.

"Babs *was* a scorcher!" Samantha laughed. "As a matter of fact it was Babs who embroiled me into this marriage with Morgan!"

"She did what?" Courtney's eyebrows peaked into an arch.

"Uh-huh." Samantha grinned, rising to fill their cups. "It was shortly after my father died," she explained, sliding onto her chair. "I don't suppose you ever heard anything about the terms of my father's will?" she asked wryly.

"No." Courtney frowned. "Were the terms unusual?"

"You might say that," Samantha drawled—in much the same way Morgan did regularly. "The terms stated that I had to marry, an American citizen, mind you, before my twenty-fifth birthday —which was only five months away at the time." A tiny smile hovered on her lips as she waited for Courtney's reaction.

Courtney's cup hit the table with a thump. "But that's ridiculous!" she exclaimed in shocked tones. "Surely you challenged the terms?"

"I had planned to, until my lawyers informed me the challenge would come to nothing." Samantha drank deeply from her cup, then leaned back lazily in her chair and smiled. "Needless to say, I was furious."

"Well, I should say so!" Courtney exclaimed.

149

"But, love, what does that have to do with Morgan?" she asked, frowning. "And Babs?"

"Only everything." Samantha laughed. "But in reverse. It was Babs first, then Morgan."

"Sam, really!" Courtney cried in utter exasperation. "If you don't explain, I'm going to take an absolute fit!"

"Wellll . . . if you're positive you won't be bored?" Samantha said teasingly.

"Samantha!" Courtney fairly screamed. "If you don't tell me at once, I'll murder you!"

"What a grouch!" Grinning, Samantha settled herself more comfortably in her padded chair. "Okay, here goes . . . and no interruptions, please. As stated, the terms of the will could not be broken, and I was frantic and cursing mad!" As she spoke, her beautiful eyes grew opaque with memory. "I *could* have married any number of eminently suitable young men. The problem was, I didn't *want* to marry any one of them. I was worrying the situation to death when I received a letter from Babs asking if I'd stand as godmother for her second child. I agreed at once, for several reasons. For one, I simply gave in to the urge to run away—and put some distance between my bad temper and my family. And two, I'd missed out on being godmother to Babs's first baby, because I'd been out of the country at the time."

"Are you getting to the part about Morgan soon?" Courtney inquired politely when Samantha had paused to drink.

"Actually, the whole thing is about Morgan, as you'll soon see . . . if you'll be patient?" Samantha taunted sweetly.

"Oh, carry on, please," Courtney rejoined with

equal sweetness. "You won't hear another croak out of me!"

"I'll bet," Samantha muttered. "Now, where was I?" she asked in a tone of contrived innocence. "Ah, yes, the christening. Well, as Babs was and is my dearest friend, I cried out my tale of woe to her immediately upon arrival at their home. Babs, being not only the mother of her children, but of hare-brained ideas, came up with—in her words—the perfect solution to my dilemma."

"Morgan?" Courtney interposed in surprise.

"Morgan," Samantha concurred softly. "Lord, we were antagonists from our first sight of each other!"

"You and Morgan?" Sheer disbelief laced Courtney's tone.

Samantha smiled gently. "Oh, yes. I suppose I must have recognized my match—or master—in him at once." Her smile became misty. Then, straightening abruptly, she went on. "At any rate Babs hatched this dubious idea of an arranged marriage between me and Morgan." She grinned at Courtney's shocked face. "The exchange being, my money for his name," she said, deliberately adding to her cousin's shock.

Courtney looked at Samantha in disbelief. "Morgan was broke?"

"No." Samantha shook her head. "But he allowed his friends to *believe* he was, for reasons we won't go into. And, of course, I believed it also. In truth, it did seem like the perfect solution; I could continue with my world-trotting existence, and Morgan could continue to work himself to death on this ranch; I with his name, he with my money." Samantha laughed easily. "In theory it sounded perfect. The catch came when Morgan

151

informed me that he expected a real marriage—in every sense of the word."

"He—ah—asked you to sleep with him?" Courtney asked in carefully couched words.

"No, he never *asked!*" Samantha's laughter filled the spacious room.

"Oh!"

"You might well say 'oh.'" Samantha grinned. "Of course, as I was already in love with him, I didn't offer too much of a struggle."

"Incredible" was the only comment Courtney could rake out of her stunned mind.

Samantha wore a wondering expression. "Yes, it is, rather. You can't imagine how many times I've thanked God for the urge that brought me to Nevada at the time. *Time!*" she repeated in a ladylike yelp. "Good heavens, will you look at the time! I've got to meet Babs!" Jumping out of her chair she dashed to the sink to deposit her cup. "Darling, you don't mind if I run, do you?" she asked anxiously.

"Not at all, Sam," Courtney responded absently, still caught up in her cousin's story. "I'll see you when I get back from Las Vegas."

Samantha started from the room, then paused in the doorway. "I'll arrange for someone to fly you into Vegas in the Cessna, Courtney, and for somebody to drive you to the airstrip." Sam smiled, then waved her fingers. "Good luck at the tables, love."

I would do better to hope for luck on the examining table! Such was the silent retort that rang in Courtney's mind as she entered the plush office of a prominent Las Vegas obstetrician some hours later.

Lady luck must surely hate blondes, Courtney

decided still later—after hearing the results of the pregnancy test. The test had proved positive—which really came as no great surprise to Courtney, as she'd been positive since being sick to her stomach early that morning. The question that tormented her now was: What in the world was she going to do about it?

There were several options open to her, and Courtney was aware of every one of them. As she was only approximately three weeks into the gestation period, she could marry at once and have no one the wiser at the time of the baby's birth. Or, she could remain single, have her baby in due course, and thumb her nose at traditionalists. Then again, she could go off somewhere on her own and have an abortion.

The mere thought of the third option gave Courtney the shudders, so she immediately discounted it. That left marriage, in all probability to Phillip, or single parenthood. Strange as it might seem to anyone else, Courtney was positive Phillip would still want to marry her even knowing she was carrying another man's child. But Courtney did not want to marry Phillip, even if it did mean upsetting her father, which she knew she unquestionably would.

As there was no blazing necessity for an on-the-spot decision, Courtney left the doctor's office. She mentally played with the pros and cons of her situation as she physically played the various games of chance in Las Vegas. And if her father at times looked at her oddly, wondering at her more-than-usual reserve, he attributed it to her recent ordeal and spoke even more gently to her than before.

The following afternoon Courtney left her father with a kiss, an embrace, and an admonition that he join her at the Wade ranch by the beginning of the next week at the latest.

"It may even be sooner." Charles smiled ruefully, returning her embrace. "It would appear that luck has deserted me."

Must be a family trait, Courtney thought with sudden tiredness, smiling in defiance of the tears that brightened her eyes. With a final wave of her hand she stepped into the cab that would deliver her to the airport and the waiting Cessna.

By the time Courtney returned to the Wade ranch, she was completely exhausted from her day. Never could she remember having felt so utterly weary, not even after her sojourn into the Texas hills. Courtney spent some time talking to Sam and Morgan; then, as soon as she deemed it decently possible, she excused herself and went to her room.

After standing listlessly under the shower Courtney blow-dried her hair, then tugged a lace-and-satin nightgown over her head. She was brushing her teeth when a light tapping sounded on the bedroom door.

"Yes?" she called softly, rinsing her mouth.

"It's Sam, Courtney. Are you in bed?"

Patting her lips dry, Courtney left the bathroom. "No, come on in, Sam," she invited, crossing the room to open the door.

"I hesitated to disturb you," Samantha admitted as she entered, studying Courtney's face with concern. "But you looked"—she shrugged—"well, odd. Is there something wrong, Court?"

The strange weakness swept over Courtney again, bringing a warm mist to her eyes. Determined not to lay any more of her troubles on her cousin's shoulders, she turned away quickly with a husky denial. "Nothing I can't handle."

Circling around her, Samantha confronted Courtney with her hands resting firmly on her slim hips. "There's nothing you *have* to handle alone!" she exclaimed. "Are we not family?" At Courtney's brief nod she demanded, "Are we not friends?"

"Yes! Of course we are!" Courtney had to swallow against the sudden thickness in her throat. "But . . ." she began.

"But nothing!" Sam overrode her objection with a vigorous shake of her head. "Something is obviously troubling you, and I want to help if I can."

Courtney stared into Samantha's compassion-filled emerald eyes for several seconds; then she caved in . . . inside. Lifting her chin with unconscious pride she met Samantha's gaze directly.

"I went into Las Vegas to consult with a physician," she said evenly. "I'm pregnant, Sam."

"Oh, Courtney!" Samantha murmured sympathetically. "Phillip?"

"No." Courtney shook her head, a wry smile shadowing her tremulous lips.

Frowning, Samantha stared at her an instant, then her eyes flew wide with horror. "My God! Was it one of the kidnappers? Were you afraid to tell us?"

"Oh, no! Sam, I was telling the truth when I said I was not raped!" Courtney hastened to relieve Samantha on that point.

Now Samantha's eyes widened with confusion. "But then, darling, who?" she asked in bewilderment.

"Rio McCord." The name came off Courtney's lips distinctly.

155

CHAPTER SEVEN

"Rio?" Samantha repeated the name in a whisper. Then, very clearly, "Rio!" she exclaimed. "But, Courtney, you were only with the man one night!"

"Exactly." Courtney wet her suddenly parched lips, and she moved to sit down on one of the comfortable chairs at the window facing the patio.

Her expression revealing bemusement and confusion, Samantha moved to drop onto the matching chair she'd occupied that morning, opposite Courtney. "Courtney," she began slowly, "I know it's really none of my business, but what in the world happened between you and Rio?" Before Courtney could respond, she pleaded, "And please don't tell me *he* raped you!"

"No, of course he didn't rape me!" Courtney said adamantly.

"But, dammit!" Samantha exploded with frustration. "Then, what happened?"

Briefly Courtney explained to Samantha—or attempted to explain—her feelings of that night. As Samantha listened, her expression softened with understanding and compassion, and she nodded encouragingly several times.

"I . . . I felt like an object, Sam! Like an inanimate thing!" Courtney had to pause to swallow repeatedly. The panic was clutching at her chest again with the restored memory, tightening her throat and chilling her bloodstream.

Leaning across the table that separated the chairs, Samantha grasped Courtney's cold fingers. "You don't have to continue if it causes you pain, Court," she said anxiously.

"I'm all right." Courtney drew a shuddering breath. "But you see, Rio was so kind, so gentle with me, so very *real* and human, not beastly like that Ben!" She lifted her shoulders helplessly. "I suppose I needed his very realness to make me feel real too."

"Yes," Sam whispered in understanding. "Yes."

Lost in their own thoughts they were quiet for some minutes; then Sam asked gently, "What are you going to do, Court?"

Courtney's chuckle had more the sound of a sob than of laughter. "I haven't quite decided," she admitted. "Except that I'm going home next week."

"What?" Samantha cried, her eyes wide with shock. "Courtney, are you saying you're planning to leave this country without telling Rio?" she demanded in amazement.

There was no need for a verbal response; the answer was clear on Courtney's face. Springing to her feet, Samantha paced the room, then spun to face Courtney challengingly.

"I am not going to let you do it," Samantha threatened decisively. "Half—hell, more than half —the responsibility lies with Rio," she declared.

"Besides which, the man has a right to know that he is going to be a father."

Naturally, Courtney had given considerable thought to the question of Rio's right to know. But how the devil to go about telling him? And, more unnerving still, how the devil would he react to the information? Courtney certainly didn't relish the idea of facing an exasperated Rio McCord! Unaware of doing so, she began shaking her head slowly back and forth.

"Courtney, you must tell him! He *does* have rights here!" Samantha's sharp tone snapped Courtney to attention. "And even if he didn't, you simply cannot have this baby single!"

"Why not?" Courtney demanded, feeling cornered. "It's done all the time these days."

"Yes, it is—but not by us! I will be the first one to admit that our family can lay claim to more than one skeleton tucked away in closets in an assortment of town houses and country estates," she argued heatedly. "But every one of them was legitimate!"

Courtney winced, as if physically struck. Realizing her advantage Samantha charged on bluntly.

"Up until now you have gone your own way with impunity; defying all advice to the contrary by financially backing every nonviolent cause going; flaunting convention by living precisely as you chose; lifting your chin imperiously to any detractors. And I've applauded you for it." Samantha smiled at Courtney's startled look. "Oh, yes, I've kept track of your career and exploits. But in this instance you are wrong."

"But you don't understand!" Courtney protested.

"I understand perfectly," Samantha countered.

158

"And I understand even more. *I* understand and accept the ramifications. Do you wish to see your child grow up with the handicap of speculation about his parentage?" Samantha shook her head, red mane flying like angry flames around her shoulders. "Dammit, Court! The child will be referred to as the Tremaine-Smythe bastard, and you know it!"

"Yes, I know, but . . ." Courtney closed her eyes, and her voice dropped to a whisper. "I—I can't tell him, Sam."

"Why not, for heaven's sake?" Samantha retorted in exasperation. "Court, what the devil happened to you up there in those hills? You are simply not the same person anymore. The Courtney I knew was not afraid of anything or anybody."

"I'm not afraid of Rio!" Courtney denied at once. Not in a physical sense, at any rate, she amended silently.

"Well, then, what is this nonsense about not being able to tell him?" Samantha demanded, frowning.

How could she explain, make Sam understand the weight of responsibility she was feeling? Courtney shrugged her shoulders in an uncharacteristically vulnerable way.

"I feel it simply would not be fair of me to burden Rio with what is, in all honesty, the result of my own precipitous action." Lifting her chin, she faced Samantha squarely. "Sam, what I failed to mention in my recounting was that I literally begged Rio to make love to me."

Samantha quickly swallowed the gasp of shock that rose to her lips; she found it impossible to imagine Courtney begging for anything! Then again, Samantha reminded herself, she had never

159

been exposed to the traumatic events that her cousin had been forced to endure. Breathing deeply, she fought for a calm tone. "I really do understand your position now, love, but it doesn't change the fact of your pregnancy, or Rio's right to be informed of it."

Courtney closed her eyes as if in pain. "I . . . I simply cannot tell him, Samantha." As she opened her eyes again a curl of uneasiness shot through her at the confident expression stealing over Samantha's face.

"All right," Samantha murmured, too easily. Her emerald eyes betrayed nothing of her thoughts: *Maybe you can't, but Morgan can.*

The dawn was heralded by a freshening gust of cold air. Lying opposite the open window, wrapped within the folds of the sea-green bedspread, Rio stared sightlessly into the grayness beyond the broad pane of glass.

After a total of three and a half hours of sleep Rio had wakened over an hour before, and had been staring out, while looking in, ever since. The regimen was not unfamiliar; it had been the standard every night since he'd returned from Nevada.

The lack of sleep, and the work pace Rio set for himself during the daylight hours, were beginning to show. The fuse to his temper grew shorter with each successive sunrise. He had dropped some weight from his already finely honed body, and his increased physical activity had hardened muscles and sinews into rippling cables of steel. His features had sharpened and were set into a mask of austere remoteness. Rio was fully aware that the majority of his men actively avoided contact with him.

Impatience rode him relentlessly; impatience with his crew, impatience with Cleat, impatience with prevailing weather conditions, but most of all, impatience with himself.

Never having known the mental and physical discomfort of emotions tied in knots by thoughts and memories of any one woman, Rio was at a loss how to deal with it. Being in a near constant, almost painful, state of sexual arousal was another previously unknown irritant.

"Dammit all!"

Rio threw back the spread and rolled off the mattress, unmindful of the cool air rushing over his naked flesh. He was tired both physically and psychologically, a combination he had experienced only once before in his life—during the weeks he'd spent caged up like an animal after he had been captured in the jungle in South America.

Now, free as he was to roam at will over the land he loved, Rio's cage was mental, and of his own devising, the bars constructed of silken threads, the memory of a woman with the taste of wild strawberries on her softly sculpted mouth.

How was she? Rio had grown used to speculating about Courtney's well-being—it nagged at him on the average of twice an hour. Was she still at the Wade ranch, or had she returned to England . . . with the ever-so-handsome Phillip? Rio's jaws had developed a constant ache from grinding his teeth over the thought of Courtney—with Phillip.

Courtney with Phillip. The connotations contained in the coupling of the two names seared Rio's mind and body like a branding iron straight from the flames.

If he touches her he is dead! Rio made that vow, and other promises of a lethal nature, concerning

Phillip, when he was at his most tired, and thus vulnerable, moments. The intensity of these feelings shook him to the core.

This particular morning, with the cool air coiling around his body, Rio felt extremely tired, annoyingly vulnerable, and eager to destroy . . . anyone or anything with the temerity to look at him sideways.

As he thrust his legs into well-worn jeans, and stomped his feet into scruffed boots, Rio concluded that he was feeling almost mean enough to reenlist in the hired-gun business. And *that* thought shook him as much as his lethal feelings against Phillip.

Maria greeted him with a tentative smile as he entered the kitchen. "Good morning, señor." Having been born and raised in West Texas, Maria spoke English without a trace of an accent, yet she persisted in addressing Rio as "señor."

"Good morning." Rio's raspy tones contained a gentleness he was far from feeling. Yet no other kind of response would have occurred to him. The sun had never risen on the day Rio could force himself to be less than gentle with Maria—the woman who had cared so lovingly for his mother throughout Luz's ravishing illness.

"Mr. Wade is on his way in to the ranch, señor." Maria offered the information with the mug of steaming, dark coffee she set before him as he seated himself at the table.

"Morgan?" Though he felt a shiver of alarm, Rio's expression remained closed, his tone mildly inquiring.

"Yes. Frank, the mechanic on duty, called from the airfield when Mr. Wade's plane landed"—she glanced up at the wall clock—"twenty minutes ago." Her coal-black eyebrows arched slightly. "Would you like your breakfast now, or would you prefer to wait for Mr. Wade?"

"I'll wait," Rio murmured absently, sipping at the hot brew. Musing, he swallowed the coffee without really tasting it. Morgan would be arriving shortly, especially if Frank was driving him in, because Frank drove as if the devil were breathing down the Jeep's exhaust pipe!

Frank was driving—Morgan sauntered into the kitchen while Rio was nursing his second mug of coffee.

"I wonder if Frank could be distantly related to Samantha," Morgan quipped, as he dropped into the chair Rio indicated opposite his own. "Morning, Maria," he continued. "Thanks, that smells good," he added, inhaling the scent of the coffee she had placed on the table in front of him.

"Good morning, Mr. Wade." Maria smiled softly. "What would you like for breakfast?"

"Oh, whatever ole blabbermouth over there is having." Flashing white teeth in a grin, Morgan nodded at Rio. "That is, unless he's having bent rusty nails and sweaty saddle leather."

"Humph," Rio snorted into his mug.

Slanting an amused glance at her employer, Maria turned to go to the gleaming almond-colored stove. "The señor always eats the same breakfast," she said blandly, "—a steak so rare it yells ouch when he cuts into it, covered by two eggs, over easy, and refried beans on the side."

"Now you're talkin'." Morgan gave an appreciative sigh. "Please, throw those steaks under the broiler, sweetheart. I've been up and moving since three this morning, and my stomach's beginning to feel like a deep well at low water."

163

"How's the family?" Rio drawled sardonically when Morgan flashed his laughing gaze to him.

"Fine." Morgan matched the drawl exactly.

A tiny warning smile curled one corner of Rio's upper lip. "And your houseguests?" he inquired politely.

Acknowledging Rio's tone, Morgan changed his own. "One of them has a problem," he murmured for Rio's ears only. "That's why I'm here now." Sliding smoothly to his feet, he relieved Maria of the two large plates she was carrying to the table, letting a smile suffice as an answer when she murmured her thanks.

While the small exchange went on, Rio was busy fighting a welling sense of panic. Was Courtney ill? Had she been hurt? Surely not the kidnappers again? At the thought of the kidnappers rage swelled to smother the panic. In his mind Rio could see the overweight Ben, slobbering all over Courtney as his hands clutched at places Rio now thought of as his exclusively.

His expression revealing nothing of the emotions exploding inside, Rio fixed Morgan with a glittering stare as he slid the plate in front of him.

"There's been more trouble from the kidnappers?" His cold, remote tone was as unrevealing as his expression.

"No." Morgan shook his head. "As a matter of fact, the law has one of them behind bars." The slice his knife made into the rare piece of beef was a clue to the anger he felt at the felon. "Wait till you hear it," he said sourly, forking the meat into his mouth. Between bites of his breakfast he related the events of Henderson's arrest.

"Stupid bastard," commented Rio when Morgan had finished speaking. Then, calmly, as if his patience wires weren't frazzled and humming dangerously, he nudged Morgan verbally. "So, what then is the problem *one* of your guests has now?"

"After we've finished eating," Morgan murmured. "Privately."

The ice broke on Rio's features; he frowned. What the hell was all the mystery about? He didn't like it. Morgan's whole attitude bothered him. With enforced coolness, he slowly ate his food.

Closing his office-study door quietly Rio crossed to the intricately carved, Spanish-style credenza and withdrew a black-labeled, square-shaped bottle. Holding it aloft, he raised his eyebrows at Morgan.

"Why not?" Morgan agreed.

Dropping two ice cubes into two short glasses, Rio splashed amber liquor over them, then handed one of the glasses to Morgan. Without fanfare or toast both men drank deeply from their glasses. As he lowered the glass from his lips, Rio's dark eyes stared levelly into Morgan's.

"Okay, what's the story?"

"Courtney's pregnant," Morgan responded bluntly. "She claims that you're the father. Are you?"

"It's possible." Rio's tone betrayed none of the thoughts rioting in his mind. He had been the first man with Courtney; he *knew* that as an irrevocable fact. But . . . had she slept with that pretty boy after she'd returned to Nevada? Rio raised his arm to sip at the whiskey he now really needed. "It's even probable," he added softly. "So?" he was feeling none of the iciness coating his tones.

"So, she'd like her child to have a name." Morgan was relaying Samantha's words to him exactly.

"Mine?" Hoping the fire in the drink would banish the tremors in his insides, Rio drank again.

"If not yours, it will have to be some other man's," Morgan observed curtly, obviously losing patience with his friend. "If it is your child, don't you want it to have your name?"

"Hell, yes!" Rio ground out the agreement fiercely, breaking the chill barrier for the first time.

"That's what I thought." Morgan smiled easily as he raised his glass in a silent salute.

Courtney and Samantha were lounging on the patio after a late-afternoon dip in the pool when Morgan called Sam into the house. Frowning at the edge of command in his tone, Courtney watched Samantha jump to her feet and hurry toward the sliding glass patio doors. Mildly surprised at her cousin's display of wifely docility, Courtney let her heavy eyelids droop with a sigh. Morgan had been away from the house all day; perhaps Samantha had some news about their sons to impart to him.

Mentally shrugging off speculation, she shifted into a more comfortable position; why *was* she so listless and sleepy lately? In the next instant her speculations and her laziness were swept from her mind by a chill tingle of awareness. There had not been the faintest murmur of sound, yet she knew she was no longer alone. His very silence announced his presence.

Rio! Here? Frozen, almost afraid to breathe in case she'd conjured him in her mind and not in substance, Courtney slowly raised her long, gold-tipped lashes. Inching, devouring, her gaze crawled up the imposing length of his long muscled body, almost indecently clad in the briefest of navy-blue swim trunks. Her eyes caressed his slender waist, then moved to the dark hair on his chest. Struck by the sunrays, the metal nestled among the curls seemed to wink at her wickedly.

Startled by her own imaginings, Courtney glanced up abruptly and found her gaze ensnared by the steady regard of Rio's dark, contemplative eyes.

Strangely nervous, wildly excited, Courtney blurted the first thing that came to mind.

"You came all the way from Texas for a swim?"

Rio's quiet laughter brought a tinge of pink to her cheeks. What an absolute asinine thing to say! She was searching her mind for something a little more intelligible when he saved her the effort.

"I came to claim what's mine." His tone was unusually low, the rasp unnaturally heavy.

For one wild, improbable moment sheer joy leapt in Courtney's heart and mind. As Rio continued speaking the joy died a painful death.

"It is my baby, isn't it, Courtney?"

Controlling her expression with every ounce of will she possessed, Courtney met his stare directly. "Yes. The child is yours."

At her admission a light appeared to click on in the depths of his dark eyes; then it was quickly doused. "What are we going to do about it?" he asked in a maddeningly even tone.

"We?" Incensed, Courtney stared at him arrogantly.

With the agile swiftness natural to him, Rio dropped to kneel beside the lounge chair. "Yes." His voice contained an angry hiss. *"We."*

167

Her own flash of anger was subdued by the sudden flare of fury from him.

"What—what do you suggest *we* do?" she inquired unevenly.

Obviously pleased at having the advantage, Rio lifted one hand to trail the tips of his fingers over her flushed, warm cheek. A hint of a smile touched his lips at her involuntary tremor of response.

"I suggest we get married at once." The hint of a smile tilted cynically. "And make the little one nice and legal."

Courtney bit her lip to keep from crying out in protest against his cynicism. A moment later she was glad she'd kept silent as he went on in an excitingly dark tone:

"We are worlds apart, Courtney, *literally* worlds apart. But we do share the life now inside your body." Watching for her tiniest reaction, he slid his thumb over her lips, smiling again when they parted with her indrawn breath. "And we do share this electrifying physical attraction."

Before she could refute or even argue his assertion he was on his feet in one fluid motion. "Would you like me to take care of the arrangements?"

"If you like," Courtney murmured, frustrated by her inability to glance away from his hard body. "You're more familiar with the proper procedure."

"Right, I'll set the legal wheels in motion tomorrow morning." His rare grin flashed momentarily. "But right now I'm going to have a swim." With a minimum of body action he moved to the edge of the pool. He stood perfectly still for a moment, preparing his dive, then slanted a glance at her over his shoulder. "Who knows," he whispered. "We might even make it work."

With a pretense of deferring all and any suggestions to Courtney, Rio went about making simple plans, then executed them with a like simplicity. The legalities were dealt with with a swiftness that aroused Courtney's suspicions. It was obvious, at least to her, that Rio had called in favors from some high places.

Without flair Courtney, with Charles, Samantha, and Morgan in tow, was ushered into the private study of a very prominent Texas judge. Less than fifteen minutes later the judge, smiling benignly, ushered them all out again, and on exiting Courtney was no longer a single woman.

From the judge's home they all went directly back to the ranch for the party Maria had arranged for them. Never before in her life had Courtney witnessed the sort of exuberance Rio's crew displayed. But the absolute highlight of the entire day came with the sudden and unexpected arrival of Rio's father, the legendary flamboyant Irishman, Patrick McCord.

The man was a veritable giant! Well, perhaps he merely looked like a giant, due to the muscular width of his shoulders and the breadth of his burly chest. At any rate Rio, her father and Morgan all appeared reed thin beside Patrick.

Patrick lived up to his name on his very entrance onto the walled patio where the party was being held. Courtney, breathless from being swung in an incomprehensible dance in the arms of one of Rio's slightly drunken men, heard the lilting bellow of Patrick's voice before she caught her first glance of him.

"Where is she?" he demanded in a tone that

169

easily carried above the clamor of the festivities. "Where's my new daughter?"

The music stopped so abruptly, Courtney's senses reeled. As the spinning world settled, her gaze focused on the remotely amused expression of her husband as he sauntered toward her, the giant by his side.

"Courtney, I'd like you to meet your *new* father, Patrick." Rio's dry voice was in variance with the hawklike watchfulness of his eyes. "Pat, my wife, Courtney."

"Well, now, she is a beauty!" Patrick exclaimed —loud enough to be heard in El Paso, Courtney felt sure.

Not in the least intimidated by his size or booming voice, she smiled and extended her hand. "Mr. McCord, I'm delight—" That's as far as she got before she was swept off her feet and into a bear hug that expelled the breath from her body with a whooshing sound.

"Not nearly as delighted as I am to meet you, girlie!" The big man laughed, swinging her around as if she had no more substance than a rag doll. "I'd just about given up hope of a grandbaby from ole Silent-in-the-Saddle there." He flashed a grin at Rio as he set her on her feet.

Had Rio told his father that she was pregnant? Even as the question registered in her whirling mind, Patrick bellowed the answer.

"I only hope he doesn't fool around too long. I ain't getting any younger, you know!"

"You ain't getting any quieter, either," Rio remarked, saving Courtney the effort of a suitable response.

Patrick's laughter seemed to bounce off the patio walls, enveloping everyone in its merry, echoing waves. "What the hell is there to be quiet about?" he roared. "Is this a wedding or a wake?"

"Would it make any difference?" Rio inquired wryly.

"Not a lot," his father shot back, along with a grin.

Feeling like a spectator at a tennis match, Courtney shifted her gaze from father to son as the exchange continued. Within seconds Courtney decided that for all Rio's austere attitude, and Patrick's audacious verbal shots, the two men loved each other fiercely. For some unknown reason the knowledge pleased her greatly. They were still exchanging mild insults when Samantha and Morgan joined the trio.

"Hey, Morgan!" Turning with incredible swiftness for a man of his size, Patrick flashed hard white teeth in a breathtakingly beautiful smile. "How the hell are yah?" But before Morgan could open his mouth to do more than return the smile, Patrick spied Samantha . "Well, hot damn!" he said in a subdued, awed tone, his sky-blue eyes darting from Samantha to Courtney to Morgan and then Rio. "Leave it to you two throwbacks to corral the most beautiful women I've laid these tired old eyeballs on in years!"

"You didn't do too badly for yourself." Rio's observation was voiced in a near whisper, and had an immediate sobering effect on his father.

The change in Patrick was startling, and for an instant Courtney could see the son in the father, as the older man appeared to freeze emotionally before her eyes. Then a gentle smile relieved the tightness of his lips.

"No, son," he murmured softly. "I didn't do too badly. I just didn't have her with me long enough." For a millisecond Courtney witnessed pure anguish in Patrick's face. "Love her well, son," he advised quietly. "You never do know how much time you've got."

Later, sitting in the quiet bedroom, Courtney thought back to the scene. What an extraordinary man her father-in-law was, she mused, smiling mistily. And how very startling was his ability to leap from one emotion to another with no effort. For, immediately after charging Rio with her care, he'd created that smashing smile for Samantha while demanding Morgan introduce them.

The party had continued for what seemed like ages to Courtney, who'd been twirled around the patio at least twice by every man there—excluding her own husband, who stood back watching everything through shuttered eyes. Amazingly, by the time the party finally wound down to a natural death, Patrick had retired to a corner with, of all people, her father! Shortly after Sam and Morgan had left to go back to Nevada, Patrick took his leave also—bearing Charles with him!

Shaking her head in bemusement, Courtney kicked her slim-heeled sandals off her aching feet and stood up to begin undressing. A light tap on the door stilled her fingers on the side zipper of the ice-blue, raw-silk sheath she'd chosen to be married in. The sound of the knock forcefully reminded her that this was her wedding night. But would Rio knock on his own bedroom door? Courtney seriously doubted it.

"Yes?" she called softly, padding in stocking feet to the door. "Who is it?"

"Maria, señora," the older woman said quietly. "I have a message that was just delivered for you."

Swinging the door open Courtney muffled a sur-

172

prised gasp at the sight of Rio gliding silently down the wide hallway toward her bedroom. Tearing her gaze from him, she fought to control the sudden tremor in her hands as she accepted what appeared to be a greeting card from the housekeeper.

"Thank you, Maria, and good night," she said softly, turning back into the room as Rio came to a halt beside the woman.

"Good night, señora, señor," Maria murmured, a smile hidden in her tone, as she started back down the hall.

Clutching the large white envelope, Courtney retreated to the far end of the room as Rio shut the door with a muffled click.

"Another card of congratulations?" He stalked her to the window chair.

"Apparently so." Keeping her back to him Courtney skimmed her tongue over her tension-dried lips.

"Are you going to open it?" Supreme indifference laced his tone.

"Yes, of course." With ridiculously shaky fingers Courtney broke the seal on the envelope and, frowning, withdrew a single square of paper, folded once. Flipping the fold open she began to read the blocked, hand-printed message, her eyes widening with horror as they skimmed the lines.

So, the big horse rancher is going to ride you now, is he? Is your body his reward for rescuing you? Well, that's okay because all he'll be doing is warming you up for me. But you best tell him to watch his back because I'll get him. And I'll get you too. Only I don't plan to shoot you. I plan to ride you to death.

There was no signature, of course, but then none was necessary; Courtney knew who had written it. With a low, frightened moan she reached out blindly for the chair back to steady her trembling body. Her hand was caught and held firmly in Rio's hard grasp.

"What is it?" Plucking the paper from her nerveless fingers Rio shot her a sharp stare before glancing down at the message. Eyes narrowing, he scanned the lines, cursing from the first words his glance encountered.

"How—how did that thing get here?" she choked, fighting the urge to run, anywhere. The panic was back, chilling her blood, numbing her reason. "Rio!" she cried wildly. "That man is going to kill you! And then . . . and then . . ."

"Stop it, Courtney!" The soft command was accompanied by a sharp shake as he grasped her by the shoulders. *"You are safe here."*

Courtney moved her head from side to side frantically. Her eyes had a haunted look. "But how did he know I was here?" she cried. "Rio, the note is from that Ben. I *know* it! How did he know I was here?"

Biting off another curse Rio circled her shoulders with one arm and drew her with him to the door. He shouted for Maria as he urged Courtney into the hallway with him.

"Yes, señor?" Maria's voice revealed her concern; Rio never shouted at her.

"Get Cleat up to the house at once," Rio instructed, leading Courtney to his office. "And make a pot of coffee, please." Not waiting for a response he practically carried Courtney's trembling body into the office.

"What . . . what are you going to do?" Stark

174

terror broke through the restraint Courtney was trying to impose on her voice.

"The first thing I'm going to do is pour a brandy into you." Suiting action to words, he crossed to the credenza. Grasping the brandy bottle, he released her to fill a pony glass to the rim. "Sip," he ordered as he handed the liquor to her.

Courtney obeyed him instantly, welcoming the warmth that spread from her throat to her chilled insides. "Rio, how *did* Ben know I was here?" she asked in a strained whisper, as she handed the empty glass to him.

"Not by any mysterious method," he chided, refilling the glass and tossing the fiery drink back neat. "Whew!" Rio expelled his breath sharply as the drink hit his throat. "It's sacrilegious to drink this stuff like that." But even as he spoke the words, he tipped the bottle to fill the glass with more of the aged brandy. After taking a small swallow he held the glass out to her. "We'll share this one," he said, his lips curving up at the corners.

"Rio . . ."

"Drink, Courtney." The tone he used left little doubt in her mind that he meant to be obeyed; still shaking, Courtney complied—convincing herself it was *only* because she was still shaking.

"Now," Rio said as he led her to the leather sofa in front of the fireplace, "as to how he knew you were here." After seating her he went to stand before the grate, leaning indolently against the mantelpiece. "I don't know, but I can think of several ways he might have found out."

"How?" she demanded tremulously.

"If you weren't so rattled, the answer would be obvious, babe." If Rio hadn't glanced down into the brandy glass at that moment, he'd have caught the spark of hope that lit Courtney's eyes at his casual endearment. By the time he looked up it was gone, replaced by the fear crawling through her. "I told you you're safe here, Courtney. I can and will protect you."

"I know that, but—" Courtney began.

"Will you trust me?" Rio rapped the question out with unusual impatience. Courtney was too scared to notice the tension tautening his lean body; she merely responded automatically and with complete honesty.

"I'll trust you with my life." Courtney was also too distracted to notice the tension ease out of him, or even the softening of his tone.

"Good." Savoring her admission, Rio was quiet a moment, then went on. "As to how that slob knew you were here"—he shrugged—"although we were married quietly, for all I know there could have been a notice of it in the papers." His lips twisted wryly. "I am Patrick McCord's son; and Patrick McCord is news."

"I like your father, Rio." Courtney offered the information softly, earning for herself a genuine smile.

"So do I, as a matter of fact." His smile disappeared as he returned to his subject. "Then again, Ben might have picked up the information in town. Maria began planning our party over a week ago. She needed some supplies and, well"—he shrugged again—"men talk—even my men."

"Sad, but true." The observation came from the doorway, from Cleat Jamison, who stood there waiting respectfully to be invited into the room. "You sent for me, Rio?"

"Yeah." With a motion of his hand Rio indicated

the sheet of paper he'd dropped onto his desk. "Have a look at that—ah—charming note. But handle it carefully, there may be prints on it."

Frowning his confusion Cleat sauntered into the room and to the desk. Bending over he read the note without touching it at all. His reaction reflected Rio's of a short while before; Cleat began cursing softly. Then, finished, he glanced up, a stain of red flowing from his neck to his cheeks.

"Excuse me, ma'am," he apologized gruffly.

"She's heard the words before, Cleat," Rio drawled. "My reaction was the same."

"You call the authorities?" Cleat asked.

"Not yet." Rio smiled. "I'm giving Pat and Courtney's father time to get back to Odessa. I want to inform them first."

"Father is going to insist that I immediately return to England." Courtney said dully, fighting an overwhelming weariness.

"Insist?" Rio repeated, too softly. "Charles can insist until the Big Bend is underwater," he added in a hard tone, referring to the desert area west of the Pecos. "You are *my* wife, and I'll protect what's mine."

Inside Courtney's tired mind echoed Morgan's voice of a few weeks previously as he'd made the same ironclad statement. *Patrick was absolutely right*, she mused sleepily, *Rio and Morgan are "throwbacks."*

"Did you hear me, Courtney?" Rio demanded when she failed to respond. Sighing, she forced her heavy eyelids up.

"Yes, Rio," she murmured. Losing the battle against fatigue, she closed her eyes again. "Whatever you say," she added in a sleepy mumble. She never saw the tender smile that briefly softened Rio's hard lips.

Listening to, but really not absorbing, the conversation between Rio and Cleat, Courtney clung to consciousness for a few minutes longer, then curled more comfortably into the corner of the couch and dropped into oblivion. She stirred restlessly sometime later as she felt herself lifted, then carried a short distance. Her lashes fluttered at the intrusive sound of a door closing sharply, and she murmured incoherently as she was swiftly divested of her clothing. But she didn't fully awaken, and slid back into deep slumber the instant she was carefully placed on the bed.

Fortunately, Courtney was beyond hearing the frustrated mutter from her new husband as he left the room.

"What a hell of a way to spend my wedding night."

As always Rio came awake instantly, every one of his senses fully alert. He was lying on his side and he frowned at the dark, rich-looking paneling on the wall he was facing. It was still the middle of the night, yet something had wakened him. What had it been? Motionless, he waited, then it came again, and a shiver feathered the length of his spine as Courtney's warm breath caressed his naked skin.

A sensuous smile curving his lips, Rio luxuriated in the feel of her as she curled closer to him, seeking his warmth. Courtney needed the rest, he thought, trembling as her breath whispered over his flesh once more. She needed the sleep, but, oh, hell, he needed her! Giving in to the demands of his hardening body, Rio carefully turned and drew her into his arms.

"Rio?" Courtney murmured sleepily, moving instinctively, sweetly, into his embrace.

"Yes." His pulses beginning to hammer, Rio inserted a hand between them to stroke her naked, silky skin. "Courtney?" he whispered urgently against her sleep-warmed lips.

"Oh, yes!" Lifting her head, she parted her lips for him.

Tiny explosions flared throughout Rio's body as he took her mouth forcefully and sought the honey inside with his thrusting tongue. The explosions created a river of fire that ran through his veins as, murmuring deep in her throat, she gave herself up to his hungry mouth and stroking hands.

The warm satin feel of her tested the bounds of Rio's control. Desire clawing at him, he slid his lips from hers, tasting her neck, her shoulders, her breasts. Taking her puckering nipple inside his mouth, he brought it to tight arousal with his flicking tongue, and felt his own nipples tighten with excitement when Courtney gasped and arched her body into him, silently demanding yet more pleasure.

Murmuring in both English and Spanish, Rio praised her beauty as he explored every inch of it. His own tension mounting, he dipped the tip of his tongue into her navel before gliding his burning lips over her abdomen. Suddenly remembering the life unfurling inside her beautiful body, Rio pressed his open mouth against her skin to whisper, "Rest easy, my child, I will keep you and your mother safe."

So intensely protective did Rio feel at that mo-

179

ment, so awed by the reality of *his* child inside Courtney's body, that the tight coil of passion gripping him began to cool; but the delicate movement of Courtney's arching hips rekindled the fire into a blaze and his mouth greedily sought the moist heat of her.

Courtney was a living flame against his hungry mouth, a flame feeding the fire inside him. With open-mouthed kisses and flickering tongue Rio loved her until he felt her entire body grow taut; then, grasping her tightly with his hands, he absorbed the shudders that rippled through her body as his senses drank in her throaty cries of satisfaction.

And now it was his turn. Passion throbbing through him, Rio retraced his trail of kisses back to her mouth, his pleasure increasing as she began to move sensuously against him again. With his hands caressing her soft breasts, he brought his open mouth to hers, nudging her lips farther apart as he parted his wider, and yet wider.

A shudder tore through his already trembling body as Courtney went wild beneath him, urging him with low moans and hot, wet kisses. His mouth fastened to hers, he positioned himself between her thighs, groaning in pleasure when her soft fingers curled around his pulsing arousal.

"Yes," he growled, "bring me to you, Courtney."

Spreading his long fingers over her slim hips, he lifted her, and then, his body following the urging of her hands, he slowly moved inside her. Closing his eyes, Rio hesitated an instant, savoring the velvet sheath of her. But then, driven by the heat scorching every inch of him, he began a rhythmic stroke, moving faster and faster until, like shattering glass, his senses spun out of control and he cried her name through gritted teeth an instant after she gasped his own.

Dawn was turning the sky to mauve when Rio woke again. This time it was a numbness in his arm that woke him. Shifting carefully, he freed the arm, then resettled Courtney's relaxed body even more closely to him, amazed at the sense of possessiveness gripping him.

But though he was amazed by it, Rio accepted it calmly. Courtney was his. And after the weeks of aching for her, longing for her, he fully intended to keep her.

Though Rio had been deeply infatuated before, he had never truly been in love. Now, at daybreak on a morning in early July, Rio wondered curiously if he could possibly be in love with his wife.

It might help if he knew who exactly his wife was, he thought. Was Courtney the scared but fiercely determined young woman he'd brought out of the hills? Or was she the cool, remote aristocrat he'd delivered to Nevada? Then again, was she the pleasant, easy-to-get-along-with person he'd come to know during the short period of time before their marriage? Rio sighed. Perhaps she was really the warm-blooded, sensuous woman who had twice shared his bed.

Tilting his head, Rio glanced down at his sleeping wife. Merely looking at Courtney heated his blood. He wanted her again, wanted her exactly as she'd been with him the night before, hot and eager and ready for him, and only him.

Hell, maybe he was in love with her! Rio gave a mental shrug. Time would tell. Meanwhile, he would keep her, and protect her, and maybe, someday, she would even come to love him.

The consideration sparked another, exciting

trend of contemplation. What would it be like to be loved by Courtney? What would it be like to know that all her arrogance and fierceness and fire and love were there just for him? The answer sprang into his mind instantly. It would be like all the heaven he had ever hoped to find. And, Rio mused, after all the hell he'd known in Asia and South America, he could happily wallow in Courtney heaven! He was laughing softly to himself when the celestial body woke up.

"Rio?" Even as she murmured his name, Courtney wriggled closer to him.

"Umm?" Rio caught his breath at the picture she made with her lips swollen from his kisses and her hair wildly disarrayed by his tangling fingers.

"What time is it?"

"Early. Too early. Time to go back to sleep." Rio silently damned the betraying huskiness of his tone; she was pregnant, for heaven's sake! The last thing she needed after a few hours rest was more sexual action!

"I don't want to go back to sleep," she said adamantly.

"Are you hungry?" he asked, belatedly remembering how very little she'd eaten the day before. "Should I ask Maria to get some breakfast for you."

"Yes, I'm hungry." Courtney yawned prettily; Rio experienced an odd, anticipatory thrill. "But you don't have to bother Maria," she continued in an exciting purr, raising her arms and curling them around his neck. "You'll do nicely, thank you."

At the touch of Courtney's lips on his, Rio exploded all over again. Yet deep inside the heart of the explosion echoed the sound of his father's soft voice. "Love her well, son. You never know how much time you've got."

An unfamiliar fear urging him on, Rio loved Courtney with the fire of near desperation.

CHAPTER EIGHT

Courtney rose from the depths of deep, restful sleep, her mind refreshed, her body replete, and her stomach complaining of a lack of nourishment. Warm beneath the covers, she moved slowly with the sensuous grace of an awakening feline. Drawing a deep, contented breath, she opened her eyes —and froze.

Rio was standing before the wide window looking larger than life in the glare of the midday sunshine, his expression veiled by the smoke rising from the cigarette between his compressed lips.

In an instant the dreamlike memory of the night was shattered, exposing her mind to the stark reality of her situation. She was a woman with a husband who had been pressured into marriage and, because of it, was now a hunted man.

Courtney felt a sudden longing to roll over, bury her face in the pillow, and escape back into unconsciousness, preferably with Rio's warm body next to hers under the covers.

"Hungry?" he asked with his usual taciturnity.

Afraid to trust her dry throat to speech, Courtney nodded, refusing passage to the sigh that rose to her lips. Rio had not been spare of words under the blanket of darkness, she remembered achingly. His gravelly voice had whispered exciting, erotic phrases in English and Spanish.

How many others before her had thrilled to those exact same erotic words?

Appalled by the pain induced by speculation about Rio's previous partners, Courtney sat up abruptly, then immediately wished she hadn't. Color tinged her cheeks at the realization that her nude body was bathed in sunlight and exposed to his narrow-eyed gaze.

"I've seen it all," he reminded her coolly, moving to scoop her robe from the foot of the bed. "You didn't seem to mind at all last night," he observed wryly, handing the garment to her.

"I . . . I . . ." Was she supposed to respond to his taunt? she wondered, hastily shrugging into the robe. What could she say, other than the truth? She hadn't minded his searing gaze on her body; she had reveled in it! Avoiding a reply, she headed for the bathroom, tossing over her shoulder, "I'll be ready for breakfast in a few moments."

"Don't let it throw you, Courtney. Most mornings I'll be long gone by the time you wake up."

Courtney halted her headlong rush in the center of the large bathroom. Did Rio consider her a slugabed? A pampered socialite, whiling away her days in mindless pursuits? Well, he obviously did! Anger and frustration vied for supremacy over her emotions. Frustration won.

Stepping under a steaming shower, Courtney expelled a sharp breath in a sigh of agitation. What had she expected, for heaven's sake? Until now

Rio had only viewed her in one light—that of the daughter of the brother of an English lord, on extended holiday in the States. Good grief! Pictured in the light of the British aristocrat, Rio's conclusions about her were understandable, if rather insulting.

Well, she decided briskly, twisting the faucet shut, she would simply have to educate her husband as to her usefulness as a human being. Hadn't the man heard that most females even of the British elite, were holding down meaningful jobs these days? Practically all the young women she knew worked, and not merely as charitable volunteers, either, even though they did that as well.

Would her occupation as a haute-couture designer alter Rio's opinion of her? Probably not, Courtney decided, fighting a swamping sense of despair as she patted herself dry. Would any man who lived close to the earth give genuine credence to the work of creating expensive clothes for wealthy women? Not bloody likely, she admitted ruefully, slipping into the robe again, and most especially not a man like Rio.

Courtney my girl, she mused, *I'm afraid your upper lip is going to atrophy from stiffness, for you are surely in for a long, uphill battle if you hope to make this marriage work.* She was reaching for the doorknob when Rio's voice filtered through to her.

"Breakfast, Courtney."

Closing her eyes for a moment she rested her forehead on the smooth oak panel, giving in to a longing to hear him call her *querida* in the passion-filled voice he'd used during the night.

"Courtney!" The morning sound of Rio's impatience held not a hint of that passion.

As she straightened away from the door a self-mocking smile feathered her lips. The nighttime Rio was one person; the daytime man was apparently someone else altogether. And, in truth, hadn't she had fair warning about the man who struck at night?

Courtney's meandering thoughts stirred memory, and a shiver skittered down her back. That note! How had she ever forgotten it? Yanking the door open, she rushed into the bedroom and straight to the table at the window where Rio had placed their breakfast.

"Rio, the note!" she panted. "What did my father and yours have to say?" The sight of him stole the little breath she had left.

He was sprawled lazily on the chair, a pair of faded jeans his only concession to convention. The medal lying on his chest reflected glittering sparks back at the afternoon sunrays, and drew her gaze to the swirls of dark hair on his sun-browned skin. Courtney had to sit down quickly in the opposite chair to prevent herself from melting at his feet.

Rio frowned as she abruptly plopped into the chair. "Are you feeling all right?" he demanded, easing himself erect to stare across the table at her.

"Yes, of course," Courtney assured him too swiftly, earning herself another frown. "I—ah—just now remembered that disgusting note. I can't imagine how I ever forgot it!"

"Can't you?" he murmured. "I can."

Oh, dear! Courtney moaned silently, beginning to ache inside at his gravelly, sexy tone. Quite suddenly she was famished, but not for the food beneath the covered dishes neatly arranged on the table. Feeling hot, and cold, and incredibly *ready,* she sputtered into speech.

187

"But what did our fathers say? And did you notify the authorities? And—"

"They said plenty, and yes." Rio's obvious amusement at her expense instilled a needed dose of reserve in her mind.

"What exactly did the parents say?" she asked very coolly, curiously lifting the lid off the plate in front of her; her mouth watered at the aroma of broiled steak and eggs.

"About what we'd both expected," Rio replied, lifting a Thermos pitcher and pouring dark coffee into their cups. "Pat was all for making a direct call to the FBI in Washington." A smile twitched his lips, then faded abruptly. "As you predicted, your father was all for rushing you onto the next plane to England." His mouth flattened, as if from a sour taste.

"Well?" Courtney asked in exasperation when he failed to continue. "What did you tell them?"

In the process of slicing into his own steak, Rio glanced up at her, a slow grin tugging at his lips. "I told them to butt out." Calmly ignoring her shocked gasp, he slid the beef laden fork into his mouth.

"Rio, really!" she exclaimed angrily, positive she would be hearing from her very irate parent before too long.

"Courtney, really," he mimicked. "I don't need or want my father throwing his weight around, either here in Texas or in Washington," he said coldly. "And I definitely don't need or want *your* father's suggestions on how to protect *my* wife." And he infused steel into the possessive pronoun.

Men, and their blasted egos! Courtney was suddenly furious with him. Rio had received a threat to his life and all he could concern himself with

was his pride! Forcing back her anger she methodically chewed the bite of delicious homemade bis-
cuit she had in her mouth. When she swallowed,
she decided to take the tack of reason.

"Perhaps it would be wise to allow your father
to do as he suggests," she opined reasonably.

"No," Rio said flatly. "The proper authorities
have been informed, Courtney. Cleat left this
morning to deliver that note to them." Revealing
cool unconcern, he continued to make inroads
into his breakfast.

"But what if Ben should come here?" she asked
softly, suddenly short of breath. *To kill you and
rape me,* she added to herself fearfully.

"Here? To the house?" Rio's laughter warmed
the chill seeping into Courtney's bones. "If he
does he's even more stupid than I thought." His
laughter subsiding, Rio shook his head slowly. "I
told you you are safe here and I meant it. My men
have been alerted, security measures have been
taken, and even if I should be gone overnight for
some reason, you will—"

"Gone!" Courtney's mind got tangled up in the
word. "What do you mean, gone?" she cried.

"This is a working ranch, Courtney," Rio explained patiently. "And I have other business interests that need looking after. There will be times
when that business necessitates my absence from
the ranch for several days to a week."

"But—"

"*But,*" he went on insistently, "even when I'm
away you'll be completely safe here. Sal Alvarez
will see to that."

Sal Alvarez? Courtney blinked as he tossed the
unfamiliar name into the argument. Who the devil

was Sal Alvarez? Rio answered the question hovering on her lips before she could ask it.

"Sal is the best horse handler on the place, and second in command to Cleat." His patience was clearly thinning.

Courtney frowned in concentration; she couldn't remember having been introduced to anyone named Sal. "Have I met him?"

"No." Rio shook his head. "Under normal circumstances you would have met him at the party last night, but there was a mare ready to foal and Sal opted to stay with her." Rio smiled sardonically. "As stated, you have nothing to fear if I have to be away. Sal is part Italian-American and part Mexican-American, and all mean when he's riled." His smile smoothed into a grin. "As he is also Maria's live-in lover, he is also in the house at night."

Courtney's head jerked up in surprise. Maria? That quiet, unassuming woman had a live-in lover? she thought in amazement. Of course, Maria was also still quite attractive at fifty-odd, yet . . . Courtney stared at Rio—who took exception to her reaction.

"Maria is a warm, loving, God-fearing, good woman," he said very softly, "who lost her husband and only child to a renegade horse over ten years ago. Sal fulfills more than a physical need."

"Rio!" Courtney protested through fear-dried lips; Rio's tone had had an absolutely terrifying edge. "I don't condemn her!"

"It's a good thing." Courtney could actually see the tension ease out of him. Then he smiled—well, almost. "I'm all mean, too, when I'm riled."

Courtney felt a twinge of sympathy for the renegade horse. "What did you do?"

190

Rio didn't pretend to misunderstand her. Cradling his fresh cup of coffee he leaned back in the chair. "I tracked the stallion for two weeks, and when I found him I castrated him with my hunting knife." He shrugged. "He died, of course."

Blanching, Courtney swallowed convulsively against the nausea burning her throat. Her eyes wide with disbelief, she stared at him mutely.

"I told you I was mean when I'm riled." Watching her over the rim of his cup Rio's eyes began to gleam devilishly. "Maybe you'd better be careful not to rile me . . . umm?"

He was teasing her, surely? And, dammit, who did he think he was to threaten her? Courtney's fear subsided as her fighting spirit rose. How dare he taunt her? she thought in cold fury, reflecting his actions as she picked up her cup and leaned back in her chair. Wretched man!

"I was unusually riled once," she said mildly, smiling sweetly, "by a charging rhinoceros while on a photo safari with my father. I shot the beast, dropped him in his tracks. I'm an expert shot, you know." She arched both delicate eyebrows. "Your hide isn't quite as thick as a rhino's—or is it?"

Rio nearly choked on the laughter that erupted from his throat. "Are you really an expert shot?" he finally managed.

"Yes, actually, I am." Glancing down she reflected his action by placing her cup on the table. "Does that amaze you?"

"No, actually, it doesn't," he mocked softly; then, standing abruptly, he leaned across the small table to grasp her chin, tilting her face upward. "You know, I'm beginning to think we just might be well matched, Courtney." Bending smoothly he fastened his mouth to hers.

Courtney was instantly spun into the sensuous realm that Rio's hard mouth had the power to create. Within that molten realm there were no fears or differences or even the tiniest thought of her barely touched breakfast. In that realm was a hunger of a different sort. Curling her arms around his taut neck she clung with helpless need, her lips parting eagerly for the bold thrust of his tongue.

Rio lifted her effortlessly and carried her back to the rumpled bed, settling her gently in the midst of the disorder. Releasing her mouth lingeringly, he stepped back, hands going to the waist snap on his jeans.

"Rio, it's the middle of the day!" Courtney gasped as she emerged from her kiss-induced fog.

A smile eased the strain of desire tightening his lips. "Yes," he purred sexily, stepping out of the jeans. "And all the more exciting in full daylight."

Courtney didn't require his assurance; her eyes gave her the evidence of that. Her lips parted slightly, her breathing shallow, she gazed in fascinated wonder at his hard, naked body.

Lord, he was beautiful! And the same even nut-brown color from head to toe. Out of her control her gaze traveled slowly over the lean, muscular length of him from his neatly knit ankles to his well-formed calves to his hard-looking, long-muscled thighs and beyond until her gaze came to a startled halt on the rigid evidence proclaiming him all male. Then, acutely aware that she was staring in awe, Courtney hurriedly raised her glance to his face.

"I could feel your gaze on me like the touch of fire, *querida*," Rio said in a tight, husky murmur.

"It felt incredibly erotic. Take off your robe and lie back, I'll show you what I mean."

Middle of the day or not, Courtney was long past resistance. His use of the Spanish endearment was an added inducement. She removed the silky garment with unstudied sensuality and her pulse rate went wild at the leap of excitement his eyes flashed when she tossed the robe aside and eased onto her back on the bed.

Within seconds Courtney came to an immediate understanding of Rio's claim. The flame seemed to leap from his eyes to lick hungrily over her trembling flesh everywhere his gaze touched, igniting a responsive heat in her that quickly raged out of control, consuming her entire being.

Following an urge that refused to be disobeyed, she lifted her empty arms in invitation.

Murmuring words that she couldn't really hear, yet understood nonetheless, Rio slid into her embrace and into her body like a brilliant pillar of fire.

"Yes, *querida,* there are differences between us," his raspy voice crooned against her mouth, "vast differences. But in many ways, especially this one, we are well and truly matched."

The afternoon was lost to the delicious discoveries of conjugal bliss.

On awakening near sunset Courtney felt absolutely marvelous, except that she was alone, not only in the bed but in the room.

"Rio?" she called softly, testing to see if he was in the bathroom. Her own soft voice echoed hollowly around her.

Missing his nearness with an intensity that startled her, she scrambled from beneath the tangled covers. Where was he? she grumbled silently, striding into the bathroom. Why had he gone off like that, leaving her alone and cold in that huge bed?

Her thoughts stopped Courtney dead, one foot in the shower stall, the other on the floor. Good heavens! How was it possible? It was inconceivable even to imagine that Rio had become so very important to her feeling of well-being! Wasn't it?

Stepping into the stall she turned the hot water on full blast; merely thinking his name sent a thrill dancing crazily over her body!

Rio. Rio. Rio. Like a litany, a prayer, a longing, his name reverberated inside her head.

She loved him! Surprise parted her lips, and Courtney sputtered as water rushed into her mouth. She was in love with her husband. Backing up, she stood numbly watching the water cascade over her body. Was it possible, really possible, to fall in love so very quickly?

Without conscious command her hand slid protectively over her flat belly. Her child. Rio's child. Theirs! Oh, dear Lord! She was carrying *their* child —the child they had created! Not until that instant had the full meaning of her pregnancy hit her. Her reaction was stunning. Wild, riotous joy coursed through her, singing to her of the richness of her womanhood. She was carrying Rio's child in her body—the body he had loved so exquisitely.

Euphoric, Courtney was barely aware of turning off the water or leaving the bathroom minutes later. Still floating in a self-induced "in-love" high, she dressed in a haze of baby-blue and pink, by sheer instinct pairing a silky jewel-toned green shirt with slim-legged, buff-colored jeans.

Courtney was humming to herself as she

brushed the tangles out of her hair when his low, gravelly voice crept to her from the doorway.

"Afternoon loving appears to agree with you. I'll have to remember that."

Glancing up quickly, Courtney's gaze collided and meshed with his. Rio! *Her* husband! The singing joy was back, brightening her eyes, painting her cheeks an apricot hue. Her lover!

Rio's soft laughter had the sound of contentment. "Have I embarrassed you?" he asked teasingly.

"No," Courtney said softly, honestly. "I think the term is 'pleasured' me." To reinforce her statement she allowed her glance to drift slowly over his relaxed body as he leaned lazily against the door frame.

"Come over here, Courtney," he commanded in an enticing drawl. "I want to taste the heat coloring your cheeks."

The hairbrush clattered to the dresser surface from her suddenly nerveless fingers, and without pause she walked to him, her eyes cloudy with expectancy.

Lowering his head Rio caressed her warm cheek with parted lips and tasted her skin with the tip of his tongue. "Humm," he breathed, "you smell good." Lingeringly he slid his palms up her body. "Feel good too," he whispered raspily. "Like a woman made for loving . . . at night, at dawn, at the height of the day."

Her body softening to his touch, Courtney melted into his exciting hardness, seeking closer and still closer contact with him. Every thing she'd been yearning for all her adult life was waiting for her inside his embrace. She willingly surrendered everything female in her to everything male in

195

him by offering her mouth to his, and with it her heart and soul.

Rio kissed her deeply but without the crushing, hot demand she had come so easily to crave. As he reluctantly raised his head his dark eyes smiled into hers.

"Maria has dinner ready," he told her by way of explaining the briefness of his caress. Looping one arm around her shoulders he drew her from the doorway. As they started down the hall he spread the fingers of his other hand over her abdomen. "You must nourish the little one."

Feeling cosseted, Courtney allowed him to seat her at the large, oval dining room table. Quite used to elegant furnishings, she was nonetheless impressed with the heavy, exquisitely carved dark wood table and chairs, which were padded on the seats and backs with wine-red leather. The spacious room was bathed in soft light from a hanging lamp of Moroccan design. Courtney adored the room on sight.

The table was set with exquisite china and sterling silver on a delicate lace tablecloth. The deep grooves of the heavy crystal glasses reflected a rainbow of colors in the glow of the gently swaying lamp.

Maria entered the room—through a filigreed door set into the archway into the kitchen—just as Rio was pouring wine into their glasses. With smiling, silent efficiency she arranged the food on the table, then disappeared behind the door with a murmured "Enjoy your meal, señor, señora," leaving Courtney in no doubt who ranked first in the house.

Fingering the stem of his glass, Rio raised the

scarred eyebrow at her. "Would you like a toast to commemorate our first real dinner together?"

Surprised, Courtney smiled fleetingly. "Yes, that would be lovely," she murmured a trifle breathlessly.

He frowned in concentration as he lifted his glass and said quietly, "Then let's drink to the few qualities we do share: a determination of character, a mutual physical attraction, and the life growing inside you. It's not nearly enough, but it will have to do . . . for now." His lips curved cynically as he brought the glass to his mouth after tipping it slightly in her direction. "Salud."

As he spoke those words, he broke the euphoric bubble Courtney had been floating in. The song of joy was stilled in her veins. Deflated, she raised her glass listlessly.

It will have to do . . . for now.

At that moment Courtney felt positive that his bleak-sounding words would ring in her mind for the remainder of her life. Had she actually begun to believe their marriage might have a chance of survival? Afraid she'd cry out in protest, she swallowed whatever it was she'd unconsciously bitten into. The bit of food was hot and spicy, a fact that she was grateful for, as it excused the tears shimmering in her eyes.

"Too hot?" Rio commiserated, holding a glass of iced water out to her. "It's Tex-Mex." He grimaced. "I should have thought—"

"No, it's fine." Courtney conjured a smile from somewhere. "I like the taste. I'll get used to it." She forked another, bigger portion into her mouth to prove her claim, rather amazed to find she really did like the taste. Conversely, her action annoyed Rio instead of reassuring him.

"You don't have to prove anything to me, Courtney." Hard, discouraging impatience serrated his tone. "If you'd prefer something milder, say so. Maria will prepare it for you."

The flare of anger inside soothed the sense of dejection weighing on Courtney. Obviously Rio considered her finicky as well as a layabout do-nothing! Flinging her head up she angled her chin haughtily and glared at him.

"This meal will do fine," she said distinctly.

Rio seemed to be on the point of argument, and where it all would have ended Courtney couldn't imagine; but fortunately the low sounds of another dissension filtered to them through the filagreed door.

"The señor is having dinner," Maria said softly but adamantly.

"But this is important!" The voice was low, intense, and unfamiliar to Courtney.

"It will keep until after—"

"Come on in, Sal," Rio called, overriding Maria.

Sal? Courtney shifted her gaze from Rio's tautly set face to the door separating the two rooms. The man who pushed through the door, battered Stetson in hand, was something of a shock to her.

He was about the same as Maria's slightly below-average size, his slim frame wiry and compact. If pressed, Courtney would have guessed his age to be in the vicinity of forty-five, while admitting he could be anywhere between forty and fifty. His head was covered by a mass of black curls, badly in need of trimming. His skin was swarthy and smooth over a lean face with a defiant jaw. His eyes were the deepest, softest brown Courtney had ever seen on man or woman.

This man is mean? she thought at once, shifting

a disbelieving glance at Rio. Reading her expression, Rio nodded briefly, but firmly, as he waved one hand at the chair to his right.

"Sit down, Sal," he invited tersely. "Wine?"

"No, thanks." Startling white teeth flashed against his dark skin. "But I sure could use a beer," he added, tilting his head back to smile at the woman who'd followed him into the room.

"Sal Alvarez!" Maria hissed, her eyes sparking with warning.

"Get the man a beer, Maria," Rio ordered gently. "And a plate, too, if he's hungry."

"No, sir!" Sal shook his head. "I've had supper." A soft smile touched his lips as he ran a caressing gaze over Maria's hips, swaying gently as she swept into the kitchen.

Studying the glow in Sal's eyes, Courtney felt a jolt of emotion rush through her. Why, he loves her, really loves her! She admitted sadly that she was feeling the envy she'd experienced earlier while in Sam and Morgan's company. At that moment Courtney was relieved that Rio's gravelly voice snagged her attention.

"So, what's so all-fired important?" Rio demanded calmly.

"The law has made a positive ID on the note writer," Sal replied, smiling his thanks as Maria handed him an open can of beer. "His name is Benjamin Colten. He fits the description your wife gave the authorities a couple weeks ago." He glanced at Courtney with a fleeting smile. "Seems the bad-ass is wanted for just about everything: armed robbery, assault with intent, parole violation, *and* attempted rape." His lips twisted sourly. "A real sweetheart."

"Yeah." Rio's eyes narrowed. "I should have put him away when I had the chance."

Courtney's gasp rang loud in the silence that fell after Rio's disgusted statement. "You—you mean kill him!" she choked, biting her lips when he turned a cold-eyed stare at her.

"Yes, Courtney, I mean I should have killed him." If possible his eyes grew even colder, deadly cold. "It would have saved the law the trouble of rounding him up." Glancing away dismissingly, he fixed that cold stare on Sal. "The authorities have anything on the other two men?"

"Nothin'." Sal shrugged. "And no leads as to their present whereabouts. Looks like they've gone to ground." Lifting the can to his lips he finished the beer in a few deep swallows.

"This Colten from the Pecos?" Rio asked softly.

Sal shook his head. "From Nevada originally."

"Figures." Rio snorted. "That's probably where he hooked up with Henderson."

"That's what the tin stars figure too," Sal concurred. "They theorize that Henderson was the brains behind the plan. That son-of-a . . ." He flashed a chagrined glance at Courtney. "Sorry, ma'am. Anyway, Henderson was working as an extra hand for the spring roundup when your wife was visiting the Wades. Mr. Wade has grilled every one of his regular men and it appears that Henderson was overly curious about your wife's actions."

"Why the hell wasn't that reported to Morgan?" Rio exploded angrily, ignoring Courtney's low moan of dismay.

"He wasn't obvious about it—and"—Sal lifted his shoulders in a helpless gesture—"well, the men put his interest down to natural curiosity over foreign visitors."

Rio's smile was not pleasant. "Something like that had better not happen on *this* property." He raised his voice, which, for some inexplicable reason, now seemed sinister to Courtney.

"I don't think you have to worry on that score," Sal said quietly. "But I'll pass the word around anyway."

"I'd appreciate it," Rio drawled, his rasp more pronounced. "Anything else?"

"No." Pushing back his chair, Sal got to his feet. "Cleat and I will be keeping lines open to the law. If there is anything, you'll know as soon as we do."

"All right, and thanks, Sal." Rio dismissed him with a sharp nod of his head.

Sal nodded back before shifting his gaze to Courtney. "Sorry I interrupted your dinner, ma'am." Without waiting for a reply from her he strode from the room, leaving a constrained silence behind.

Courtney finished eating the now almost cold food. The conversation about the disgusting Ben had unnerved her, yet she admitted to herself that Rio's flatly cold statement that he should have killed the man had unnerved her more. She had always had an absolute abhorrence for violence, and the very idea that Rio could talk so calmly about taking a life, a human life, chilled her blood. Her feelings were evident to Rio.

"You're shocked?" he asked coolly, sipping his wine.

"Yes." Courtney was beyond dissembling. "I hate the thought of killing."

"Yet you told me you'd shot a rhino," Rio taunted softly.

"The beast was charging!" Courtney insisted. "It was either the animal or me!"

201

Rio smiled. "It may come to that with Ben," he reminded her smoothly. "I could have prevented all the hassle we're having with him now."

"By killing him in cold blood?" Courtney cried.

"But you admitted to wanting to kill him." He shrugged. "I don't see the difference."

"At the time he had hurt me, Rio!" Courtney argued. "He never actually gave you reason to kill him." Without thinking through her charge she rushed on, "Is that how you acquired the name Night Striker . . . by killing?"

Rio withdrew, closing himself off from her completely. If Courtney had thought he'd been cold before, she now learned the true meaning of the word.

"What do you know about the Night Striker?" His voice had the consistency of ice crystals forming into words.

Courtney gathered her composure around her like a shield and met his frigid stare with deceptively cool eyes. "Very little, actually. Morgan was not exactly forthcoming."

"Morgan?" His quiet, almost pleasant, tone had a sinister ring. "I never knew Morgan to be overtalkative."

Courtney squirmed in her chair. Had she seriously been afraid of Ben for Rio's sake? she thought wildly. Now, mesmerized by the deadly stillness of her husband, she almost pitied Ben for having "riled" Rio.

Her husband! Courtney's thought reverberated in her head loudly. The connotations connected to the phrase were too overwhelming to consider at the moment. Slowly inhaling a calming breath, Courtney attempted to thaw some of his ice.

"Rio, Morgan was *not* overtalkative," she placated. "I was naturally curious about the man who rescued me." She lifted her shoulders in what she hoped was a light is-it-really-so-important shrug. "I questioned him; his answers were sketchy at best."

"Umm."

What was "Umm" supposed to mean? Dammit! Rio was no more enlightening than Morgan had been! She was his wife. She had entrusted not only her future but that of her unborn child into his care. Feeling as cold as he looked, Courtney decided she deserved some answers.

"Rio, how did you get the name Night Striker?" Courtney would not have believed it possible, yet he seemed to withdraw even more. Suddenly fury born of uncertainty seared through her, and flared from her trembling lips. "Damn you! Did you earn the name by taking human life?"

"Yes." Rio's response was devastatingly calm, and shatteringly remote.

Slumping against the chair, Courtney unconsciously slid her palm over her abdomen. Rio observed her action through eyes devoid of expression—or even life.

"I did what I was paid to do, Courtney. I was tagged with the stupid title simply because I preferred to execute my assignments at night." Rio's tone was as devoid of life as his eyes, which flickered only once—when Courtney shuddered at his use of the term *execute*.

"And . . ." Courtney wet parched lips. "And those assignments were to . . . to kill?" she choked out.

Rio's lips curved sardonically. "If necessary." The smile faded. "And it usually was."

Courtney felt sick to her stomach; still she kept

203

on, inflicting deep pain on herself while lashing out at him. "You were paid to execute?"

"I was paid to rescue," he corrected her in a jagged-edged tone. "In much the same way I was hired to rescue you." Rio smiled naturally for the first time since their confrontation had begun. "Even though taking a leisurely ride into the hills was a piece of cake compared to crawling through some damned jungle."

Though spare, Rio's description was enough to set her meal rumbling in her stomach. Grasping her wine she swallowed convulsively in an effort to drown the nausea stinging the back of her throat.

"You—you were no more than a hired gun," she accused.

"There you're wrong." Rio studied her pale face unemotionally. "The companies I worked for had the wherewithal to hire any number of guns. *I* was hired, and paid very well, for my expertise." Not a hint of conceit or ego colored his even tone.

"But why?" Courtney cried.

"Why what?" he queried softly.

"Why did you ever even consider *that* kind of work?"

"I've already told you," Rio replied. "I was more than adequately compensated for my skills."

"But your father is a wealthy man!" she exclaimed, feeling at the end of endurance.

"And I'm my own man."

Emotionally spent, her stomach upset, Courtney closed her eyes and rested her head against the back of the chair. His own man. Of course, she really should have known. Out of all her male acquaintances Rio was, with the exception of Morgan Wade, unquestionably *the* most definite "man."

204

"I almost feel sorry for that beastly Ben." Court-ney murmured her earlier thought aloud, her eyes flying open when Rio laughed quietly.

"Would you like my word that I won't kill him?"

He was serious! The evidence of her probing gaze left Courtney in no doubt whatever that Rio was dead serious. And, without questioning how she knew, she was positive that once given, Rio's word was unshakable.

"Yes, I want your word on it, please," she pleaded.

"You have it," he promised unhesitatingly. Then a dry smile tilted his lips. "I might bend him a mite, but I swear I won't break him."

"Thank you for that, at least." Courtney could not know that the excessive weariness shading her tone came across as disgust to the man sitting opposite her, and so could only wonder why when the shutters were again drawn over his expression.

"Like it or not, you are going to have to learn to live with it, and me, Courtney." The ice was back, double thickness. "At least until the child is born."

"What?" Her mind and body beginning to succumb to the effects of too little food, too little rest, and an abundance of sexual activity, Courtney shook her head in confusion.

Rio misinterpreted the gesture as one of rejection. Fluidly surging to his feet he rounded the table to her. "You heard me," he said grittily, bending to lift her out of her chair and into his arms. "You wanted a name for the child," he growled, carrying her along the hall to his bedroom. "We both wanted the correct name for the child," he amended grimly.

The bedroom door swung shut at a short, backward kick of his foot. Intent on his purpose Rio crossed the deeply piled carpet to the large bed.

"Okay," he grunted, settling her gently on the bed. "You've got what you wanted; you'll take what goes with it."

Snuggling into the mattress Courtney sighed as she closed her eyes. She was so very tired; what was Rio talking about? With an effort she roused herself enough to open her eyes a smidgen. Rio's face, set into unrelenting lines, sent a shiver over her arms. He seemed so terribly intense.

"Rio, I don't—" Courtney started to tell him she hadn't understood what he'd said, but he cut her off harshly.

"It's too late now, Courtney." His light touch in variance with his rough voice, he began to remove her clothes. "*You* set the rules by sending Morgan to me. And now you'll live with them. When you accepted my name you accepted everything that entails." He stepped back as he stripped her last piece of clothing from her and began divesting himself of his own garments. Moments later he slid onto the bed beside her.

"You are my wife, *querida*. The marriage has been consummated." Gathering her into his arms he drew her to the hardness of him. "And you'll be my wife in every way, including—no, especially— in the bedroom." He paused, then repeated his earlier remark. "At least until after the child is born. Do you understand?"

Courtney didn't, not fully, yet she was so sleepy, she breathed, "Yes, Rio. May I go to sleep now?"

"Yes, Courtney," he returned, mockingly.

CHAPTER NINE

Holding Courtney captive in a close embrace, Rio lay awake long into the night. Although the night was warm and the house comfortable, he shivered from the chill of his thoughts.

Courtney thought him a killer, probably of the same ilk as the lumbering Ben and his buddies. No. Rio's lips twisted. She considered him even worse than the men who'd kidnapped her. She considered him a cold-blooded killer, a hit man, a hired gun. And Courtney of the social elite hated violence and killers.

Feeling suddenly old and used up, Rio sighed. For a few brief hours he had seriously begun to believe their marriage might have a chance of working. Now he knew better.

The loving had been so unbelievably good, it had bordered on the perfect.

Damn! Why had Morgan—Rio cut off the condemning thought abruptly. If Morgan hadn't said word one it wouldn't have made any difference, and he knew it. Courtney would have learned the truth about him at some point, and her reaction would have been the same.

It was as he'd known from the beginning: they were from two vastly divergent worlds. Now Courtney had suffered the trauma of emotional shock as well as of cultural shock. Added to the hard-baked earth of West Texas, she found herself with an equally hard-baked man.

Shifting, Rio inched onto his side to gaze on Courtney's sleeping face. Why did she have to be so very special? he reflected achingly. Why couldn't she have been like any other of the many nice, pleasant, yet ordinary women he'd known? What made Courtney special, anyway?

She *was* stunningly beautiful—but it was more than her surface beauty that appealed to him. Outwardly caressing her features with his brooding gaze, Rio examined images of Courtney with his inner eye.

There was the image of the first time he'd seen her, after stepping into that bedroom in the cabin. Even then her physical beauty had stopped the breath in his throat. But it had been her expression that had caused a cold, murderous rage in his body. Her expression had revealed a variety of emotions, the uppermost being stark terror. Yet, even in the watery light from the moon, he had been able to read revulsion, hatred, and fierce determination in her face as well.

Rio had known instantly what she'd been determined about. It was as plain as if she had shouted it aloud; she would die before enduring the rape of her body by the animalistic Ben.

Courtney's resolution had been quixotic perhaps, possibly even foolish, but Rio had understood it at a gut level.

Then there was the image of her tenaciously holding on to the horse, and holding herself together, while he'd led her out of the hills. Though suffering from shock, reaction, sheer exhaustion, and physical discomfort from the cold, Courtney had clung to the saddle and her composure grittily, without complaint, arousing in Rio regret for not having eliminated the kidnappers, and thus any future threat from them.

On arrival at the ranch Rio had discovered yet another Courtney: a vulnerable woman pleading for reassurance about her attractiveness and realness as a person. That woman had stirred compassion in him.

But it had been the woman he had held in his arms, the passionate, giving woman, who had stamped a tormenting image in Rio's mind and senses. It was that Courtney who compelled his body and lured his thoughts.

Of course, there was also the Courtney he had observed for a few enlightening hours after he'd returned her to the haven of her father's arms and her cousin's home. That Courtney was arrogant and haughty, a true representative of the British aristocracy.

Gazing bleakly at her shadowed features, Rio sighed; damned if he wasn't intrigued by every facet she'd revealed to him. In truth he couldn't even fault the woman who deplored violence . . . even though it meant she naturally deplored him, and the way he'd earned his living as well.

Shifting position again Rio cradled her form closely to his own, feeling the warmth of her in the depths of his body and soul. He wanted her. God how he wanted her! But he wanted all of her. He wanted every facet of her attuned to every facet of him. The muscles of his throat tightening, he spread his open hand over her flat belly. His child. The concept awed Rio. *His* child! If they could never share anything else, they would forever share the living proof of their time together.

Lowering his lashes, Rio kept his eyes shut tightly as a spasm of pain moved over his rigid features. Damn! Falling in love was a bitch!

As the chill of dawn pervaded the room, Courtney snuggled against him, seeking warmth. The silky skin on her cheek teased the hair on Rio's chest and tangled his libido and emotions.

Once again his hand sought her abdomen. However deep her antipathy for him, he would keep Courtney with him until her pregnancy was over, Rio decided. He *would* see his only child come into the world!

Living with Rio McCord was like trying to set up housekeeping on a seesaw, Courtney concluded after a month of the up-and-down relationship. To all appearances Rio had donned the role of husband with aplomb, wearing it with the ease with which he wore his faded jeans and scuffed boots. And, to the casual observer, the marriage would seem to be working very well, Courtney felt positive. But appearances aside, she knew their marriage was a sham; there simply were no lines of communication open between them.

Courtney and Rio lived in the same house, ate at the same table, slept in the same bed, and monitored the growth of the child they had created. And they were still strangers to each other.

By the time the merciless summer sun softened its grip on the parched land, Courtney knew Maria, Sal, Cleat and most of the rest of Rio's employees better than she knew him. In his silence Rio remained an enigma.

As the weeks accumulated into months Rio maintained a consistent attitude toward Courtney. He was considerate, he was polite, he was often kind, he was remote—except in the bedroom, in the bed. When he made love to her, as he did most nights, Rio was a living, breathing flame, a flame that burned away every trace of the reserve Courtney used as a defense during the daylight hours.

Despite a growing sense of futility Courtney never considered refusing his nighttime advances. She loved him, and against all her attempts at rationalizing her feelings away, her love for him deepened with each successive day. Even on her most depressed nights it was always the same. Rio had but to reach for her and her resistance melted like an ice cube exposed to the Pecos summer sun.

With an eerie sensation of existing somewhere in limbo land, Courtney drifted in the ebb and flow of Rio's tide, her chin angled regally, her sapphire eyes cool, her upper lip stiff as the starched collar on Sal's Sunday go-to-church shirt.

There were many times when Courtney longed for the release of tears, but she never once gave in to the temptation. She was a Tremaine-Smythe, and she'd be damned before she'd ever again betray her weakness to Rio McCord!

Fortunately Courtney had her work. The week following their marriage she requested transport into El Paso to do some shopping. When he found out what she wanted to shop for, Rio himself flew her to Houston, where, within a few hectic hours, she was able to purchase all the materials she needed to set up her own studio in the ranch house. The work was her only means of escape from the reality of the situation.

Through the weeks that followed, Courtney worked long hours in the room Rio allocated to her. It was only while working that she could lose herself, and the pressing sense of failure that haunted her waking hours.

Curiously the line of clothes she eventually sent off to her father was the best she'd ever designed. Utilizing mainly the tweeds and soft wools that were produced at the mills owned by her father, Courtney poured out her soul onto the detailed drawings that came to life under her talented hand.

While sitting, standing, pacing, before her drawing board in a ranch in West Texas, Courtney never dreamed that the exquisite fall and winter fashions she created from her own unhappiness would electrify the entire world of haute couture when they were unveiled the next spring. At the time all she thought of was surcease from her own conflicting emotions.

If there was any bright spot at all during those never-ending weeks and months, it was the apparent disappearance of Ben and his cohorts.

The arrest of the man named Henderson had necessitated several trips to Las Vegas for Courtney for the purpose of identification and depositions. Rio accompanied her, supplementing her story with his own.

Henderson had absolutely refused to name his accomplices, and was languishing in the county prison awaiting trial.

In early November Courtney was again called back to Vegas for additional (in Rio's words) "legal red-tape unwinding." As her body was beginning to show the proof of the child growing within, Courtney was uncomfortably aware of the speculative glances she received from the representatives of the law. Though the question was delicately couched, she was once again asked if she had been violated by one of the kidnappers.

The connotation was not lost on either Courtney or Rio; the authorities believed that she *had* been raped but, as often happened, was too ashamed and embarrassed to admit it. And though every man who spoke to her was gentle in approach, the speculative gleam was there in the glance that shifted from her body to her husband.

By the time Courtney was told she was free to return to Texas, Rio was icily furious. He bluntly informed them that he would not allow Courtney to travel to Nevada again until after the birth of *his* child. Amazingly Rio's dictate was met with sheepish agreement.

Strangely, with each successive trip away from the ranch, Courtney felt more like coming home on her return. The realization that she was coming to regard the desolate, dry Pecos as *home* instilled in her both happiness and grief, for not at any time had she forgotten Rio's words to her on the evening of their first full day of marriage:

"You'll be my wife in every way—at least until after the child is born."

Courtney didn't want to love the land any more than she wanted to love the man. But there it was, she was caught up in love for both.

The week before Thanksgiving, Courtney came to the dinner table with her mind set on a purpose. She broached the subject before Rio had finished his fruit cup appetizer.

"I would like to go shopping."

Rio's hand paused midway between the fruit cup and his mouth.

"In Houston," Courtney added coolly.

His gaze remote, Rio slowly lowered his hand to the table. "You know the doctor said no long trips before the baby comes," he said in a deliberately reasonable tone. His too cool, too calm attitude set a spark to her temper.

"Houston is not a long trip, Rio!" she exclaimed in exasperation.

"What do you need that you can't buy in Marfa?" he demanded, referring to the picturesque town in Presidio County that Courtney had fallen in love with at first sight.

"Problably nothing," she responded honestly. "But I want to shop at the Galeria."

His lips curved wryly. "Nieman-Marcus," he murmured.

"Yes," Courtney admitted, glancing down at her blossoming abdomen. "I'm growing out of even the loosest of my clothes. But that isn't the only reason I wish to shop in Houston," she went on. "With both of our fathers coming for the Christmas holiday there are some specialty foods I want to purchase."

"I don't like the idea," Rio said flatly, picking up his fork again. "Make a list of the things you want and I'll have them sent out from Houston." He resumed eating as if the subject were now closed. Courtney quickly disabused him of that notion.

"Rio, I really don't care whether you like the idea or not." Straightening her shoulders, she favored him with her most haughty look. "Nor am I seeking your approval," she continued cuttingly. "I am going to Houston, with or without you." She shrugged. "One or the other, it doesn't make the slightest difference to me." The last was an outright lie, but Courtney certainly was not about to let him know that.

Rio flew Courtney to Houston the Monday after Thanksgiving, and booked them into the city's most expensive hotel. Then he proceeded to confound her utterly by being the most considerate, charming companion she ever could have wished for.

For four lovely days and five ecstatic nights it was as if she and Rio were on the honeymoon they had never had. Stunned by his attentiveness, Courtney drank in his sudden warmth. Not only did he accompany her on her shopping binges, he offered his opinion on each and every selection.

As Rio had insisted she take her shopping in small doses due to her condition, Courtney made four separate lists, determined to eliminate one list per day. The first morning after their arrival she set off, Rio by her side, with the list containing the items of clothing she'd decided to purchase to see her through the remainder of her pregnancy. Fully expecting Rio to stand by, bored to the nines, Courtney was delightfully surprised when he took an active part in choosing the garments.

That evening as he escorted her into the very elegant restaurant in the hotel, Rio brought Courtney to a full stop by complimenting her on her appearance in the cleverly cut maternity dress he had particularly admired in the shop.

Calling herself a fool, Courtney nonetheless bloomed with his praise. As she had very recently begun to feel awkward and ungainly, Rio's timing was perfect.

The dinner they were served was delicious and

satisfying; the loving that came later that night was even more so.

The first day in Houston set the precedent for the three that followed. Together Courtney and Rio crossed off every item on her Christmas list on the second day. On the third day they shopped for the special foods and wines she wanted for the holiday. On the fourth morning, filled with trepidation, Courtney led Rio into the infants' department in a very exclusive shop.

Later she asked herself why she'd ever entertained the fear of Rio's displeasure; hadn't he made it abundantly clear from the beginning that he wanted the child? On entering the gaily decorated department Rio had merely smiled and drawled teasingly:

"What color are we going to buy—pink or blue?"

Set free of constraint Courtney indulged in an absolute orgy of shopping for the nursery she had secretly planned. But even though she went a little wild, at least her purchases were all practical. Rio, on the other hand, chose such vital items as enormous stuffed animals, a crib mobile, and a huge, hand-carved rocking horse in a dark wood that was tagged with an equally huge price sticker —discreetly hidden, of course.

By the time they flew out of Houston the next morning, Courtney was tired, but pleasantly so. The flight was smooth and uneventful. As Rio had arranged to have all of their packages sent to the ranch, their only baggage was the hand luggage they'd left with the previous Monday.

As they deplaned, Rio saw Sal, leaning negligently against the dusty Chevrolet Blazer Rio had bought a few months before.

"What are you doing here, and where's Frank?" he demanded as he guided Courtney to the vehicle.

"Maria's orders." Sal's grin revealed sparkling white teeth. "She sent Frank into El Paso for some supplies, and me out here to pick—"

Sal's voice broke on a high note with the zinging sound that cut through the air, and the puff of dust that burst from the ground as the rifle slug hit, missing Rio's head by less than half an inch.

"Je-sus!"

Courtney heard Sal's exclamation as Rio's body bore hers to the earth. After that the sequence of events happened so swiftly she was never quite sure of them in her memory.

Protecting her body with his own, Rio crawled, dragging her with him, to the Blazer and the shield of the large rear tire. From the corner of her eye Courtney had caught the motion as Sal dived through the open door of the vehicle just as another slug tore through the side window.

"Sal?" Rio called sharply.

"Missed me," Sal caroled back; then, "Comin' at ya, Rio," as he tossed a long-barreled handgun out through the door.

To Courtney's amazement Rio's arm snaked out and he plucked the weapon, butt to palm, from the air. The gun glinted blue-black in the harsh sunlight, mesmerizing her.

"Rio, who . . . ?" Courtney paused to swallow.

"I can make a pretty accurate guess," he muttered, checking the rounds in the chamber. "The bastards."

"B—but, I thought—" There was another whistling noise, then a thud at the impact of the shell into the body of the Blazer. Had she really

217

convinced herself that they had heard the last of Ben and the other kidnappers? she wondered wildly.

"Stay as far down as possible, Court!" Rio ordered tersely, pushing her head down to her drawn-up knees. "And stay absolutely still!"

Before she could utter a protest he was scrambling away from her on his belly, moving toward the protection of the front wheel. Courtney bit down hard on her lip to muffle the scream that rose to choke her. Dear God! Was Rio trying to get himself killed? An instant later Courtney did scream as another bullet whizzed through the air to sear a shallow trough in Rio's thigh. Rio's reaction was a low grunt of pain followed by a string of obscenities.

As sinuous as a reptile, Sal, the rifle in his fist looking like an extension of his right arm, slithered off the front seat of the Blazer and along the ground to Rio's side to examine the bloody wound briefly.

"I'll live," Rio snarled as Sal's fingers probed carefully. "The sons of bitches are behind the hangar."

"Right on both counts, as usual," Sal murmured. "They've got us pretty well pinned. How do you want to play this, ol' horse?"

"I'd say one of us has to make a dash for the hangar door, and since you have the rifle, it looks like I'm the one." Rio's tone was so imperturbable, Courtney had to bite back another scream.

In a continuous, fluid movement Rio was up, in a crouch, heading for the hangar, and Sal was firing the rifle repeatedly in the general direction the shots had come from. Before Rio reached the hangar doorway there was a shout of pain, then the sound of an engine starting, then the screech of tires as a vehicle drove away at considerable speed.

There was an instant's pause; then Rio and Sal were both running to the corner of the hangar and around it. Scrambling to her feet with an agility that belied her condition, Courtney was mere seconds behind them. As she rounded the corner of the hangar she came to an abrupt halt, her eyes widening with shock.

Rio and Sal were kneeling beside a man lying on the ground. There was a red stain spreading over his shirt. Courtney had never heard the man's name, but without having to be told she knew that the man she'd thought of as average would never terrorize anybody again. The low, choking sound she involuntarily made in her throat drew Rio's attention while at the same moment several vehicles came to a tire-squealing stop a few feet away. Cleat was out of the Jeep and running toward them before the vehicle's engine had stopped.

Her gaze riveted on the man's bloodstained shirt, Courtney was barely aware of Rio surging to his feet to move to her side, or even the rapid-fire questions Cleat rattled off at his employer. Her breathing shallow, her body chilled, she stared at the dead man until Rio turned her away. The sun had oddly lost its glare and her vision was narrowing when she heard the distant sound of Rio's raspy, clipped voice issuing orders.

"Cleat, leave two of the men here with Sal to wait for the authorities. You take the others and see if you can pick up a trail from behind the hangar. My wife's in shock, I'm taking her home. Sal, tell the sheriff he can talk to me there if he needs to."

Even while he was speaking Rio was leading her to the Blazer. Still dazed by the unexpectedness of the attack, and the gruesome outcome of it, Courtney didn't break free of the faintness pressing down on her mind until they were halfway back to the ranch house. As the mental fog cleared, Rio's injury was the first lucid thought that sprang to her mind.

"Rio, your leg!" She gasped, berating herself for forgetting, even though she'd nearly blacked out. She was reaching across the seat to examine the wound on his right thigh when his hand flashed from the steering wheel to push hers aside.

"It's all right—only a crease. Maria will take care of it." Rio's tone was off putting. "She's handled worse—much worse."

The chill that pervaded Courtney's body was infinitely more immobilizing than the chill of shock. Feeling like a tolerated outsider, she withdrew into the protective cloak of haughty composure.

"Of course," she murmured distantly, unaware of the pained expression that flickered over Rio's face. She didn't speak again until Rio brought the Blazer to a stop at the house. Without waiting for him she flung the door open and dashed for the door, speaking even as she fled.

"I . . . you'd better see Maria immediately to have that wound cleaned. I'll be in the bedroom. I . . . I'd like to lie down." Her eyes stinging, Courtney ran—to escape Rio, but mostly to escape the realization that he neither needed nor wanted her assistance.

In the quiet of the bedroom, however, Courtney did not think of lying down. Instead she paced restlessly, worrying about Rio's wound, and wondering what had happened to the man she had been in Houston with.

She had actually come to hope that she and Rio had made strides during their stay in Houston in closing the gulf separating them. Because of his attitude while shopping with her, and his gentle, ardent lovemaking every night, she had believed they might actually have a chance of making their marriage work.

What a foolish, naïve woman she was! The four days they'd spent together were moments out of the real world, quite like the moments they'd shared after Rio had rescued her. The real world, or at least Rio's real world, was an alien, frightening place to her, a place that contained whizzing bullets and a red stain spreading over a man's chest.

How very quickly Rio slid from the out-of-time world, to the harshness of his reality. The sound of gunfire and the scent of danger had instantly changed the Rio she had laughed with into the silent, narrow-eyed Night Striker, ready to face any challenge.

Was this the type of environment she wanted to raise her child in? she asked herself in frantic disappointment. But what choice had she? she countered her own doubt. She loved her child's father!

Courtney's thoughts soured her expression; at that moment Rio strode into the bedroom, only to come to an abrupt halt at the sight of her pale face.

He was carrying his boots in one hand and his jeans in the other. His only covering from the waist down was a swath of navy-blue. Rio did not appear ludicrous attired in a shirt and very brief shorts; he looked heart-thuddingly attractive, tough as old leather, and, amazingly after what he'd just been through, ready for action—sexual action.

A long white bandage drew Courtney's eyes from his arousal to his thigh. Embarrassed at having been staring, she forced her chin up and her voice low, and cool.

"Is the wound dreadfully painful?" Strangely, the accent that had softened over the last months rose to the fore under stress. Even to her own ears her voice had that veddy, veddy British note. Rio's face cringed at the sound of it.

"Middlin', but Maria assures me I'll survive." He drew the West Texas drawl out deliberately.

Hurt by his taunting, Courtney spun around to walk to the window. Why, why, had this had to happen now, when they were at the very brink of understanding one another? There was no answer, only the silent presence of the man behind her, the man who reacted so naturally to danger, and so casually to death. Courtney shivered with her thoughts.

"You hate it, don't you?" Courtney started at the sound of Rio's voice close to her ear; she hadn't even heard him move! Before her rattled mind could form an answer he was speaking again. "You kept your wits together very well out there. You didn't panic or go all screaming hysterical. But you hated it, didn't you?"

"Well, of course I hated it!" Courtney exclaimed, twisting around to face him. "Any normal person would have hated it! Rio, a man is dead!"

"That's right," he agreed. "Now there are two down and two to go."

Courtney knew she went white because she could actually feel the blood drain from her head. "Rio! You're not going after them? You're not going to take the law into your own hands?" She clamped her lips together at the rising pitch of her voice. "Rio, you promised!"

A confusing sadness seemed to cloud his eyes for an instant; then it was gone and his eyes were as flat as dark stones. "And I'll keep my word," he said tightly. "I won't personally kill either one of them, but I do intend to join the hunt." He smiled sarcastically. "If it bothers you, Courtney, think of it as you might a hunt at home . . . only you kill the fox, don't you?" He turned and strode into the bathroom, leaving her staring after him, her eyes mirroring a wound that went much, much deeper than the one on his leg.

Why now? Why now? The question had been Rio's steadfast companion for the entire week he'd spent with the Rangers, fruitlessly trailing the two remaining kidnappers. Damn! Ben and the lowlife he hung out with couldn't have picked a worse time to surface!

She was his! Rio had felt it in his bones during their stay in Houston; Courtney had been all warm and loving during those four days they'd had together. And now she'd froze up on him again. And he hadn't even had the pleasure of seeing Ben and the other man run to earth.

Disgusted, Rio turned the Jeep over to Cleat and, after giving a brief account of the unsuccessful chase, strode into the house to confront Courtney. Tired of the lack of communication between them, he intended to resolve their differences, one way or the other. To Rio's way of thinking, marriage should not be a state of undeclared war. While trailing around in the hills, he'd decided it was either going to be a real marriage or none at all.

Besides, he'd had it with being regarded as little more than a cold-blooded killer. Rio had never regretted his decision to work as a private covert agent, and he wasn't about to start now. Courtney was going to be given the choice of taking him as he was, or leaving him the hell alone.

As Rio followed the sound of Courtney's voice into the living room he thought he was prepared to meet anything—anything, that is, except their respective fathers. As he stood momentarily unobserved in the threshold of the Spanish-style room, a wry smile played over his face. The way his luck had been running lately, he thought resignedly, he really shouldn't have been surprised to see Pat and Charles. Pat spotted him first.

"Well, it's about time you got back," Pat boomed, springing out of his chair. "How did the hunting go?"

Rio glanced at Courtney, his spirit sinking at the anxious expression on her face.

"Hello, my dear." Rio planted a kiss on Courtney's cheek, then turned back to his father. "As for the kidnappers, we lost them in the hills," he answered him. "I can't imagine where the hell they're holed up now." Extending his hand, he headed straight for Charles. "How have you been, sir?" Rio asked, as if he really cared.

"Somewhat concerned, I'll admit." Charles smiled. "I was rather hoping those men would be incarcerated by now."

"I was kinda hoping they'd be dead," Rio said bluntly, ignoring Courtney's soft gasp as he strolled to the liquor cabinet in the corner. "It would save a lot of time and trouble on a trial," he

224

added, pouring amber whiskey into a short glass. As he turned back to the room, he tilted the glass to Courtney. "Your health, ma'am, and how are you feeling?" His gaze holding hers, he raised the glass and emptied it in a few deep swallows.

"I'm—fine—thank you," Courtney murmured with quiet dignity.

"Glad to hear it." Rio favored her with a half smile, then turned back to the whiskey bottle. He was baiting her, and he knew it, and he couldn't stop. He was tired, and suddenly hurting like hell, and what he really wanted to do was pull her into his arms and beg her to love him. But he couldn't do that—so he baited her, for the entire remainder of the evening, and the length of Pat's and Charles's stay through the Christmas holiday.

Oh, thank heaven it's over! The phrase taunted Courtney as she watched the plane carrying her father and Charles East become a dot against the brazen Texas sky.

Turning to walk to the Blazer, she flinched as her shoulder brushed Rio's arm. An odd expression, part smile and part sneer, tugged at his lips, causing her to cringe inside. Averting her gaze she hurried to the vehicle, slid onto the seat, and stared stonily through the side window. Rio eased silently behind the wheel. Courtney's thoughts were her only real company throughout the drive back to the house.

The holiday she had awaited with such anticipation had been a complete debacle. Courtney would have had to be blind to miss the contemplative looks her father had leveled on Rio, or even the swift, sharp glances Patrick shot at his son when Rio's tongue had held a certain bite. In her own mind Courtney was sure that it was, without doubt, the worst Christmas any one of them had ever lived through.

Now, in early January, tense and stressed from weeks of forced gaiety for the benefit of Charles and Patrick, and coping with Rio's remote attitude and cynical comments, Courtney felt on the very edge of shattering into tiny shards composed of bitterness and tears.

She was so ghastly tired. Staring sightlessly at the desolate terrain Courtney wondered again, perhaps for the thousandth time, why she simply hadn't left this unfriendly land and her equally unfriendly husband to return to her homeland with her father.

Because Rio would not have allowed her to leave, that's why, Courtney acknowledged wearily. Oh, he didn't want her anymore. Rio had established that fact in several ways, the most telling being his lack of interest in her in the bedroom; Rio had not touched her in any personal way since their return from Houston over six weeks before. Every night he came to their bed long after she was asleep, and was always gone when she awoke in the morning.

But Rio had a reason for keeping her at the ranch. He was determined to see his child come into the world. He had informed Courtney quite coolly that he had every intention of being in the delivery room when her time came. Courtney could not even speculate on what Rio would decide concerning their relationship—or lack of it— after their baby was born.

Two months. Sighing, Courtney closed her eyes. How could she manage to survive two more months in Rio's company? Her doctor had predicted the middle of March as her time for delivery. The mere idea of enduring Rio's remote companionship for that length of time sent a shudder through her.

"You can stop cringing away now"—Rio's raspy voice drew Courtney from the contemplation of the bleak weeks facing her. "You can run inside and escape now. We're home."

Before she could argue, or even protest his unfair analysis of her feelings and desires, Rio was slamming out of the Blazer and striding toward the stables.

As the weeks went slowly by, Courtney found herself smiling in self-derision at her January fears. Rio had discovered a variety of reasons (she was positive they were false) to be away from the ranch for long periods of time, and she tormented herself imagining Rio in the arms of another woman. The image made *her* both physically and emotionally ill.

Pure, soul-destroying jealousy was a completely new and thoroughly uncomfortable emotion for Courtney. Born to beauty and privilege, she had never found cause to be jealous of anything or anybody. The closest she had come to it were the twinges of envy she'd felt for the near perfect happiness her cousin Samantha had found with Morgan. But that mild envy was as nothing compared to the searing pain and anger she experienced at the thought of Rio caressing and loving another woman as he'd caressed and loved her.

Fortunately Rio was in between "business" trips when Courtney went into labor three weeks before her projected time. During the pain of childbirth Courtney had not the time or inclination to consider Rio's reaction. It was only later, as she lay exhausted but proud of the tiny, beautiful daughter she had helped create that she mused that not even the agony and messiness of giving birth had the power to rattle the ever-so-cool Night Striker. The closest Rio came to revealing any emotion at all was in the huskiness of his tone when he spoke to her after it was finally over.

"Thank you for my daughter, Courtney. She is perfect."

Having murmured his appreciation, Rio walked from the pastel-painted room, shutting the door gently. Courtney had more than earned a long rest. Pausing in the hospital corridor he drew a slow, deep breath; then, straightening, he strode down the gleaming corridor. As Rio passed silently by, observers saw only the hard set of his features and missed the bright sheen of tears in his eyes.

Once in the Blazer, Rio allowed his facial muscles to relax for the first time in what seemed like ages. The strong, callused hands gripping the steering wheel betrayed the tremors rippling in waves through his tough body.

With every atom in his body Rio thanked his maker that he'd been at home when Courtney had gone into premature labor. A soft smile gentled his expression as a vision of his perfectly formed, beautiful daughter rose in his mind.

Luz. Rio's smile faded at the thought of the name he was positive Courtney would never agree to. And Courtney had her rights, he acknowledged. More than most, after his behavior of the last three months.

Flicking the ignition key, Rio drove off the parking lot and to the hotel he'd be staying in until Courtney was released from the hospital. Looking

228

neither left nor right, yet missing nothing that went on around him, he went directly to the hotel bar-lounge. Over a double Jack Daniel's he decided he'd offer no objections to whatever name Courtney chose for their child; in his mind he would always think of his daughter as little Luz.

What would Courtney do now? Refusing to give in to the thickness that tightened his throat, Rio signaled the bartender for another drink. He had calls to make—to the ranch, to Nevada, to his father, who was presently in Dallas, and to England. How he longed to make those calls joyously, with all the pride and delight of a true husband. But he wasn't a true husband; he wasn't a husband at all except in name. During all the nights spent alone, whether at home or in some unfamiliar hotel room, he was longing, aching, for the passionate warmth and wild strawberry taste of his wife. He was irrevocably in love with Courtney, would be in love with her till the day he closed his eyes forever, and she was lost to him, if in fact she had ever been his at all.

And, though Rio granted Courtney her rights, he would allow himself none. He would abide by her decision in whatever she chose to do. What choice had he? Courtney thought him a killer.

The barren prospect of his own future had Rio motioning for the bartender to refill his glass.

She would have to leave. Rocking the chair gently with the toe of one foot, Courtney gazed down adoringly at the infant suckling greedily at her breast. The natural sensation radiating through her body by the action of the tiny lips was intensified by memories of a similar action by a strong male mouth.

Rio. The rocking stilled as Courtney rested her head against the chair's padded back. He was gone again, on yet another of his mysterious business trips. In the two months since their child's birth Rio had spent more time away from the ranch house than in it. His attitude spoke loudly enough. She didn't need the actual words to know that he wanted to be rid of her.

The sucking action ceased, drawing Courtney's attention to her daughter. Luz was sleeping soundly, her tiny lips slightly parted. She was glad she had acted on impulse in naming the child after Rio's mother. Each passing day the child grew more and more in the image of Rio, and thus like his mother. Rio's surprised and obviously delighted reaction to her choice of name had made it worth forgoing the one she had previously chosen —which she couldn't even remember anymore.

The occasion of the baby's christening had been the only time Rio had displayed any kind of warmth during the entire eight weeks following the child's birth.

Yes, Courtney decided, rising to lay Luz in the canopied crib she'd fallen in love with in Houston, she would have to leave.

With her decision finally made, Courtney left the nursery and strode purposefully to the bedroom. For all its desolate dryness she had come to love the land that had spawned Rio. Before she said her good-byes to Maria, Sal, Cleat, and all the friends she'd made, she would say a silent good-bye to the land—from the back of a horse.

Fifteen minutes later Courtney approached Sal in the stables with all the regal bearing befitting her position. Sal merely sighed in apology when she requested he saddle a mount for her.

"I can't allow you to ride out alone, Miz Mc-Cord. Sorry, but I have orders straight from the boss."

Suddenly all the months of hurt and rejection and frustration welled up to overwhelm Courtney's innate good sense. Drawing herself up even straighter, she stared down at the sorrowful Sal out of eyes glittering glacial-blue with fury.

"I told you to saddle a mount for me," she enunciated coldly. "And, when your 'boss' returns, from wherever he is, you may tell him Courtney Tremaine-Smythe said he can go to—"

"Do as she asks, Sal, and throw a saddle on Hot Foot while you're at it," Rio's cool voice cut in. "I will accompany the lady," he drawled with just a hint of sarcasm.

Courtney was tempted to tell Sal to forget it and turn on her booted heel and walk back to the house. But, her pride somehow challenged, she stood rigid, trading Rio stare for stare.

In antagonistic silence Courtney rode beside Rio into the grasslands of the Marfa Highlands in the direction of the escarpment known as the Rimrock. In other sections of the grasslands she knew that herds of cattle grazed, but here, on McCord land, all was quiet now that Rio had thinned his own herd of horses.

As the sun moved steadily toward its zenith, and the heat rose in enveloping waves, Courtney requested a short respite near a rock-rimmed, spring-fed pool. She had not been astride a horse since the early months of her pregnancy and now her muscles were complaining painfully.

Shrugging his unconcern one way or the other, Rio reined in Hot Foot and stepped out of the

231

saddle, standing absolutely still as he watched her moved stiffly toward a flat rock.

Her leg muscles protesting, Courtney carefully lowered herself to the rock. A soft "Oh" whispered through her lips at the sight of a small flower valiantly lifting its blossom to the light of the sun from beneath the rock. She was bent over, reaching down to touch one tiny petal with her fingertip, when Rio's low, raspy voice froze her in place.

"Don't move, Courtney."

Although she automatically obeyed his command, Courtney glanced up, eyes widening at the taut, coiled look of him.

"W-what?" she croaked, suddenly frightened.

"I said don't move. Don't talk." His motion fluid, Rio raised his right arm and carefully slid the rifle from the saddle scabbard. "Don't even breathe." Seemingly in slow motion he turned to face her while bringing the rifle butt to his shoulder.

Every living cell inside Courtney ceased functioning as she found herself staring fixedly at the tiny black hole at the end of the rifle barrel.

"Steady."

Panic exploded inside Courtney's head at the deadly calm tenor of Rio's whispery voice.

Oh, God! My God! Has Rio gone mad? He is going to fire that thing at me! Her dry mouth stung with the metallic taste of fear as her final thought screamed through her mind.

Rio is going to kill me!

In a frozen state of terror Courtney watched helplessly as Rio's finger eased the trigger back. She felt the bullet zing by her ear an instant before she heard the rifle's report. Stunned, she watched as he ejected the shell casing from the weapon. Then she glanced up and saw his eyes. And Rio's

232

eyes were more terrible than the fear she'd felt seconds before.

"You can breathe again," he said too softly as he walked to where she was sitting. "I usually hit what I aim at." With the barrel of the rifle he indicated a spot behind her hand.

Dragging her gaze from his, Courtney glanced down and around and felt sickness rise to close her throat. Partially hidden under the rock was a copperhead, minus the head. Springing to her feet she dashed for a low bush edging the small pool, into which she emptied her stomach of the breakfast she'd eaten a few hours previously. When she at last backed away from the bush Rio thrust a handkerchief, moistened in the pool, into her hands.

"If you're recovered, I'd like to go back to the ranch now." His tone was so devoid of inflection or life, it caused a thrill of dread along Courtney's spine.

What had she done? Oh, Lord, what had she done to him? The insistent question tormented Courtney all the long, silent way back to the house. Her horror at what she'd believed Rio was going to do had been transparent to him; Rio's cold, lifeless withdrawal was all the proof she needed of that. He *knew* that for an instant she had actually thought he was going to kill her. Her shame was endless, and Courtney fully realized she would live with it for the remainder of her life.

Rio walked away from her as soon as they'd dismounted at the stables. Denying the urge to run after him and plead for forgiveness, Courtney spun on her heel and retreated into the house to spend what was left of the afternoon rocking and crooning to her daughter, who slept peacefully through most of it. There was work she could have busied herself with. There were designs to be completed for the next spring line. Still she sat on, numbly rocking, rocking.

Courtney went to the dinner table freshly showered, with her hair brushed to a golden sheen. But she was devoid of makeup and attired simply in a flowing caftan in muted shades of blue. Her appearance was a true barometer of her distracted state, for even in Texas she had insisted on always dressing for dinner.

Rio joined her after she was seated, nodding at her but saying nothing. He was in dark slacks, and a dark shirt, and an even darker frame of mind. He said little throughout the meal, and then only in response to a comment from Maria, who made no attempt to hide the glances of confusion and concern she slanted from the "señor" to the "señora."

After eating less than half of his meal, Rio pushed his chair back so abruptly, Courtney looked up at him in startled reaction. His smile was an insult.

"If you'll excuse me?" His shuttered eyes were a burden. "I have work to do in my office."

Courtney followed him moments later; after bracing herself she walked to his office to apologize. Her timid knock on the office door was answered by what sounded like an impatient grunt. Squaring her shoulders, she opened the door and entered the room.

Rio was not sitting at his desk working. He was standing by the window, a glass half full of amber liquor in his hand. At Courtney's entrance he turned and stared sardonically. Loving him until it hurt, and more than a little afraid of what he might say to her, Courtney plunged into speech at once.

"Rio, I want to apologize for my hysterical behavior this afternoon." She really couldn't blame him for the sneering smile that briefly tilted his lips; even to her own ears her words rang of the finest finishing-school correctness.

"What for?" he drawled heavily. "Your reaction mirrored your true feelings."

"Rio, no!"

"Yes, Courtney," he mocked in an oddly sad way. "You actually thought I was going to fire that rifle and watch the slug slam into your body." The eyebrow inched higher. "Didn't you?"

"But . . . but, Rio! What was I to think when I glanced up to see you pointing that thing directly at me?" she cried desperately.

"You could have immediately thought that I was protecting you," he shot back harshly. "But, no, you wouldn't think that, not when you've always thought of me as a killer." Raising the glass he swallowed three quarters of the contents. A sigh hissed through his lips as he lowered the drink. "You've said your piece. Was there something else?"

"Rio, I've apologized," she cried, chilled by his remoteness. "What more can I do? Do you want me to grovel?"

"No, Courtney," he responded tiredly. "I want you to leave."

Everything was packed. Glancing around the room Courtney bit her lip to keep from crying aloud. She didn't want to go. She didn't want to take Luz and leave Rio. Now, when it was too late, she wanted to run to him and beg him to let her stay. But it was too late, he didn't want her around any longer.

Before going to Luz's nursery Courtney gazed around the room where she had lost her virginity and found her love. She had slept in the guest room since the night Rio had told her he wanted her gone. Stifling a sob, she quickly left the room.

When Courtney discovered the nursery empty she smiled and walked along the hall to the living room; Maria had taken to laying Luz on a blanket in there the last few days. Entering the archway into the room she came to an abrupt halt at the sight that met her startled eyes.

Propped up on one elbow, Rio was lying on the floor, talking softly to his daughter, who kicked and cooed and understood not a word of what her father was saying.

". . . and I want you to be a good girl, you hear? Eat your cereal and fruit so you grow big and strong and beautiful like your mother and grandmother." His voice dropped to a whisper. "I'll miss you, little love. I love you very much, and . . ."

Tears burning her cheeks, Courtney backed out of the archway.

CHAPTER TEN

"Are you sure this is wise, Samantha?" Morgan Wade asked his determined wife. "It's been almost six months now. If Rio was interested in Courtney, don't you think he'd have contacted her by now?"

"Rio? The man whose own father refers to him as Ol' Silent-in-the-Saddle?" A mocking smile curved her full lips. "You have got to be joking, darling. I feel quite certain ol' Rio would go to his grave with sealed lips before admitting he'd made a mistake by sending Courtney away." Sighing with exasperation she lifted the telephone receiver from the cradle. "The man loves her, you know?" Sam didn't look at Morgan as she punched in the long-distance number.

"Well, at one time I thought so too," Morgan said, shrugging. "But now I just don't know."

"We'll see." Samantha's grim tone altered. "Yes, hello, Maria, may I speak to Rio, please?" Her chin setting determinedly, she picked a sheet of stationery off the desk. "Rio, it's Samantha. I want to read something to you."

Rio's insides clenched with apprehension the instant he heard Samantha's voice. Mutely he gritted his teeth and listened as she continued.

"This is a passage from a letter I received from Uncle Charles. Please listen carefully."

Carefully? Rio almost laughed; every nerve and molecule in his body was straining to hear the contents of the letter.

"Charles writes: *Samantha, I am deeply concerned about Courtney.*"

"Is Courtney ill?" Rio broke in, imagining all sorts of terrifying things, from a serious accident to a more serious disease.

"Rio, will you please just listen?" Samantha's tone held a suspicious note of satisfaction.

Eyes narrowing in contemplation, Rio said, "All right, but get on with it, will you?"

"Of course. Now, where was I?" Sam went on too smoothly. "Oh, yes. Though Uncle Charles is concerned, he is also relieved that Morgan and I are flying over there next week. He continues: *I pray you can talk some sense into your cousin, for I'm afraid she's got in over her head this time. As I'm sure you're aware, Courtney does have this penchant for financially backing any cause that even smacks of passive action against violence. As she has both her own mind and her own fortune, I have never interfered. But this time I'm truly concerned for her personal safety.*

"*Courtney has been sponsoring a young man lately, an Irishman named Bryan Quinn, and although the man is personable enough, there are times he's simply much too intense for my tastes. I mean, really, the man has actually told me he intends to unite Ireland into a whole nation. A*

worthy cause, certainly. But in my experience vio-
lence seems to always surround these would-be
peacemakers, and I do not want Courtney hurt by
any peripheral turbulence.

"There is more to the letter," Samantha said
softly. "But I assume you get the drift?"

"Yes, I get the drift." Somehow, from somewhere, Rio found a steady tone. The phone moved
in his sweat-slick palm and, frowning, Rio glanced
down and grasped it more tightly. "When are you
and Morgan planning to leave for England?"

"We have seats booked on the Concorde depart-
ing from Kennedy next Wednesday."

"If I can arrange passage, I'll meet you at the
airport."

The following Wednesday found Rio, sprawled
with deceptive laziness on a plastic chair in the
departure lounge, scanning the faces of the crowd
for Sam and Morgan. As he waited for his friends
to arrive, Rio mentally reviewed the endlessness
of the months that had passed since he'd asked
Courtney to leave the ranch. Had it really only
been six months? It seemed six times that long.
Every day had felt like a week, and every week a
month. And the only contact he'd had with her
were the pictures of Luz she sent with scrupulous
regularity.

Why hadn't Courtney petitioned for a divorce?
Despite Rio's assurances to her that he would not
contest any action Courtney instigated, he had
had no notification of a suit from his lawyers. Secretly he was glad.

Where the hell were the Wades? His indolent,
relaxed appearance masking the impatience eating at him, Rio scanned the faces more closely.

There were still no signs of a beautiful redheaded woman escorted by a satisfied-looking tall man.

Sighing silently, Rio closed his eyes and let his mind wander. Courtney. Immediately an image of her rose to his mind, exciting him, hurting him. God, how he missed her—and the daughter whose growth he monitored periodically through snapshots. Luz was sitting up by herself now, and he hadn't been there to observe her struggles to do so.

At first Rio had eagerly looked forward to Henderson's trial, simply because he knew Courtney would be summoned back to the States to testify. Henderson himself had dashed Rio's hopes a month and a half after Courtney had returned to England. The word Rio had received was that Henderson had become involved in a scuffle in the prison yard, and had come out of it with a crudely made, six-inch blade in his chest; he had died en route to the hospital.

How many nights had Rio lain awake, aching for her, longing to hear the cultured sound of her voice blurring into the universal sound of sensual murmurings? Rio laughed wryly to himself; he had slept in snatches every night for the entire six months. Hell, he even missed the two-A.M. squalling from the nursery.

A chill of apprehension trickled down Rio's spine. Was Courtney safe? Was Luz safe? Dammit! They belonged with him, protected and cared for, not on the fringes of some fanatic's dreams of glory!

Fear tightening his throat, Rio squirmed in the small seat. He had decided months before that he would have to go to her, beg her if necessary to give their marriage another chance to work. He wanted the marriage with Courtney more than he'd ever wanted anything before in his life. Had he waited too long? A fine sheen of sweat beaded his brow. Why had he hesitated on the most important decision of his life? Rio inhaled deeply and exhaled slowly. Had it been his stiff-necked pride or simply because it was *the* most important decision of his life? There was always the distinct possibility that Courtney would turn him down.

And now that beautiful, burning flame he'd held so carelessly in his arms, *his* Courtney, was in all probability courting danger by aligning herself with a would-be crusader!

Clamping his teeth against a shudder, Rio glanced up, sighting Sam and Morgan as his will settled into unyielding steel. He would bring Courtney and Luz home, back to Texas—at any cost.

Samantha was still unsuccessfully hiding a smug smile after the plane had reached cruising altitude. Unusually edgy, Rio continued his barrage of questions.

"What else do you know of this Bryan Quinn, Sam?"

"Very little." The mention of the Irishman's name sobered her. "Other than that my uncle is obviously very worried about Courtney's involvement with his cause. I do know that she's been introducing him to some important people, along with making large monetary donations to him."

"Dammit!" Rio's anger got the better of him. "I might just decide to end the fool's cause myself. And I will, if Court gets hurt!"

"Correct me if I'm wrong but, didn't you send

241

Courtney away in the first place?" Morgan asked blandly.

"Yes." The admission came out with a hiss.

"Might a friend ask why?" Morgan's tone was bone dry.

"No."

"Rio!" Samantha glared at him. "We want to help! You *do* love her—don't you?"

"Yes." This time his voice was a whisper. "Yes, I love her." Rio moved uneasily in the seat; he wasn't in the habit of discussing his emotions with anyone. "I sent her away because of the way she looked at me," he finally admitted.

"The way she looked at you?" Morgan and Samantha exclaimed simultaneously.

"Rio, really!" Samantha shook her head in confusion.

"That's about as clear as mud, ol' son." Morgan frowned. "I don't understand."

"She questioned me about the stupid nickname you two so very helpfully told her about." Rio related the fact with a hint of accusation. "I was honest with her. I should have lied." A ripple of emotion moved over his face, hardening his features. "She considers me a killer."

"What?" Morgan barked.

"Rio!" Sam exclaimed.

"Oh, Courtney's cool," he murmured. "Her breeding shows." Cynicism tinged his smile. "But it was there, in her eyes. I couldn't miss it."

Sam stared at him in astonishment. "Couldn't miss what, for heaven's sake?"

"The waters are still muddy, friend." Morgan inserted.

"Revulsion. Disgust." Rio's shoulders lifted in a shrug. "Courtney hates violence, remember?" He tried a smile on for size; it didn't fit. "When she looks at me, she doesn't see Rio. She sees the Striker: a killer."

"I don't believe that, Rio." Sam's tone held firm conviction.

"Neither do I," Morgan concurred.

Rio dragged deeply on the cigarette, exhaling a sigh with the wisp of gray smoke that spiraled off into nothingness. "I hope you are both right. I want to bring her back with me. I want to bring my wife and daughter home to Texas." His smile hurt Sam's heart. "Even though I know my hot, dry land is as alien to Courtney as my former employment, I want her there with me."

On arrival in England, Rio found London the exact opposite of his native land—the air was chill, a misty rain was falling, the sky was pewter gray.

During the long drive into the city and his father-in-law's home near Berkeley Square, Rio's nerves tautened and his stomach muscles clenched. How would Courtney react to his sudden appearance? he wondered, retreating still farther into himself with each passing mile. Would she object to having him show up unannounced? Come to that, how would Charles react? Might both father and daughter frown at his uninvited visit?

The hell with it. Rio dismissed conjecture with a mental shrug. Courtney had never attempted to deny him his rights as a father. Rio longed to hold his baby in his arms while she still *was* a baby.

Charles welcomed his niece with open arms, her husband with a strong handshake, and Rio with a blatant smile of relief.

"I cannot tell you how delighted I am to see you,

all of you." Charles looked directly at Rio. "I had not dared to hope you'd come." A smile flickered over his lips. "Even though I prayed that you would." As he ushered them into the sitting room, his smile tilted apologetically. "I'm sorry, but Courtney and Luz are not here."

Stark alarm snaked through Rio, freezing him from the inside out.

"Where are they?" The inner freeze coated his raspy voice with ice.

"In the country, at Sterling."

Rio needed no further explanation; he knew all about Charles's country estate in Kent. His eyes narrowed dangerously as Charles continued.

"I was planning to leave tomorrow"—he paused to smile at Sam—"with Samantha and Morgan, to join her there. We've invited guests for the weekend. A hunt has been arranged."

"Will Quinn be there?" Rio's tone produced an effect different for each of the other three people in the room. Sam shivered. Charles frowned. Morgan smiled.

"Yes. In fact"—Charles wet his lips nervously— "Bryan is there now."

Now Rio smiled—a sight that increased Sam's shiver, deepened Charles's frown, and widened Morgan's smile into a grin. Rio's smile was a visible harbinger of what was to come; the Night Striker was ready to prowl.

Meanwhile, in a manor house in the county of Kent, Courtney paced, crooning to the fretful child in her arms.

"If you weren't such a little pig," she murmured into her daughter's silky dark hair, "you wouldn't have a bubble tormenting your tummy."

244

Rubbing the child's back gently, she circled the room that had been the library and was now her workroom. All the tools and clutter of her art made dedicated pacing difficult, and as she skirted around her design board, Courtney frowned.

The design on the board was only partially complete, yet it showed exquisite promise of a breathtaking ballgown. Halting her steps, but continuing to sway easily from side to side, Courtney ran a critical gaze over her creation. A soft sigh whispered through her lips; she had so wanted to finish the design before the rest of her guests arrived. So intent was her perusal of the incomplete work, Courtney didn't hear the low click of the door opening.

"Itching to be working, are you?"

A smile smoothed Courtney's pursed lips at the sound of the lilt that all his years and schooling in England had failed to erase from Bryan's voice.

"Yes," she admitted, shifting Luz in her arms. "But this little pig has a tummy ache from gobbling up her bottle too greedily."

At that moment Luz emitted a loud burp for such a tiny thing, and immediately her eyelids began to droop sleepily.

A hint of irritation flickered over Bryan's features as he observed the child; she was much too dark and foreign-looking for his tastes.

"Why do you insist on keeping the child with you throughout most of the day?" he demanded roughly. "Taking care of her is the nanny's job. That's what you pay the woman for."

Crossing the room he came to a stop less than a foot from Courtney, staring down at her fiercely. "Everyone knows you are a devoted mother,

245

Courtney. You have nothing to prove by spending nearly every waking moment with the babe."

Courtney was fully aware of Bryan's feeling on the subject of her method of motherhood. She was also aware of his hesitation to refer to Luz by her given name. How often had he urged her to bring two lawsuits—one of divorce, the other to legally change her child's first name? Courtney had stopped counting, simply because she hadn't the slightest intention of doing either.

"I'm not trying to prove anything, Bryan. You see, I don't feel at all as if I should spend time with Luz for appearance's sake. I *want* to spend time with her." Courtney's smile softened her firm tone; she genuinely liked Bryan, but she adored Luz, and loved Rio—another name Bryan found distasteful and foreign.

"And what of your guests?" Bryan's flash of anger revealed the rebel inside. "Are you planning to neglect them? There are some very important people coming for the weekend and the hunt; they could be of enormous help to me!" Raking a hand through his shock of auburn hair, Bryan spun away, then back to face her again. "I had hoped we would announce our engagement this weekend."

"Bryan, that is out of the question, and you've always known it. I do not have any feelings like that for you. I am still very much a married woman." Sighing, Courtney carefully carried her child to the large American-made playpen, and settled the now sleeping Luz on the padded floor of it. "I do not want to discuss the subject again. I already have a husband and my daughter has a father. You and I are just friends with the same political concerns."

"I intend to change your mind about that," Bryan argued.

"Oh, Bryan." Straightening away from the playpen Rio had had shipped to her from the same exclusive store in Houston where they'd shopped to outfit the nursery at the ranch, Courtney smiled sadly at the fiery Irishman. "How could you hope to be a father to Luz? You can barely force yourself to either look at her or say her name."

"Her name can be legally changed," he said mulishly. "As easily as your own can," he added with a glimmer of hope.

Her movements betraying weariness with the continuing argument, Courtney walked to the liquor cabinet along the one wall, raising her brows in question as she poured wine into a fragile tulip-shaped glass.

"Whiskey," Bryan responded to her silent invitation.

After handing him his drink Courtney, sipping at her wine, studied him over the rim of her glass. In appearance Bryan represented his homeland perfectly, with his auburn hair and eyebrows, and his muscular body, and his ruddy good looks. Oh, yes, Bryan Quinn had turned more than one young, and not so young, maiden's head. It was a pity, really, that he'd had to set his sights on her, Courtney mused. For, good or bad, like it or not, she was, and always would be, irrevocably Rio's, whether he wanted her or not.

"I am not going to change my name. I will not, even if Rio decides to divorce me," Courtney responded at length. "I do not love you, Bryan. And that is that."

"I won't give up even though you insist on ending this conversation." His tone had an underlying pout.

At that moment Bryan looked quite like an overindulged young man. Courtney nearly choked on her wine as a vision rose in her mind, a vision so sharp it made her ache all over—quite the way she did each and every night when she was finally alone in her bed. The comparison between her vision and the man scowling at her was so ludicrous, she almost laughed aloud. In comparison to the dark, silent, self-confident man of Courtney's vision, Bryan appeared little more than a petulant boy.

With a harsh shake of her head Courtney swung back to the cabinet, splashing wine into her glass with careless abandon. She didn't want to think of Rio, didn't need the proof of comparisons. Rio was the only man she wanted in her life, in her arms, in her bed; if she couldn't have Rio, she would sleep alone for the rest of her life. And, as it was patently obvious that Rio didn't want her, Courtney had resigned herself to an empty future and an equally empty bed. But she would not change her mind about Bryan and it was a pity, she mused again, raising her glass in salute to him. She really did like him.

Amazingly, Courtney did finish the design on her board before the rest of her guests began arriving for the weekend. It was a good thing, too, she reflected later that night when she'd finally bidden good night to the last of the night owls. If the evening was a sample for the weekend, she was in for a rather hectic time of it!

It was not until after luncheon the following day that Courtney realized exactly how hectic the weekend was going to be.

Courtney had joined several of her guests in a motor tour of the surrounding countryside. On her return to the house a smile lit her face at the sight of her father's Rolls-Royce parked in splendor before the wide steps. She was laughing up at Bryan as she entered the large reception hall. The living vision that met her gaze widened her eyes and dried the laughter on her lips.

Rio was sitting, lounging, on the third to last step of the grand staircase that curved majestically up to the first floor, his long, jean-encased legs stretched out in front of him, booted ankles crossed. His elbows were propped indolently on the step above the one he was sitting on, his broad, slender hands dangled over the edge of the marble riser. But most shattering of all to Courtney, for some odd reason, was the fact that he was wearing his Stetson—inside the house!—the brim tugged low over his glittering dark eyes.

"Rio!" In her shock and surprise a hoarse squeak was all Courtney could manage. But even in her shock she could feel Bryan stiffen beside her at the intimate tone of voice with which Rio responded.

"Hello, Courtney."

Moving in that boneless, effortless way that was uniquely his, Rio swept the hat from his head and surged to his feet. At the same instant the rest of the touring party came clattering, chattering, into the reception hall behind Courtney and Bryan. As if as one, the members of the group seemed to sense something awry and fell silent for a tense heartbeat of time. Then a voice, cultured, authoritative, broke the electric tension.

"Rio, my boy! When did you arrive?"

There was a collective gasp from every throat, including Courtney's. His narrow-eyed glance slicing through the dozen or so people now surrounding his wife, Rio drew another gasp from them with the grin that slashed his face and the familiar greeting that passed his lips.

"How goes it, Jamie?"

Jamie? Courtney thought blankly. He refers to her uncle, James Tremaine-Smythe, the Marquis of Ravenburn, as Jamie? Even *she* only ever called him Uncle James in private! Good grief! There were only a handful of people in the entire world privy to the affectionate family sobriquet, and her father was the single person ever to use it!

Loose-limbed and easy, his grin softening to a warm smile, Rio sauntered toward the tall, gauntly imposing figure standing near the open entrance doors. Blind to the expressions of shock and the gasped murmurs of the assemblage, he moved through them purposefully, extending his hand as he drew near the older man.

"I swear—Rio McCord!" James breathed unbelievably as he grasped the proffered hand.

"My lord Ravenburn." Rio nodded respectfully, clasping the hand firmly. "It's been a spell."

"It has indeed, seven years in fact since we met in Hong Kong." A delighted smile broke his somber countenance.

"My lord!"

The confused gathering turned to the new voice that rang from the broad staircase. As Courtney's face lighted in welcome, Samantha swept down the stairs and directly into the open arms of her mother's brother.

"Well, now, what have we here?" Ravenburn demanded, holding Samantha at arm's length to gaze into her glowing face. "Ah, I do believe it's that rebellious chit my sister brought into this world!"

"The same, my lord." Throwing back her glorious red hair, Samantha smiled up at him mistily.

"And every bit as lovely as her mother was—God rest her soul," Ravenburn murmured. Then he frowned. "Where is that cowboy you married?" he demanded arrogantly.

"Ever close to her, my lord," Morgan drawled, strolling toward them from the foot of the stairs. "Ravenburn," he greeted, grasping the man's hand with the same panache as Rio had.

"Wade." Ravenburn managed a passable drawl. "You do know Rio?" It was more a confirmation than a question.

Morgan smiled slowly. "We've spoken, a time or two."

"Quite." With a sharp nod of his white-maned head Ravenburn waved languidly toward an enormous set of double doors, while fixing a frown on Courtney. "Isn't it time for tea?"

"What?" Bemused by the incredulity of the scene she'd moments before witnessed, Courtney blinked. Then, coming to her senses, "Oh, yes!" Flustered, she spun on her heel to lead her guests into the large lounge, tugging the cord to summon the butler as she swept by.

Hanging back, Ravenburn leveled a coolly assessing glance on Rio. "In getting his man, the Night Striker's record remains unblemished." One thick eyebrow peaked arrogantly. "Will he now allow his woman to get away?"

"Can't have that." Rio smiled lazily. "It

251

wouldn't do to blot my copybook now, would it, sir?"

Inside the lounge Courtney wondered at the cause of her uncle's sudden roar of laughter.

CHAPTER ELEVEN

"What is he doing here?"

Clamping her lips against a startled yelp, Courtney jerked around at the sound of barely contained anger in Bryan's voice. She was standing in the shadows of the draperies that outlined the wide French doors leading onto the formal rose gardens. It had been nearly an hour since she'd ushered her guests into the lounge. Although her mind was still reeling from the events in the reception hall, her training had served her in good stead as she saw to the comfort of her guests. She had only moments before slipped into the protective shadows of the draperies for a breather; the absolute last thing she needed was a confrontation with Bryan.

"And why this particular weekend?" he continued harshly.

"It's really none of your business, but I assume Rio has come to England to see his daughter," she responded with a sigh.

Bryan wasn't listening. "Damn it! Besides your

uncle there will be several men here this weekend who could be of inestimable help to me in my campaign." He brushed the hair off his brow. "I need your support to enlist their aid." Bryan pinned her with a fiery gaze.

She returned his angry stare with blue eyes flashing. "It's unfortunate that Rio chose this weekend to visit, I agree. But I cannot deny him his parental rights."

"He obviously knows your uncle very well," he observed enviously.

"Yes," Courtney murmured, distracted by the same consideration. She glanced back into the long lounge, her gaze homing in unerringly on the dark man seated in the midst of a group that included her father, her uncle, and Morgan. As if he could feel her frowning regard, Rio glanced up. His dark-eyed gaze tangled with hers, refusing to release her.

Fingers curling into her palms, Courtney silently fought the sensual intimacy flaring in the depths of Rio's eyes. Her breathing shallow, painful, she received the message he was sending to her as clearly as if he'd shouted it the length of the room.

I want you, Rio's intent gaze whispered, *and I intend having you.*

Confused, wary, Courtney started when Bryan muttered close to her ear, "Damn him! I wish I could think of some way to get him out of here."

Alarm shot through her. Suddenly concerned, Courtney whirled to face him. Was he mad? she thought wildly. If Bryan started something! Oh, Lord! Courtney's cheeks flushed with anger. Bryan was foolish to think he had any say in her private life.

254

"Bryan, please." The fingers she placed on his arm trembled with inner tension. "Don't make a scene. I will arrange another weekend for you." She smiled placatingly. "You must accept the fact that Rio is my husband and he has every right to be here."

"Don't you understand? Time is valuable!" Bryan ground his teeth in frustration. "Dammit! I *needed* this weekend to raise financial support!" His movements jerky with suppressed anger, he strode away from her, his face working into an expression of geniality as he approached one of his targets.

Throughout the rest of the afternoon, and the entire evening, the hours blurred for Courtney, testing her exclusive-boarding-school training in deportment and gracious entertaining.

Her adroit efforts to avoid any personal contact with Rio left her tense and jumpy. Courtney's heart ached when he joined the rest of the party for drinks before dinner to see Rio in the same pearl-gray suit he'd worn on their wedding day. Sighing with a longing that clawed at her to her very soul, she lifted her chin, smiled at her guests, and averted the dark-eyed gaze that seemed intent on consuming her alive.

Would the evening never end? Courtney had asked herself that same tiresome question countless times before she smilingly bade the last of the guests good-night. Turning from the curving staircase wearily, she stared at the closed doors to her father's study. The four men—her father, her uncle, Morgan, and Rio—had been closeted in the study since shortly after dinner.

Tired beyond belief from the strain of Rio's sudden appearance, she squared her shoulders and

255

walked purposefully to the doors; she would tap lightly, open the door a mere crack, bid them all a soft good-night, then beat a hasty retreat.

The study doors opened even as she was reaching for the knob. As the men exited the room, they bade *her* a soft good-night. Rio wasn't one of them. Frowning her confusion Courtney trailed behind the three men as they mounted the stairs.

When had Rio retired? she wondered, turning into the hall that led to the suite of rooms she'd redecorated for herself on her return to England six months previously.

As she did every night, Courtney walked past her own bedroom to visit the nursery before retiring for the night. Moving with extreme quiet so as not to waken Luz's nanny, she crept into the room —and stopped dead, one hand flying to her shock-parted lips.

The scene her wide eyes absorbed was illuminated by the soft glow of a small night-light. There was no sign of the nanny. The small cot upon which she usually slept had been moved from its place along the far wall and placed directly against the side of Luz's crib. Positioned exactly like his daughter's, Rio's long form sprawled face down on the cot. His upper torso was naked and one arm was thrust between two of the crib bars. His splayed hand rested protectively on Luz's tiny, vulnerable spine.

Feeling herself an intruder, as she had on the day before she'd departed Texas six months previously, Courtney fought the sting of hot tears and backed stealthily from the room.

The image of Rio and their child haunted Courtney throughout that endless night. Not at any time had she doubted Rio's love for their child. But

256

now, for the first time, she forced herself to consider what being separated from Luz was doing to Rio's soul.

Courtney wept, for herself and her hopeless love; for Rio and his guiltless entrapment; and for Luz and the life she faced with her parents separated by half a world. Dawn found her staring red-eyed and exhausted from weeping and lack of sleep. Dragging her body from the bed, she tossed off her nightgown with a sigh.

The day would be a long one, with precious few moments for Courtney to rest. There was the hunt to get through, and then the hunt breakfast, and then dinner, followed by the traditional hunt ball.

Standing under the stinging shower spray, Courtney shuddered and wished she were back in Texas.

The din of excited voices and metal horseshoes striking cobblestones greeted Courtney as she strode onto the courtyard where the hunting party was gathered. At any other time the scene, with its noise and colorfully attired hunters, would have pleased her. This morning she tapped her riding crop against her buff-colored riding breeches impatiently; all Courtney wanted was to have the weekend over with.

Responding automatically to the greeting called to her, she walked directly to a group that included her father, her uncle, Samantha, Morgan, and several grooms, all of whom were holding the reins to horses stamping and snorting in impatience to be off. There was not a sign of Rio.

After exchanging greetings of the morning, Courtney was on the point of asking after Rio when he sauntered across the courtyard toward the family group. His concession to the traditional

257

hunting attire were boots that rose to his knees, breeches hugging his muscle-corded thighs, and a small cap perched on his head. In comparison to the abundance of red jackets in the yard, his snowy-white, full-sleeved shirt blazed like a beacon.

As Rio joined the group a groom led a huge horse from the stables and across the cobblestones to him. Inattentive to the conversation around her, Courtney was the first to notice the horse. But before she could open her mouth to question the groom, her father spotted the animal.

"What is this?" he demanded sharply, pinning the groom with a cold gaze.

"The horse that was ordered for Mr. McCord, sir," the groom replied respectfully.

"Ordered by whom?" Charles exclaimed, thus causing the spirited animal to dance excitedly.

"Why, I don't know, sir." The groom visibly gulped, uncomfortably aware of the silence that had fallen like a stone in the yard.

"Take that beast back at once," Charles ordered. "And bring a suitable mount for Mr. McCord."

Throughout the exchange Courtney was fully aware of Rio's narrow-eyed gaze studying her speculatively. *What now?* she thought tiredly, facing him with defiant eyes. Rio spoke and at that instant she realized he believed she had ordered the horse.

"What's wrong with that horse, Charles?" His low voice didn't penetrate beyond the immediate family circle.

Charles could barely control his voice. "The beast cannot be broken to the saddle. I've made arrangements to sell him." He again glared at the

258

groom. "Think, man! Who dared to order Stomper saddled for the hunt?"

"I—I—" The groom sputtered.

"He's well named," Rio murmured, running a glance over the big animal, who was forcefully living up to his name. "Isn't he, Courtney?" His glittering dark gaze came to rest on her, piercing her composure like a laser.

"Rio, I—" Courtney broke off in shock. In avoiding the accusing gleam in Rio's eyes, she'd caught sight of Bryan; his smug expression explained everything. "Bryan!" she called, intent on chastising the jealous man, but Rio overrode her voice.

"A favor, Morgan?" he asked very softly.

"Anything," came the prompt reply.

"Get that English gear off that bastard." Spinning on his low heels Rio strode back to the house.

On the edge of her consciousness Courtney heard the murmured comments from her family members and the ripple of excited questions from the rest of the crowd milling in the courtyard; she was even aware of Morgan as he relieved the groom of the reins and led the horse back to the stables; but her entire concentration was leveled on Bryan. As she stared furiously at him, his smug expression grew into a smirk. His taunting remark proved he hadn't heard the exchange between Rio and Morgan.

"Well, now"—he chuckled, mounting up—"as it would appear the Texan has an aversion to good horseflesh, I suppose we'll have to ride without him."

Some members of the party had already mounted. The others moved to do likewise. Some were up, some still standing, and some were halfway between, when Ravenburn, mounted on a

259

gleaming chestnut, turned his head arrogantly to stare down his aristocratic nose at Bryan.

"I will decide when it is time to ride," he informed the Irishman frigidly.

Bryan's expression was an open book, revealing chagrin, and remorse, and sheer panic, at the fear of his career lost for the game of one-upmanship over a rival.

Courtney could not work up one ounce of sympathy for him. The stupid fool had actually attempted to embarrass Rio, and possibly even injure him! She turned away from the sight of Bryan's flushed face; but her eyes flew wide at the more upsetting sight of Morgan, leading Stomper back into the yard. On the animal's back was a familiar, well-worn saddle. Did Rio drag the tack with him wherever he went? she wondered, spinning to the swell of murmurs in the courtyard.

Dressed much the same as he had been when lounging on the stairs the day before, Rio retraced his steps over the cobblestones to Morgan, and the unbreakable, uncontrollable Stomper, his slanted bootheels ringing loudly on the cobbles.

"Back it up, folks." Rio issued the terse warning as he approached the large animal, who was regarding him with wildly rolling eyes.

Amid the gasps and exclamations of the assemblage Ravenburn's cold voice enforced the advice. "Pull your mounts back at once."

Fluidly, smoothly, Rio stepped into the saddle. There was an instant of absolute stillness, during which Courtney saw a smile flicker over Rio's thin lips; then the horse exploded into action.

There were female screams and male outcries as Stomper set about living up to his name. Bucking, twisting, kicking, and stomping, the maddened animal fought wildly to dislodge his rider. Gripping the reins firmly Rio maintained his seat. When all his tricks failed him, Stomper gave up the battle. Educated by a master the horse stood panting and docile.

As the mob closed in to offer congratulations on a superb performance, Rio glanced at Ravenburn. "Now we ride!" Ravenburn commanded.

The hunt master's horn called the group to order, and within seconds they were dashing across the fields after the braying dogs. Giving her mare its head Courtney automatically joined the chase, grasping the reins with one hand while dashing at the tears on her cheeks with the other. A simple fact revolved around in her tired mind: Rio might have been injured or even killed. Hardening her heart she vowed that Bryan would never again receive support from her of any kind.

Then, through the jumble of chaotic emotions hammering in her head, she heard the thunder of Stomper's approaching hoofbeats. As Rio drew the magnificent animal alongside her mare, Courtney glanced at him quickly. One look at Rio's set features was enough; feeling another kind of fear Courtney kept her eyes averted for the remainder of the chase.

When it was over, and the fox cornered, Courtney surrendered to the compelling force of his gaze. Lifting her eyes, she felt a spear of ice shaft through her. Rio's dark eyes were filled with contempt and disgust as he shifted his gaze from her to the trembling fox, then back to her. His cynically twisting lips spoke with silent eloquence of his opinion of their "sport."

Shamed and unable to endure his accusing stare, Courtney wheeled the mare, startling her into a gallop with a crack of her quirt. As she shot away from the milling group, Bryan's head jerked up and around.

"Courtney?" he called anxiously, unaware of the narrow-eyed man inching the big horse into position beside him. "Courtney, wait!" Bryan called again, gathering the reins to turn his mount. His action was stilled by a firm hand grasping his. Feeling the pain shoot up his arm Bryan looked up, and into a pair of dark eyes glittering with warning.

"You've had your chase," Rio rasped icily. His Stetson tilted in the direction of the retreating horse and rider. "That one's mine."

Releasing the other man's wrist by flinging it from him, Rio turned Stomper, setting him into a trot until he'd cleared the other riders; then, loosening the reins, he set the big animal free.

"Okay, bastard," he crooned. "Let's see what you're made of."

Stomper's long, powerful legs stretched mightily, covering the rolling countryside in a blurring movement. Pumping easily, steadily, he closed the distance between Rio and Courtney's flagging mare. As Rio drew the barely winded animal alongside the mare his arm shot out to grasp the reins and jerk the horse to a shuddering stop.

Apprehension tightening her throat, Courtney watched as Rio swung his leg over the horse, then slid to the ground.

"Dismount, Courtney." The coldly delivered order snapped her out of the freezing fear.

Flinging her head up with defiant arrogance, Courtney glared her refusal at him. An instant later she was standing on the ground before him. Had she really forgotten how very swiftly and silently he could move? she asked herself in amazement. Then sheer fury at his manhandling directed her actions. Without hesitation she raised the quirt and brought it down and across his shoulder in one continuous, flashing movement. She cried out in pain as Rio grasped her around the wrist, twisting the crop from her fingers with one hand and capturing the back of her neck with the other.

"And you say *I'm* violent?" he demanded, drawing her face close to his by applying pressure to the back of her head.

"Rio!" Courtney gasped for breath. "Please, don't—"

His head swooped down and his open mouth fused onto her parted lips. For one mad instant Courtney struggled against his possession of her mouth. Then, with the realization that she was fighting not him, but herself, she flung her body against his.

At the inciting sound of the groan that was ripped from his throat, she speared her fingers into his hair, tugging him closer to the hungry demand of her mouth. Biting, sucking, she attempted to devour his lips, while reveling in his efforts to do the same to hers. Her tongue brushed his as it thrust into her mouth.

God! Oh, God! She loved him so terribly! She had missed him so desperately. Wanting more and still more of him, she tried to consume him with her mouth, while thrilling to the evocative thrust of his stiffened tongue and the searching grasp of his strong hands.

Unmindful of the grazing horses they moved as one, dropping to the coarse, uneven meadow grass. Courtney whimpered in protest when Rio removed his hands from her feverish body, and cried out in pleasure when his ungloved hands returned to mold her breasts possessively.

"I want you, *querida*," Rio murmured harshly. "Right now, right here, in the sunlight, in the open." His lips sought the curve of her neck; his hands sought the flesh hidden beneath the hunting jacket; his legs sought the cradle of her thighs.

"Yes! Yes!" On fire with the need to be close to him, be one with him, Courtney was way beyond considerations of propriety.

With frantic, trembling fingers they tore at each other's clothing. When at last they were both free of the confining material, they came together with urgency, straining with the yearning to be one person.

It had been too long, and the heights were scaled swiftly through a mist of flame. On his drive to the summit Rio arched his body into Courtney, tension exposing the tendons in his neck as he called her name aloud at the same instant she cried out his name in ecstasy.

Exhausted, stunned by the magnitude of the experience, Courtney stared at him in mute wonder. *How can I bear to give him up again?* She cried inwardly, blinking against the hot sting of tears. *I can't give him up again!*

Her eyes sparkling like rain-washed blue diamonds, she gazed up at him, silently begging for a place in his heart.

Feeling shattered by the incredible experience, Rio stared into Courtney's pleading eyes. *What is she begging for?* he wondered uneasily. *Her freedom?* A tremor of emotion quaked through his deliciously replete body. *I can't let her go!*

"Courtney?"

"Rio?"

Their voices blended in unison, and in unison they both fell silent.

I want her! he thought fiercely.

I need him! she thought achingly.

If she won't come home with me, I don't want to live! he realized with a shock.

If he doesn't take me back with him, I'll die! she faced the truth wearily.

The intensity of emotional passion reignited the flame of physical passion. Their bodies still joined, they stared into each other's eyes as he grew inside her.

"Can you bear to love again so soon, *querida?*" he whispered around a sensual smile.

"Rio." Courtney felt the ripple that coursed through his strong body as she whispered his name.

This time there would be no groping urgency, Rio determined, causing a shudder of pleasure in her with the gliding quest of his palm. Her damp skin caressed his hand like moist satin. Her tight, aroused nipple jabbed imploringly at his palm. Feeling himself expand inside her, Rio teased her wet lips with his teeth.

"It was always fantastic with us," he affirmed, gliding his slick tongue over the edge of her teeth. "Wasn't it, *querida?*"

"Yes, always." Courtney sighed into the curve of his neck. "Even the first time, when it should have hurt, but didn't." With the tip of her tongue she tested the salty taste of his skin, her body arching to his in response to the rotating movement he made with his hips.

Hard, callused palms caressed the underside of her thighs before slowly moving to the sensitive

265

skin on the insides. As her breathing grew shallow, then labored, he trailed his fingers upward, watching the passion on her face.

"You belong to me, Courtney," he said raggedly, his body thrusting reflexively to her arching hips. "You will always belong to me." He drove himself into her as if to underscore his assertion.

"I—I know!" Courtney gasped, trembling in reaction to his powerful possession. Her eyes were tightly closed to savor every nuance of pleasure, and when he went suddenly still she blinked in confusion. The expression on his face was impossible to decipher, but it seemed to be a mixture of incredulity, wonder, and sheer awe.

"You know?" he repeated roughly.

"Yes." There was a stillness about him that brought a fine frown line to her brow. Why was he so still? "Rio, what is it? What have I—"

"How long have you known?" he demanded.

Confused by his intensity, Courtney tried to withdraw by pressing her body into the ground.

"Answer me, Courtney."

"Almost from the beginning," she blurted, shaken by his threatening whisper. "Rio, I never really wanted any man before I met you. And—and after that night we spent together, I knew I'd never want any other man."

"You wanted a killer?" he asked very, very softly.

"You are not a killer!" Suddenly incensed, she grasped at his hair and shook his head. "Dammit, Rio McCord! You are not a killer! I would not love you if you were!"

"Whoa! Honey, hold it! Are you trying to shake

my head off?" Rio's rich, full laughter rang sweetly in the clear air.

Though her hands stilled, her fingers flexed against his scalp. "I should, but I won't." Fingers pressing, she urged his mouth to hers. "But only because I like the way it looks attached to your body."

His lips brushed hers tantalizingly. "Personally, I like my body attached to yours." The tip of his tongue teased the tender skin on the inside of her lower lip, then dipped into her mouth at her responsive moan. "You're coming home with me, Court. You must. We'll work out the differences between us. Maybe it won't be all roses. In fact I'm sure it won't, but it will be good. We can make it good." Pulling his head free of her grasp, he gazed at her with eyes so full of tenderness that Courtney's throat closed. "*Querida,* I can't live alone in that barren land without you. Come home with me."

"Rio?" Courtney could manage no more than a breathless whisper. "You *are* telling me you love me—aren't you?"

"Yes, I love you." Leaning to her he kissed her fast, and hard. "Of course I love you." The action was repeated. "I've always loved you." When she sought his mouth again he pulled his head back. "Now please tell me," he asked.

"Yes, I love you." Slipping her hand around his neck she drew him to her. "Of course I love you." Tugging him closer she brushed his lips with hers. "I've always loved you." Curling her other arm around his neck she clung fiercely. "I even love that barren land of yours. Yes, darling, we'll make it work." Her lips touched his again. "We could begin right now."

And there, beneath a brilliant midday sun, Rio proceeded to prove to Courtney how well they could work together.

CHAPTER TWELVE

Courtney woke to cool Texas air and the feather-light brush of hard male lips over her brow. Boneless with satiation, she forced her eyelids up and smiled lazily into her husband's love-softened dark eyes.

"Is it time to get up already?" She sighed, glancing over his shoulder at the faint gray of predawn beyond the window.

"Not yet," Rio murmured, gliding his lips from her brow to her temple. "In a little while."

"What woke you?" she mumbled into the warm curve of his hard shoulder.

"Need." Demonstrating, he gripped her by the hips to slide her body over his blatant arousal.

Deliberately tormenting him, Courtney wiggled her hips, laughing softly at the groan she elicited from him. "Honestly, darling, you are the greediest man!" She gasped as his hand found her naked breast.

"Yeah." He nipped at the sensitive skin along the side of her throat. "And you love it."

"Quite true," she admitted on a satisfied sigh, shimmying her body up his to allow his mouth access to her throat, and her own lips free rein to explore the hard planes and angles of his face.

"You smell of expensive perfume . . . and a long night of loving," Rio muttered, stabbing into the hollow at the base of her throat with the tip of his tongue. "It excites the hell out of me."

"Everything excites the hell out of you," she taunted, dropping biting kisses over his high cheekbones.

"Not everything," Rio corrected gently, sinking his teeth into her silky shoulder. "Only everything about *you.*"

As if to prove his point he skimmed his hands down her sides, outlining her curves with his palms. At her responsive shiver he stroked her thighs from her knees to her rounded bottom.

Gasping with pleasure Courtney arched her back for him, fingers digging into his hair to tug him closer. "I think"—she gasped again as his teeth scraped over the sensitized bud—"I think I'd want to kill anyone who dared to hurt you!"

Releasing her breast, Rio laughed aloud. "Blood-thirsty little devil, aren't you?" he teased, grasping her around the waist to draw her down and onto the throbbing heat of him.

"Where you're concerned, yes. Now I understand how you felt about protecting me," Courtney confessed, moaning as he thrust into her.

For long moments conversation ceased. The only sound that disturbed the first morning chirping of the birds was the occasional cry of appreciative pleasure.

With the strength of ever-renewing hunger

Courtney and Rio took possession of each other fiercely, wildly, joyfully.

Rio's soft laughter broke the sweet languor induced by completion.

"Whatever," Courtney queried around a yawn, "are you laughing at?"

"The memory of how you attacked Quinn that day." He grinned wickedly. "When we finally did return to the house." His grin widened. "To partake of the hunt breakfast after partaking of each other."

Courtney smiled dreamily. "That day was marvelous." She sighed, gazing into his gleaming eyes. "You told me you loved me that day."

"I've told you the same a million times since," Rio reminded her indulgently. "As you've told me."

"Yes," she purred. "We both do lap it up like kittens with cream—don't we?"

"Umm," Rio murmured, laughter erupted from him again. "Which doesn't change what you said to the crusader. You went after him like a riled rattler, hissing and striking."

"I never struck him!" Courtney denied indignantly, bolting into a sitting position to glare down at him.

"Well, no," Rio allowed, grinning again. "But you came damn close."

Courtney felt the warmth of a flush wash over her cheeks. "I was tempted," she admitted contritely. Then, raising her chin with inbred arrogance, she decreed, "But the fool deserved it, damn him! He had no idea of your expertise in the saddle when he ordered Stomper for you! For all he knew, you might have been badly injured or even killed by that beast!"

271

"Hey, lady," Rio chided. "That 'beast' is a damned fine piece of horseflesh."

Courtney shuddered delicately. "Let's not go into *that!*" she pleaded. "I don't even want to think of that animal taking up residence in your stables."

"Stomper is a fantastic stud," Rio maintained stoutly.

"Somewhat like his new owner?" Courtney asked sweetly, setting the spark to Rio's laughter again. "At any rate," she continued quellingly, "I really did not have to strike Bryan."

"Damned straight!" Rio choked on another bout of laughter. "Ravenburn did it for you!"

Courtney fought to control the twitch at the corners of her kiss-brightened lips. "I never thought to see the day my lord Ravenburn would raise his fist at another man." Still struck by the wonder of it, and Bryan's ignominious departure from Sterling, she shook her head slowly from side to side.

"It was a great hunt ball, though," Rio observed musingly.

Her spine stiffening, Courtney peered down the elegant length of her patrician nose at him. "For whom?" she inquired icily.

"I had thought for everyone." Rio's laughter subsided as he eyed her tenderly. "You looked ravishing," he remembered, smiling softly, "with your beautiful hair and your white skin in that delicious midnight-blue confection of a gown."

"And you were quite devastating," Courtney gritted, "in your exquisitely tailored tuxedo and that frilly white dress shirt, contrasting so appealingly with your dark skin." Her tone grew colder. "Throughout the evening, whenever I glanced in your direction, it was to discover yet another lovely woman either draped on your arm, or snuggling on your chest while supposedly dancing."

"Courtney?" Rio jerked upright to sit facing her. "Are you serious?"

Having lived with the hateful, childish jealousy for the three weeks since that wretched ball, Courtney merely stared at him. The avowal of his love had come so suddenly, she was still very unsure of herself.

"*Querida!* Has this been festering in your mind all this time?" Rio's brows drew together in a frown. Courtney's anguished eyes betrayed her. And, before those eyes, his face set into unrelenting lines. "I will say this once, and only once. You are the only woman I see, regardless of how many I glance at. You are the only woman I ever want draped on my arm, or snuggling on my chest, or in my life, or in my bed." His face seemed carved from stone. "You either trust me or you don't."

For an instant a scene flashed into Courtney's mind and she could see his face on the day he'd shot the snake to protect her. A tangle of love for him, and regret for her own stupidity, brought a rush of tears to her eyes.

"Oh, Rio, I do trust you," she sobbed, flinging herself into his chest. "I trust you with my body, and my life, and the life of our child!"

Rio was quiet for some moments; then, very softly, he asked, "Are you willing to prove your trust?"

"Yes, yes, I'll do anything!" Courtney cried, clutching his hard warmth close as if in fear he'd withdraw as he had the other time. "Tell me how I can prove it."

"Will you ride out with me again?" he asked

quietly. "Out to that same spot where I killed the snake?"

Leaning away from him, Courtney lifted a trembling hand to wipe at the tears on her face. "That's all you want me to do? Ride out with you to that place?"

"Yes. Will you come?" Though his face remained closed to her, she could read traces of remembered pain in his eyes.

"I hurt you very badly—didn't I?" she whispered achingly.

"Will you ride with me?" he asked, refusing to answer her.

"Rio." Reaching out with both hands she stroked his face lovingly. "I would happily ride to the very ends of the earth with the Night Striker."

The sun had not yet made its appearance on the eastern horizon when Courtney and Rio rode again into the grasslands of the Marfa Highlands. Comfortable in the Western-style saddle, and Hot Foot beneath her, Courtney observed Rio's seat astride Stomper with appreciation. When mounted, he seemed to become one with the horse under him.

Noting her perusal, Rio smiled into her sparkling blue eyes, loving her with his gaze. Behind the glow of near adoration his mind still whirled with the echo of her fervent declaration: "I would happily ride to the very ends of the earth with the Night Striker."

Residual tremors still rippled through his body from the quake of relief her assertion had sent shuddering through him. With her soft assurance Courtney had forever banished his belief that she

274

reviled and loathed his former occupation, and him personally.

Courtney loved him! Rio shivered with the import of the thought. *Courtney loved him!* A bubbling joy unlike anything he'd ever experienced before in his life hummed along his veins. God! Rio had to fight the urge to leap into the air, whooping and hollering like a wild cowboy on a weekend rip! Rio controlled himself by making love to her with his eyes.

Courtney's breathing went slightly haywire as she gazed into the smoldering depths of Rio's eyes. Helpless against the emotion tightening her chest, she gave in to the shivers of pleasure his caressing gaze sent tingling over her flesh. Incredible, impossible, as it seemed, she had the overheated sensation of actually feeling his touch on her body.

Her melting reaction was slightly amazing to Courtney—considering the fact that, up until little more than a year ago, she'd had no experience and didn't understand sexual contact as an expression of love! A pleasurable warmth suffused her body as she recalled how very passionately she'd expressed her love for Rio.

Love him? Courtney restrained the desire to laugh aloud at the tame expression. The word *love* barely defined the way she felt about Rio. Searching her mind, Courtney sought a more definitive term to apply. The only word she could come up with that even came close was *worship.*

To the lullaby of creaking saddle leather, and the visual expression of mutual adoration and worship, they came eventually to the spot Courtney thought of as "the snake place."

After removing his work-scarred gloves Rio stepped out of the saddle, then held his hand out to her in silent invitation. Without hesitation Courtney dismounted and slid her palm into his. The silence easy between them, they strolled to the rock-rimmed, spring-fed pool and directly to the low, flat-topped rock Courtney had rested upon over six months before. Courtney was the first to break the silence between them.

"There was a little flower"—she indicated one side of the rock—"looking like it was striving to reach the sunlight."

"It probably was." Rio's voice was even more raspy than usual.

Dropping to one knee Courtney peered under the rock. "It's gone." Disappointment colored her tone.

"It was a spring flower, love." Rio smiled softly, lovingly. "There will be more next spring."

Courtney glanced up to flash him a quick, understanding smile; Rio was telling her *they* would come back next spring also. "It was so very small, so valiant looking." Her tone tightened. "I had reached down to touch one tiny petal when—"

Courtney's eyes widened in disbelief and horror as a whizzing sound cut across her words and a bullet plowed into the earth on the far side of the rock. Staring at the furrow the bullet had made, she was barely aware of Rio's harshly expelled curse, or that he'd moved to shelter her between his body and the rock. As he dropped into a crouch in front of her the whizzing sound rent the air again and another bullet slammed into the earth, this time from the opposite direction.

"Two of them," Rio muttered, biting out a string of curses; his rifle was in the saddle scabbard! Reaching behind him he pushed Courtney roughly to the ground. "Stay down," he ordered.

He couldn't lose her now! he thought frantically, coldly glittering eyes scanning the terrain through slitted lids. His thoughts were brought to an abrupt halt by the taunting call from beyond a gently sloping sand-hill off to Rio's right.

"Just you stay where you are, cowboy." With the instruction a man scrambled around the sandhill, rifle firmly in position. An instant later another man appeared from the back of a cluster of rocks to Rio's left.

"Ben!" The name came from Courtney's throat on a sigh of sheer terror.

With flashing anger Rio had recognized both of the men at once; the terrified sound of Courtney's voice solidified his anger into an icy, deadly rage.

No. No. The denial froze to his brain. He had waited thirty-eight long, empty years before falling in love; he wasn't about to allow any two-bit, down-at-heel punks to take her away from him. A chilling smile twitched his lips. He wasn't about to die in the blaze of an orange morning sun either— he had a date, with Courtney, and a very large, comfortable bed.

Choking with fear as Ben and the ferret-faced man warily approached, Courtney nevertheless sensed the determination settling in Rio. He was so very still . . . deadly still. In that moment *he* was infinitely more frightening than the two men cautiously moving toward them.

"Rio?" Courtney whispered through fear-dried lips. "Please, don't take unnec—"

"Be quiet," he warned through lips that barely moved. "And be very still."

"Okay, big-deal rancher," Ben sneered, coming to a stop some twenty-five feet from them. "Move away from my *puta* . . . slow-ly and care-ful-ly."

Only Courtney heard the hissing sound of Rio's indrawn breath at Ben's use of the insulting term *puta*. Impossible though it seemed, he smiled. That smile was a warning for anyone with sense enough to see and interpret. Courtney was the single person there with enough sense. The realization of how very dangerous Rio was, now that he was well and truly *riled*, set her heart thumping madly.

Obeying the beady-eyed, leering Ben, while narrowly watching the silent ferret-faced man, Rio lithely rose to his feet and walked away from Courtney with a murmured "Stay put."

Tension electrified the air around her as Courtney helplessly watched the man she loved walk to almost certain death. A blur of movement to her left caught her attention and a sigh of angry regret whispered through her lips as she observed Ferret Face move at an angle to join forces with Ben. Never having been in a position even remotely resembling this one, she'd have been astonished had she been able to feel the satisfaction that rippled through Rio.

That's right, that's right. Rio's thoughts were not betrayed by his frozen features. *That's right, you stupid bastards, close ranks—please.*

Elation zinging along his nerve ends, Rio watched Ferret Face stop beside the hulking Ben. His steps measured, Rio walked to within two feet of them before Ben had the sense to order him to stop. The order came three feet too late.

Before Courtney's disbelieving eyes her soft-spoken husband, her gentle, passionate lover, exploded into a coldly precise killing machine. Employing moves she had never witnessed before, not even in films on martial arts, Rio attacked with the edge of his slashing hands and the whipping action of his long, muscular legs.

Reveling as never before in the bloodlust for destruction, Rio slashed and kicked with deadly accuracy. The two rifles went sailing through the air from suddenly numb fingers, and then he was on them, flashing back and forth from one to the other, beating them to the ground with merciless fury.

"Puta!"

Courtney heard Rio spitting the word out with a snarl as he sank his balled fist into Ben's bloated belly. With a cry of agony Ben went down, rolling into a ball before becoming still. Not even bothering to look, Rio concentrated on the ferret-faced man. Seconds later the kidnapper was nothing more than an untidy heap on the sun-baked Texas earth.

"Courtney," he called, standing over Ferret Face's prone form. "Get me the lariat from my saddle."

Springing to her feet Courtney ran to where they'd left the horses. Her trembling fingers were tearing at the rope fastening when the hoarse sound of Ben's voice stilled their action. Spinning around, she felt a sinking sensation in her stomach. Ben was on his feet, backing away to a safe distance from Rio, one of the rifles clutched to his shoulder. Loose limbed and ready, the other rifle held confidently in his right hand by his thigh, Rio stood, calmly watching every move Ben made.

"Do you want my word that I won't kill him?" The echo of his own voice whispered in Rio's mind.

"Yes." Courtney's response followed the echo. "You have it."

Barely winded by the scuffle, breathing easily as he monitored Ben's slightest move, Rio listened to remembered voices. He had so recently succeeded in gaining her trust. Could he afford to take the chance of losing it again now? No! He'd simply have to take his chances with Ben. The decision made, Rio acted immediately on it. Loosening his fingers, he tossed the rifle aside.

Sheer amazement washed over Ben's face . . . and widened Courtney's eyes. Ben raised the rifle and aimed at Rio.

What is he doing? she thought frantically. Then, the same voices Rio had heard moments before murmured inside her mind. *Good Lord! He doesn't want to break his word to me!* With the startling realization Courtney ceased consciously thinking and obeyed instinctive command.

Keeping her movements Spartan to avoid detection, Courtney slowly slid Rio's rifle out of the saddle scabbard and carefully brought the weapon to her shoulder. Coldly, unemotionally, and expertly, she captured Ben's large frame in the sight. Without hesitating she eased her index finger back against the trigger. Her body jerked at the buck of the report. With a surprised shout of pain Ben crumpled to the ground.

With an unnatural and jerky movement Rio turned to face her, his expression blank with disbelief as he shifted his gaze from her to Ben, and then back to her again. As if clearing away a mind-fog, he shook his head, then slowly walked to kneel by the fallen man.

Courtney was lowering the rifle when Rio straightened to his full height.

"Is he dead?" she asked tonelessly.

"No. You just got his shooting arm." Rio's voice

280

was hoarse from the emotions clamoring through him. Courtney had actually taken a bead on another human being and pulled the trigger! And she had done it to protect *him!* Containing the whoop of laughter crowding his throat, Rio glanced at her and nearly stopped breathing. She was setting the sight on Ben again!

"Courtney, no!" Uncaring of his own safety, Rio ran to her, pushing the rifle up even as the report sounded; the slug was sent on a harmless trajectory toward the sun.

"Let me go!" Courtney demanded, struggling to maintain her grip on the weapon.

"I'm not going to let you kill him!" Rio shouted, tearing the rifle from her grasp. "No matter what he did to you in the hills," he went on more calmly when the rifle was safely in his possession, "I can't let you do this to yourself."

"To me?" Courtney stared at him uncomprehendingly. "What he did to me! What he did to me doesn't matter!" she ranted, sending a murderous glance at the man, then gazing at Rio with anguished eyes. "He was going to kill *you! He was going to kill you!*" she repeated in a raw cry.

"It's over now, *querida.*" Though his tone held firm, a smile teased the corners of his mouth. Keeping a sharp eye on her trembling figure, he slid the rifle into the scabbard, then lifted a two-way radio from a sleeve on the saddle. As he called for assistance from whoever might be closest, he drew her to him with his free arm.

Replacing the radio, he gathered her close to his hard strength just as the sobs began shaking her slender body. "It's all over. We'll let the law take care of that scum."

Sal was the first of Rio's men to arrive on the

scene. An unholy gleam in his black eyes, a flashing smile on his lips, he'd assured Rio he'd be delighted to stand guard over the criminals until the law got there.

"You just take your lady away from here." Sal's grin was positively evil. "If I get real lucky, one of these dudes might start something—and give me an excuse to get nasty."

Chilled, as much by her own actions as the entire attack, Courtney withdrew behind a wall of cool composure. The ride back to the ranch was made in silence.

On their return to the ranch Rio took over. His arm around her waist clamping her to his side, he went first to the study, ordering her to drink the straight whiskey he poured out for her. When she'd finally managed to swallow the last of the amber liquid, he drew her with him into the nursery, where Luz was sleeping soundly, napping off her lunch. From the nursery he led her to their bedroom, coaxing her out of her clothes and into the shower with him. The stinging shower, combined with Rio's gentle ministrations, banished the last traces of her chill and shock. She didn't have to be ordered, led or coaxed onto the bed with him.

Now, free of self-doubt, and trembling from the tension curling her toes, Courtney shuddered in the prelude to ecstasy and whispered of her love and need.

"Rio! Darling, please . . . please! I love you . . . I love you . . . I love—"

Fusing his mouth to hers, Rio drank the sweetness of Courtney's cry. Then, watching her every expression, he buried himself in her flesh again and again in the most profound, celebratory act of life he could imagine.

As Courtney soared over the edge of impossible pleasure, she cried his name aloud.

Soaring right along with her, Rio closed his eyes in both pleasure and gratitude.

"I'm with you, love, I'm with you. I'll always be with you."

Long after twilight had crept into the room, Rio held Courtney tightly to his steadily beating heart, stroking her back with his trembling hands, and her lips with his own.

"That was an incredible journey," Courtney murmured in an awed tone.

"Ah, *querida*," Rio laughed softly. "Now you have ridden to the very ends of the earth with the Night Striker."

ABOUT THE AUTHOR

Amii Lorin is the pseudonym of bestselling writer Joan Hohl. The author of over thirty romances, she includes among her titles *Morgan Wade's Woman*, *Handsome Devil*, and *Come Home to Love*. She is a past winner of *Romantic Times* Reviewers' Choice Award and of the Romance Writers of America Golden Medallion Award.

Futuristic Romance

Love in another time, another place.

DESTINY'S LOVERS
By FLORA SPEER

Janina the Priestess was a maiden whose golden purity must remain untouched. Reid was the stranger whose life was spared to improve the blood lines of the village. He was expected to mate with any woman, but he desired only the one who had heralded his mysterious appearance. Irresistibly drawn to one another, Reid and Janina broke every taboo as they lay tangled together by the sacred pool. But in the heat of their heady desire they forged a bond that no man could put asunder.

_2985-5 $3.95 US/$4.95 CAN

Futuristic Romance

Love in Another Time, Another Place...

FROM THE MIST

By *Saranne Dawson*

For generations the men and women of Volas had been separated. Their only dealings were for purposes of procreation, and they were strictly scientific rather than sensual. But fiercely possessive Jorlan swore he would restore the women of Volas to their men, particularly the fiery beauty Amala, who had chosen him as her long-distance mate. But Amala wanted no man to dominate her, not even the charismatic Jorlan, who filled her with a strange longing to taste the forbidden pleasure of love.

___3083-7 $3.95 US/$4.95 CAN